FABYAN PLACE

Peter Angus

FABYAN PLACE

Copyright © 2021 by Peter Angus

Published by Dottenfritz Press
Old Tappan, New Jersey

All Rights Reserved. No part of this book may be reproduced or transmitted in any form or by any means, electronic or mechanical, including photocopying, recording, or by any information storage and retrieval system, without written permission from the author, except for use of brief quotations in a review.

This is a work of fiction. Names, characters, places and incidents are either products of the author's imagination or are used fictitiously. Any resemblance to actual events, locales or persons, living or dead, is entirely coincidental.

Author services by Pedernales Publishing, LLC.
www.pedernalespublishing.com

Front cover design: Richard Mantel

Library of Congress Control Number: 2020925944

ISBN 978-1-7364132-2-7 Paperback edition
978-1-7364132-1-0 Hardcover edition
978-1-7364132-0-3 Digital edition
978-1-7364132-3-4 Audiobook edition

10 9 8 7 6 5 4 3 2 1

Printed in the United States of America

xx-vl0

FOR THE LADS

CONTENTS

PREFACE

Most of the historical events in this book actually transpired, while some elements surrounding individuals are fictionalized. I tried to use vernacular that was common in the 1940s (including the vocabulary as well as the pejoratives). It is not meant to shock or insult but to advise the reader what it was like in the world in the early part of the last century.

One

THE CHRISTMAS AFTER

The agonizing pain that war veteran Sonny Jacobs suffered was not necessarily active in his mind, but it was a constant presence. As he headed home, it manifested itself in a slow, deliberate gait that, if he walked too briskly, exposed a pronounced limp. Like the ringing in his ears, it only disappeared when he managed not to think about it. And of course, he always felt the suffering if it was chilly enough to sting his cheeks, and today, the temperature was approaching that point. If he gave the pain a moment's thought, however, it jumped back into the present and tormented him once again. But for now, it was barely present in his mind. He had no idea how much of that agony would be dragged into the front of his mind and how soon.

He had developed a fatalistic view on life over the past twelve months, and though it appeared he was in no immediate danger of missing the Jacobs' Christmas tomorrow, he just wanted to survive another day to celebrate it with his family. It was what he lived for, what he dreamed about. To Sonny, the very idea of this upcoming sumptuous meal and the warmth of spending time with those closest to him would be a miracle. He clung to that main thread of hope of celebrating the Yuletide holiday with his parents, sisters, grandparents, and uncles through the memories of some of the most horrific torture he had ever faced. He had learned not to count his chickens. He wanted, no, needed to make sense of it all. Was there a reason for all the suffering and sadness he had experienced? Did the harrowing events of the past year happen for a reason?

Sonny's once thick, very thick, jet-black, slicked-back hair was now thinning and had some tinges of premature gray on the temples and top. He was still handsome with a chiselled nose and square jaw, but with an older look than someone who had not quite yet reached thirty years of age, and his especially very dark brown, piercing eyes had a bit of a distant stare that seemed to see something no one else could, something that haunted him.

Not much more than a year ago, these eyes were framed with laugh lines because of his constant mirth, and he had the ability to keep young women entranced with his looks, smile, and features alone, as if his wit and humor were not already enough. But the crow's feet beside each eye now did not accompany constant smiling, and they added age to his slightly paunchy face. He had been a strapping lad of five-foot-ten with a robust chest and arms for lifting—a true "Adonis"—but now his arms and trunk appeared to have somewhat atrophied in the last twelve months, and he currently walked with a limp and a very slight stoop.

The air was brisk this day; snow crunched underfoot, and people carrying Christmas trees were walking in front of his home from an unused parking lot only yards away; the lot was selling them starting at fifty cents for the runts. They were holding abundant trees for the first time in years there.

A Negro gentleman from a nearby neighborhood, wearing a worn face with the years etched in—who looked as old as Sonny but was closer to twice his age, also with a limp and a slight stoop—was leaving the tree lot wearing a warm coat and gloves and was not paying attention. He swung a tree up onto his shoulder to carry home, and as he was shifting it to his other shoulder for better balance, he nearly knocked Sonny to the ground in the process. "Shit!" Sonny said to himself as he took a slight slip back and put too much pressure on his injured feet. "God, I can't take much more of that—ignorant nig…" He didn't finish the word, and though he thought it a lot, he would never say that out loud or use the pejorative outside of mixed company. He considered himself better than that, but he had been influenced more by his family than he cared to admit.

A moment later, something else caught his eye. Walking by was a tall, recently returned naval officer, still enlisted and in uniform with an attractive young woman on either arm, each of them wearing newly available nylon stockings showing off their shapely gams. He attempted to swing around to chat one of them up (after all, the officer couldn't keep two for himself!), but his neck couldn't turn as it was still stiff from the beatings he had endured half a year ago. So, he began to turn his whole body to get a better look and took a tumble. He caught himself before he crashed to the ground and let the vision of their legs disperse from his inner vision, but he chuckled to himself. *Perfect headline: "Army veteran splits open skull bird-dogging officer's women!"* he thought. But he immediately reflected that he made the attempt due to reflex, not desire. The craving was not there as it once was, and his libido was seriously diminished from just last December. Discerning confusion, he realized he wasn't sure if it was because it would be a bit indecorous to treat the women as objects or with disrespect or if this was what "growing up" was all about. He could *not* figure out why his view of the world, previously set in black and white, had shifted to so many varied hues. Or possibly worse: Had he somehow been emasculated during German incarceration?

He didn't think about it long as he was approaching his home: 50 Fabyan Place.

It was Christmas Eve morning in 1945 on Fabyan Place in Newark, New Jersey, the largest city in the state and a stone's throw from New York City.

ॐ ॐ ॐ

Sonny had been out this day running one of the myriad errands necessary during the holiday, though not at as brisk a pace as he would have liked. At twenty-seven, he was already considered an "older" veteran of the war, but the limp was not due to age, and he winced if he put any significant pressure on his feet.

His youngest sister, Eileen, intercepted him as he walked up the front porch steps to the door.

"You got a long-distance phone call!" she called out with expectant enthusiasm, delighted to be the first to tell him.

"Christ, from who?" he said in a very low voice so that his taking the Lord's name in vain would not be heard beyond Eileen.

"Language!" yelled his mother, a gentle woman, though nosey and fanatical about religious propriety, particularly when her oldest was blaspheming and with her own mother standing right next to her in the kitchen. Sonny's grandmother, an inveterate bigot from the old country, was standing in the kitchen and was within earshot, and she too raised her voice in admonition.

Eileen continued her enthusiastic announcement of the long-distance call. "A guy named John, I think, called from Georgia. No, wait. Maybe somebody was calling as a favor for some guy—that's it. He said he was trying to reach you for days."

"Huh?!" Sonny was taken aback.

"Well, it was actually a grocery store owner named Clyde Cornpone, or something like that, in North Carolina—he talked funny. He said he was given two dollars—to deliver the message—and has been trying to get through for days! Two dollars! By a customer named John to get through to tell you he'd see you at 10:05 at Penn Station on Broad Street on Christmas morning. Can you imagine? Two dollars?!"

"Will you stop saying two dollars!" Sonny surely wasn't thinking about the gratuity paid, though if the message delivery could be guaranteed and reliable, it was still probably cheaper than a telegram.

He couldn't figure out exactly who'd made the call, but he had an idea. And for a ton of reasons didn't want to deal with it. "If it is who I think it is, I really, really don't want to deal with this….*at all.*"

Eileen went on, "You invite someone to Christmas without telling us? Is he on the invite list? The man said he'd been trying us for the last two days." Eileen said this again to reemphasize the news, once clearly being not enough. "But I didn't believe him—I'll bet he forgot." She carried on nonstop. "Is he an Army friend? Is he cute?"

"The storekeeper or guy sending the message?" Sonny asked.

"How do you know what the storekeeper looks like?"

"I don't."

"Then why did you ask me?" Eileen inquired.

"I don't know either of them. Leave me alone." Sonny gave his sister a sideways glance as he trundled past her and into the warm house. "Eileen, you're the prettiest veteran I know, but you'll be single forever 'cause there is no one out there to put up with your wit or tongue," Sonny said to her tongue-in-cheek, and then to himself, "and you're a big pain in the ass." Though he genuinely believed it, and he knew his younger sister always managed to make people laugh, Sonny's mind quickly returned to this new confusion that his mind perceived but could not resolve: the precise identity of this caller John. Sonny said to himself, "If it is who I think it is, it is just going to make a mess of things, *especially* tomorrow."

Until Eileen's newsflash, Sonny's war experiences had been pushed back farther in his consciousness than they had been in months during this first holiday after the war's end. At this moment, however, the experiences came pouring back in.

Sonny's family, the Jacobs, were half-North American Indian; his father was born a Mohawk-Iroquois in Canada and was living a somewhat prosperous life in Newark as an ironworker. His mother's side were Croatians, her parents pretty much right off the boat.

Christmas in the Jacobs household was considered legendary, if not necessarily by the family themselves, then certainly by invited guests. The family prepared and necessarily served a mixture of a native Mohawk-Iroquois repast as well as Croatian and adopted American food specialties as was the custom at this particular time of year. Sonny sat down in a warm, comfy chair, creaking under his weight, still trying to resolve the phone call in his mind, and said to no one in particular so he didn't have to think about it, "I can't believe I'm here, and we're all alive and celebrating tomorrow." Family members bustling about smiled at him indulgently and allowed him to enjoy the moment.

Wartime ration restrictions were being gradually lifted, and there was food and goods aplenty. It was a rare home in America that suffered no casualties, and while there were quite a few in Sonny's extended family who had served in the armed forces, all had come back home intact—though Sonny only barely—and he was considered the "miracle" after having been listed missing in action for five months. Captured in the Ardennes Forest in Belgium just over a year ago almost to the day, the family knew nothing of his fate until the Germans surrendered in May. The pale-yellow telegram announcing his release was framed on their living room wall next to a crucifix.

Sonny returned to the present and to his conversation with his sister, and in any case, the telephone call was news enough.

"The family's first long-distance call ever! And during Christmastime! And long distance!" She was falling over her words. "And he paid two dollars!" she said yet again. Sonny pursed his lips, glanced up at her, and briefly grimaced.

There were few phones that worked in Newark (materials and manpower had been used for the war effort and not the manufacture or repair of family phones) and the whole country, so having a working phone was a big deal to her.

Just the thought of the family celebration on Fabyan Place had helped keep him alive this past year during his incarceration by a merciless captor. There was much at home that had stayed just the same as Sonny remembered, but there was much new as well. For one, the Jacobs family had their first telephone, though as a shared party line—much to the consternation of their next-door neighbors who did not have young daughters who dominated the phone's use. One of Sonny's sisters was engaged to be married, and the other was very popular and "on the market." Between them, they both monopolized the phone's available time.

Sonny noticed that his sisters were gossiping like mad about anyone and everything, as always, in the kitchen. Sometimes interesting hearsay, sometimes petty, personal, and awful, but they only did the latter when Grandma and his mom were out of the kitchen, or they said it only in a low tone so as not to be heard. They were preparing food for Christmas Eve dinner as well as for the meal the next day. Sonny walked into the bustling, steaming kitchen—always the center of attention—with percolating pots on every oven hob and the lone window covered with moisture. He grabbed a bit of food already prepared from the table, a wonderful thing to do, having experienced so much painful hunger in the last year. Even after months of being home, the simple act of having readily available food still had an emotional impact on him. His oldest sister slapped his hand as he reached for another portion. "That's for later." And he dropped it back on the plate but picked it up again when she turned her back to tend to something on the stove. He tried to cover his actions by making some comments.

"You ever notice how Mom is thin and always smiley, nonjudgmental about nearly everything, and Grandma is, well, just so thick and just the opposite?" Sonny thought it would have been the height of disrespect to call her fat, though she was quite "matronly," and he got a sideways glance from Eileen as she scooped mashed potatoes into a larger bowl.

"In fact, Mommy is a hundred percent different from Grandma in every way. Grandma is…," he began as the kitchen door swung open and his grandmother came in, wiping his hands on her apron, looking for a completed dish to carry to the larger dining room table.

She asked, "What next?" and then, "What you say, Sonny?"

"We were talking about Mr. Applebaum, the tailor on Woolsey Street, and his . . . "

Sonny had barely finished saying the name when his grandmother said "*Zhyd*" in Croatian, meaning "Jew," as he knew she would.

He winked at Eileen, who was about to defend their grandmother. She turned her attention elsewhere. Sonny, always the needle, continued to try to get Grandma into a state.

He changed tack. "Grandma, do you know if Pesci's Grocer is still open today? I'd like to get some tomatoes and then pick up my shoes at Ike's." Ike, whom the family knew was the local Negro cobbler.

In quick succession, his grandmother spat out "guinea" and then "nigger"—she couldn't countenance anyone not White and preferably Croatian and thus couldn't hold back her acid tongue or pejorative imagination.

Sonny smiled, enjoying his ability to wind up his grandmother and clamp a stopper over his sister defending her.

Eileen tried to change the topic. After all, she knew it was heading toward a bigoted tirade, though she quickly regretted what she said because she was bringing up Italians, Grandma's particular dislike.

"Cora is dating Phil, that baseball player—"

Grandma interjected, "Dat midget *guinea*…" She had a special invective for Italians for some reason.

Eileen knew what Sonny was doing and managed a wan smile back at him in surrender. She was as cute as a button, demure with a round face and dark eyes that missed nothing. Any one of his former Army buddies would have killed to go out with her. He turned to his oldest sister, Dorothy, or Dot as she was called. He grabbed her left hand to admire the dazzling but modest diamond on her ring finger for the millionth time.

"Nice," he said, for the millionth time. "You never told me—what day did Fritzie propose?"

"You never asked. The day after he returned," she said. "He came over and asked Daddy for my hand. They polished off two quarts of beer on the front porch, and then he came onto the back porch where Eileen and I were sitting, laughing like hyenas, to give me the ring."

"But that was the day after he got back, wasn't it?" Sonny said.

"He tried to give me a larger diamond the day he returned that he said he'd "liberated"—his words—from a German he captured—his words again—and when I found that out, I told him I didn't want it. He had to go out and buy a new one. But I did say yes."

What Dot didn't know was that he had "liberated" it out of the pocket of a dead German prisoner; so, Fritz was already feeling guilty when he raced over to the Bowery that night in New York with his dad to buy a "fresh" engagement ring for Dot.

Jesus, Fritz is a loudmouth. Why'd he have to tell her where he got it? It cost him a new ring! he thought to himself.

Dot was finishing two years of college in Newark; Fritz had served with the artillery, landing in Normandy and ending the war at the Elbe River in Germany. Dot missed very few of the nuances of life that went on around her, like who was dating whom behind their girlfriends' backs and whose parents disapproved of a boyfriend or girlfriend. Dot was a classic beauty, and she had many, many suitors. With wavy raven black hair, luminous mahogany eyes and classically sculpted features combining the good looks of her Indian dad and Croatian mom, she carried a torch for Fritzie who she met ten years earlier when he visited her family Indian Reservation when a Boy Scout as a youngster. She was as suspicious as her grandmother when it came to questioning people's motives and as distrustful as a homicide detective. And judgmental. And while Dot was, for the most part, bias-free, in weak moments and from time to time, she still succumbed to her grandmother's influence and expressed a racially influenced opinion.

A knock on the door, and a young couple carried in some boxes of pre-made dishes that would need reheating tomorrow. "Here you go—our contribution." It was a French couple (the neighborhood was indeed mixed): the Balliets. Dot wiped her hands on her apron, took the box, took a quick look inside, and walked it to the back porch.

Sonny reflected, "Everybody still wants an invite to the Jacobs for Christmas from everywhere. Good to see that hasn't changed." Ever the needler, when he saw them standing in the doorway, he adorned a stern look and innocently asked, "Did we really give you an invite again this year?" The Balliets froze in their tracks and looked at him with dismay, not aware that he was taunting them. The invites were issued each year (and did not automatically renew—a truly embarrassed family stumbled upon that truth a few years back); so, local neighbors and friends would get closer to the entire family starting late October. Their hope would be to join the feast according to Croatian national custom after all their own celebrations took place on Christmas Eve or early the next morning. One concession since coming to America was that the Jacobs family shifted traditional festivities from "the evening before" to "the day of" for the coveted bacchanalia.

Sonny's face broke into a broad smile, missing a tooth or two, to indicate the jibe. The cozy room was filled with the aromas from the kitchen as well as from the evergreen from the decorated tree just nearby.

"Welcome!" he called. "Good to see you again."

13

And the Balliets relaxed and went over to the chair to greet him back.

The Christmas celebration was special to Sonny; he knew that the idea of this upcoming holiday and celebrating it with his family kept him breathing during his imprisonment. Indeed, his colorful description of prior holiday feasts kept many of his fellow captives alive with hope, as one thing they had very little of was food. Through the horrors they faced the previous year, oddly enough, it was the thought of things their body craved that kept them alive.

"Sonny, who is this guy you're picking up at the train station tomorrow? And that storekeeper had a really funny accent, like guys in the movies. I thought he was making it up. And the phone never rings, so when it did, I jumped out of my skin. It took me forever to find a pencil and paper to take the message. I almost didn't!" Eileen rambled on. "Sonny, the guy calling was not the guy sending the messages. He had to make a train."

"The guy giving you the message had to make a train?" Sonny questioned.

"No, the guy from who the messages were coming had to make a train. He said he'd been trying to reach you for a few days. It was from a guy named John, and he would meet you at Newark Penn Station Tuesday morning just after 10:00 a.m.," she repeated.

When the name sank into Sonny this time, his spine stiffened, which he felt keenly, given the beatings his back had taken.

Eileen broke Sonny's train of thought once again when she repeated "Two dollars" for what seemed like the hundredth time.

"He was kinda hard to hear, and in the middle of the call, Mr. Jorgensen next door picked up the party line to make a call and slammed it down again…yelling *Jesus*." (She whispered the last word.)

"Language!" his mom yelled from the kitchen.

"Shit," Sonny said so only Eileen could hear him. "How does she do that?"

"*Language!*" came a scream from both his mom and grandmother, both now back in the kitchen.

Sonny shook his head, then… *Who could have possibly been calling?* he thought. Maybe Eileen got the message wrong.

"I've invited no one," he said aloud. "I don't know who that is. And *please* stop saying two dollars!"

Sonny mused that the only person named John who had been invited to his home was dead to him, but now, he wasn't sure if he was being fair. Though a common name, Sonny had invited scores from that shared place of imprisonment to come to his family Christmas family celebration, and most of those were now dead as far as he knew—and under unspeakable circumstances.

His memories had started to creep, then slowly pace, and now sprint into his head.

"Who was calling me?" he asked no one in particular again. Regardless of who it was, if it was the man he was thinking about, he just knew he couldn't face him.

TWO

NEWARK PENN STATION

The only activities on Christmas Eve for Sonny's family involved the last-minute wrapping of presents, some final cleaning, and preparing for the onslaught of people tomorrow as well as midnight mass at Blessed Sacrament Church on Clinton Avenue a half-mile away.

Sitting in his pew in the church that evening, he still wasn't quite sure who could be waiting for him, if indeed someone would show up and it was not all just a wicked prank. He knew a couple of soldiers named John in the service with whom he did not serve, yet very few of them had been invited to Christmas at the Jacobs household.

"Nearly all the guys are dead. And the guys outta state are not going to come," he mused.

But Sonny had befriended a few soldiers from the South, and now he wracked his brain to figure out if he knew this guy only by a nickname, and his original moniker had disappeared from his memory.

After weighing it all in his mind and not reacting to

the Latin mass's repetitiveness being celebrated in front of him, he resolved that he would not go to the train station to be faced with something too distressing to contemplate. He put it out of his mind and concentrated on the mind-numbing chanting of memorized prayers.

His night had not been a good one. Sleeping in the bedroom of his youth, where as a youngster he had dreamed about the exciting adventure of going to war—and as he got older, chasing the local teenage skirts, his swarthy looks making each conquest relatively easy—he had a restless night. Though he fell fast asleep when his head hit the pillow, he awoke what he thought had to be soon afterward but was actually the middle of the night, after meeting the friends he'd left behind in Germany in his sleeping fantasies. When he realized where he was in his dream and with whom he was speaking, he woke up screaming, with both his mom and dad on either side of the bed holding his arms and hands in an attempt to calm his sweating body, both having been alerted by the noise of Sonny's violent thrashing coming from the bedroom. These things still raced through his mind that night as well the following day as he drove toward the rendezvous. He had caved to both his curiosity and anxiety; he needed to see who was awaiting him.

That next morning, Christmas Day, a little after 10 a.m., Sonny saw a sole person standing outside Penn Station's front entrance on Market Street. It was so bitterly cold. The wind, with bits of the dusting of snow from that morning, whipped miniature tornados that moved along the sidewalk next to the granite building. It couldn't be who he thought it might be. So much water under the bridge. He felt his palms sweating on the steering wheel of the pre-war Chevy.

As Sonny pulled to the front of the station, he saw the man, pitifully dressed for the Newark winter in lighter, cotton, tan, short pants stopping just below the knees, a white shirt buttoned at the top but with no tie, and a light, zippered jacket with a simple print—all items meant for a far warmer climate. He was wearing what appeared to be homemade woven cotton sandals with white cotton socks—comfortable but somewhat inappropriate for the cold—and he was looking quite lost.

Once Sonny saw his face, his identity fell promptly into place. "God, I'm gonna regret this," he said out loud.

He pulled up in his borrowed Chevy coupe, then leaned across, opened the door, and motioned him in. The man looked left and right as if seeking assistance or another offer.

"I'm waiting for someone, sir."

"I think you're waiting for me. Are you Mr. Chalmet?" Though he intentionally mispronounced the gentleman's name as "Shall-met" because that was how, when printed, it looked like it should be pronounced, Sonny knew exactly how to say it properly ("Shall-may").

Too cold to argue, the man jumped in and closed the door. Sonny released the parking brake, and they drove toward the parking lot exit.

"How do you know it was you for whom I was waiting?"

The man had a peculiar way of talking and an unusual accent Sonny found vaguely familiar. Sonny stared at him for a moment as if to question the veracity of his query before returning his eyes to the road and shifting gears. It was a rhetorical question, and Sonny decided not to answer.

"You Sonny?" the man added.

"Yep. And you John?" asked Sonny.

"Yep. You got my message?"

"Of course. Your son's named after you?"

"Well, yes. My name, though, is Jean." It sounded like he was saying John, only very quickly and abridged. "A French name. Jean," he said again. "Jean-Claude, actually. You call me JC. Everybody else does.

"My son told me a lot about you, Sonny, mostly in notes I received from overseas after he got out. I hope you don't mind, but he told me about your Christmas festival—thought I should go. He said so much about you I just had to meet you—and it seems that you meant so much to my son at one time. I didn't want to miss Christmas on Fabyan Place."

Sonny was ambivalent, and he knew he certainly would not be prepared for any type of emotional disruption on this Christmas day. And he was still angry with John for a multitude of reasons.

As Sonny looked to the end of the parking lot and into the street, he gave the engine a bit more gas and drove forward a bit faster now. Though thinking through his current situation and passenger for a moment, he realized he had a more immediate problem—he knew he could not take this man into his family home.

"Let's find a place to warm up first and get a little something in your stomach. I'm sure you're exhausted," Sonny offered.

JC nodded agreement and was just thrilled to be somewhere away from the cold.

❧ ❧ ❧

With few taverns open on Christmas, Sonny knew he would have a challenge finding a place in Newark to sit down and get something to eat, let alone a place for JC to spend the night before he could bundle him off back to the South. But he would think about that later. At the moment, vivid memories were screaming into his brain.

Whenever Sonny got nervous or didn't know quite what to say, he babbled and babbled. "Okay, JC," he said as he pulled onto Market Street. "You wouldn't know it, but this is Market Street, and we're headed toward McCarter Highway—it bisects Newark."

JC could not have cared less. The few moments he had spent outside had frozen him to the core, and he was just enjoying the blowing heater of the car and not really paying attention to Sonny.

As he drove along, Sonny thought it unusual that a small convoy of large commercial trucks now occupied the lane next to him—some were dump trucks and others were for refuse—and it reminded him of a military procession.

"JC, this group of trucks alongside us reminds me of my own unit, the 89ᵗʰ Quartermaster Division." He immediately regretted bringing up the war. Right away, he realized he'd be tiptoeing through this minefield for the rest of the day. JC looked out the window absentmindedly, warmth only now seeping back into his extremities. One of the trucks hit a pothole in the road, and the back dump-bucket jumped inches off its bed and slammed back down. It sounded to Sonny more like an ordnance explosion than metal banging on metal.

And just as soon as it entered his mind, it left again, too traumatic to keep in his active memory, though it happened frequently since he'd returned from the war—his family had noticed startled jumps from him quite a bit in recent months. He was constantly on guard; in fact, he had previously "hit the ground" many times after a loud backfire from an exhaust pipe or even a heavy book being dropped. And the night terrors—screams during the night of which he many times had no memory of their cause in the morning. But his family knew.

JC and Sonny approached the establishment.

"Here, this place is open. Good food. We'll have the meatballs, best in Newark. Everybody minds their own business." Sonny was lost in thought as he parked the car and went a few steps ahead, leading JC toward a tavern he knew served food and would be open on Christmas. Sonny was initially greeted with a smile, but when the bartender saw he had someone in tow, he made a disagreeable face, shook his head, and pointed in an exaggerated fashion over his and JC's shoulders toward the door.

Sonny and JC walked back to the car, the crunch of the snow giving a distinctive sound as their feet sunk an inch or so into the frozen top layer of powder frozen from the night before, and for Sonny, it triggered yet another memory. He glanced down at his ill-clad companion's sandals, the white socks within them already wet and soiled from slush on the street and the sidewalk. He looked at his own warm, snug shoes, but he only thought of what JC was wearing, and in them, he saw the rags that he wore in the wet and soiled snow in Belgium last December.

As they walked to his car, another empty dump truck fell again into a pothole large enough to make it bounce, this time on nearby Route 21, and when it resumed immediately on the solid road, a heavy back box banged once again against its chassis, and it sounded like yet another explosion in Sonny's mind's eye. He hadn't always paid attention to the banging before, but now, it made the exact same sound of a howitzer shell exploding into frozen hard ground, and it startled him.

His consciousness jumped back to Belgium in 1944. It had only been twelve months and a universe apart from the present, but the memories frightened him.

THREE

SONNY

Sonny had been drafted to serve the US armed forces late in 1943 for the duration, and after arriving at the draft board in Newark, filling out some paperwork, and taking a several-page sit-down test, he was immediately assigned to the Quartermaster Corps. The information and the test indicated an unusual acumen for numbers and remembering random facts, and he seemed to be a natural for that branch of the armed forces.

"The quarter-what corps? Are they soldiers?" he had asked the sergeant who had a cigarette dangling from his lips, a crew cut, and a slight paunch from little exercise and working as a clerk.

"Yeah, stupid. Open your ears: *the* Quartermaster Corps—supply soldiers. You're going to be part of the supply group."

"How is that fighting? I thought I was enlisting to fight."

"Look, stupid. We're gonna teach you to fight, but

somebody has to supply food and ammo for the guys carrying guns. Your civilian work makes you perfect for that type of work. Plus, it is way safer. No bullets being fired at your fat ass." The sergeant behind the desk, pointing out where Sonny had to sign his life away, was already looking at the next guy in line.

"Well, what exactly do they do?" was his follow-up—and unanswered—question as Sonny moved down the line of soldiers processing the inductees.

Sonny obviously had never heard of the Quartermaster Corps, and he didn't get helpful answers from the sergeant behind the first counter, so he had to ask the next desk jockey in the following room distributing skivvies. They knew each other from high school, so he was a bit more kindly. "Look, Sonny, the group you just got planted in arranges for supplies all within the armed forces: management of materials, distribution, procurement, and all the field services to sustain fighting soldiers, their units, and their equipment. They're responsible for gas, all fuel, water, and even the cataloging and burying of dead soldiers. To be honest, the Quartermaster ranks are massive, and they are the largest and most important part of the Army. The ratio of Quartermaster soldiers to fighting soldiers is six to one—a big force."

"And it sounds like, most importantly, no bullets being fired at my fat ass," Sonny said to the nodding and smiling complaisant clerk.

"Your training starts in Philly in two days. Take these orders. Get your picture taken, go home to see your folks

24

before you're sent to parts unknown, and head to the train station.

And after he was sworn in: "Get a move on, soldier."

❧ ❧ ❧

During and after the war, very few stories appeared in the newspapers about the Quartermaster Corps, and as a result, they became only minor characters in the great battle for the victory of freedom over fascism. If it were not for the Quartermaster Corps, there would have been *no* victory because the soldiers would not have had bullets or the guns with which to fire them; the artillery would not have had shells, nor the machines with which to hurl them. There would have been no transport for those soldiers, no gasoline to run the vehicles, no clothing for their backs, and no food for their bellies. The Allied advances would have ground to a halt.

Even after the few months he'd been home postwar, Sonny realized the dichotomy between the fighters (who were few) and those who made it possible for them to fight. *Hey, I did my part, though I'm pissed not everybody sees it that way. I haven't seen any movies about the Quartermaster Corps,* he thought. Though strangely, it still pleased him that he had done a big part, albeit somewhat anonymously.

Frankly, what put his nose out of joint was the disdain that some showed the supply soldiers. Sonny could see no reason for this, especially given what he'd seen and experienced.

ﾞﾞﾞ

Before that, Angus "Sonny" Jacobs (some called him Jakes because of his surname) worked as a truck dispatcher and union shop steward at the Ballantine Brewery in Newark, New Jersey. The building was a vast complex located near the municipal airport and had just managed to avoid bankruptcy and sale a little over ten years previously when Prohibition was lifted and they could manufacture beer once again in strength and quantity—for the duration of Prohibition, they had gotten by on processing and selling malt syrup. The brewery, somehow considered necessary to the war effort, had exemptions for nearly all the employees. However, young, able-bodied men were gradually replaced by women in the plant's manufacturing and delivery aspects as the war progressed and the Allied invasion of the European continent and the ground war in Asia grew nearer.

Sonny's mother, Antonia Mary, known simply as Mary, was originally a US citizen but relinquished that status when she married a North American Indian from Canada (that country being as far from her own parents as she could decently imagine and escape to). When she moved back to the US, she had to officially become an American citizen once again. She had already absorbed and exhibited a state of racial tolerance by marrying an Indian. She had found her husband to be so, well, ordinary, which led to an epiphany that bled away her ingrained parental prejudice—instilled mostly in those who had little contact with people outside of their own race, ethnicity, or religion.

Her parents, on the other hand, had left a trail of disappointed and bitter spouses in their hometown in Croatia. They were a bit self-loathing about the disposition of their prior marriages, and were also relatively intractable when it came to ethnicity other than their own. Mary's father, Ferdinand, was a gentle though mischievous soul, revered by the entire family because of his calm and nonjudgmental nature in family matters, though not so much regarding race or skin color. His wife, Sonny's grandmother, Giovanna Maria, was the opposite except for the same bigotry. She was a fault-finding, judgmental, emotionally controlling, hypercritical, bigoted zealot. Other family members loved the grandfather and feared the grandmother.

૰૰૰

This was the background of Sonny's ethnic education. He knew, as a "half-breed Indian," he was to some people an ethnic "undesirable," though to most he was merely an "invisible minority." If they gave his race a second thought at all, however, with his thick black hair and dark complexion, they might have thought he was the child of Italian immigrant parents, slightly more acceptable than American Indians to the White unwashed masses. If they heard his first name, "Angus," it threw them off entirely—and his last name, Jacobs, made them think perhaps he was a Jew.

He had seen and enjoyed Western movies in the theater, though Indians were always the bad guys; they killed the White man and were brutal warriors. But they were also easily defeated (after a setback or two) by the might and right of whoever they were facing: White soldiers, White settlers, or "friendlier" (to the White man, at least) Indian foes.

The conversations he had in the schoolyard growing up were as stereotypical as they were inaccurate.

"Jakes, you mean to tell me your dad is a hundred percent Indian?"

"Yep."

"Like…" And then the other boys put two fingers up behind their heads for feathers and popped their hand on their mouth while howling.

"Yep. But you know, Indians don't do that anymore."

"Bullshit."

"Okay, wise guy, where does he hunt for food? Does he make his own clothes? Eat buffalo meat?" a schoolmate asked.

My friends are as humorous as they are stupid, Sonny had thought. And after a bout of teasing, during which they would exhaust their wit on the topic, most people forgot he was a "half-breed" anyway, and it was often overlooked because of his handsome looks and the fact that his skin color was much like theirs. They simply forgot he was Indian after they drained the humor from the topic and the "fun" had run its course.

If Sonny gave his own race a second thought, it was

because occasionally some of his schoolyard friends as he grew older spat this invective upon him, undoubtedly learned from their own parents, and thus he was pretty relieved that it was not readily apparent he was an Indian. He was thankful for this, but it did not prevent him from participating in and supporting the occasional bigoted comment made by friends, neighbors, and colleagues regarding the more obvious racial minorities with whom he came into contact, most notably Negroes.

Their bigotry always perplexed him because it seemed to hold such a strange conviction, though he still played along so that he would not be next in line to become a target. In this respect, he was a bit of a coward. Nor could he connect the fact that he was doing the exact same thing regarding Negroes that his schoolmates had done to him.

అలంలంలం

"Hey, Sonny! Sonn-ee!" called out one of his fellow foremen from the warehouse floor. His voice echoed in the cavernous space.

"What?!" Sonny was strolling across the loading dock floor.

"Boss wants to see you."

He made an about-face and walked toward the boss's office. Narrow steps, two flights, bricks on either side. A flimsy green door. He opened it slightly, knocked, and then fully opened the door all in one move. He made a quick turn and faced the wide and high window overlooking the loading and shipping dock and the boss's desk in front.

The boss was sitting at the desk, an ubiquitous, malodorous lit cheroot dangling from his lower lip. He was adding something up on a multi-key ancient comptometer. He didn't glance up.

"Sit down, Sonny." He looked out over the boss's shoulder through the big window but could only see the moveable cranes on rails for moving unusually awkward pallets.

The boss stopped his additions, wrote down a number off the register, put down his pencil, and stared thoughtfully at Sonny. He had his hand folded across his extended stomach and stared for a significant moment.

"Sonny, you know I like the ponies, right?" The boss's predilection for betting on horses, even before the first legal track opened up earlier that year in New Jersey, was well known. And he generally monthly lost a fortune between the infrequent jackpots, receiving emergency loans (which he always—usually—promptly paid back) from his employees when his bookmaker was present. He perpetually had a pencil with a chewed end over his ear and a small spiral notebook in his hand.

"No, sir. No clue. You actually bet on the horses? Like, who will win? For money?" asked Sonny.

"Cut the crap."

Sonny went mute.

"Look, Sonny, I already know you've been seeing my boss's woman on the side. I seen ya arm in arm on Broad Street one night last week. Hell, if I didn't think I'd get killed, and it wasn't my boss's wife, I'd give her a go too. And in order for me to keep your secret safe with me, I need a favor."

Nearly all on the shop floor knew Sonny was a Casanova, so he let his boss continue with little protest.

"I got a guy who I'm into for a lotta cash, and we're going to hire his son—he's a 'Darkie.'" The boss thought it was being old-school elegant by using that turn of phrase since, he thought Sonny, being Indian, was pretty close to being a Negro.

"He is smartly-dressed, unusually articulate, and has no hair. Bald as a baby's butt, so he really stands out. Name's Mike Jefferson."

Sonny would not have cared if he was from a different planet or worse, a rival brewery. He just wanted to make sure to please the boss, his guarantor of steady employment and promotion (such as you could achieve in a brewery), and prevent his boss's boss from finding out he was romancing his girl. He knew he would just have to deal with his colleagues' racism, but as he felt he wasn't a bigot in any case, he'd be able to deal with it.

Nor did he care about the boss's motives for wanting to hire this guy, Jefferson. Subsequently, because Sonny was motivated to have Michael "work out," he hired him not to load the trucks, which was a bit of work fiercely protected by the teamsters already on the loading dock, but employed him ironically as a "white-collar" worker, keeping track of inventory coming into the plant at the docks and the outgoing finished product. Sonny reasoned he could easily do this because he was already keeping track of his father's betting book in his head, whereas writing it down and having it confiscated by police would surely get him thrown in jail. Sonny put him in that job because it was non-union and he wanted to keep Michael *out* of the union, where Sonny knew racial discrimination would come to the forefront. The teamsters hired Negroes frequently throughout their organization; however, they did it to achieve a political edge rather than any type of racial equality.

As time went on, Sonny mostly laughed along with the group at the racial comments said behind Jefferson's back because it was what everyone did at the time, and so he could feel like part of a group, and because he did not dare oppose it. Sonny took a secret liking to Jefferson because, aside from his skin color and appearance, he found him an incredibly amiable, charismatic, and friendly person—not as bad as Sonny perceived most Negroes.

"Who's the nigger?" a loading-dock bull asked the day Jefferson started work.

"It's *Negro,*" Sonny replied, the pejorative word somehow wounding both himself and Jefferson as well, "and he is assigned to our team." Though he used the word nigger all the time in telling jokes, not realizing its power to hurt, it strangely annoyed him when others used the label to insult.

"Hey, I heard him and Tony," a fat white guy who drove a forklift at an adjacent loading dock began, "were going to put their heads together and make a black and white ass of themselves! *Ha!*"

This was good for a hearty laugh among the crew, and even Sonny chuckled.

"He is not loading our goddamn trucks with us," one of the teamsters said.

"Fine, I've got another job in mind," replied Sonny.

And that is how Michael got the job as inventory supervisor.

No matter how many times he had seen it, Sonny was still completely baffled by what he considered overt bigotry, even though he harbored an ingrained prejudice that he just didn't recognize in himself.

What is wrong with these guys? he thought. *They don't even know this new fella yet, and they insult him before they meet him, and with their idiocy, they gave away a better-paying, cushier job. What dopes.*

࿔࿔࿔

With his distribution and logistics background, Sonny was uniquely qualified to work in the Quartermaster branch of the military to which he was assigned—his time at the brewery working with facts, figures, and products, as well as his directing and managing all types of folks, including different colors, came into play. Sonny had a unique ability to keep hundreds if not thousands of figures and bits of data in his head, and he could put his hands on the location of individual fifty-five-gallon drums of oil (it turns out) as quickly and as easily as he could find particular bulk beer orders for individual wholesalers in northeastern New Jersey. He was exceptionally skilled in this area, though this prowess and ability to remember information would ultimately nearly get him killed.

FOUR

NEWARK: WHERE TO GO?

Sonny was driving around aimlessly now, having tried three taverns already, looking for a place he could plant and feed and then gently get rid of JC so he could return to his family Christmas. How he was going to do that, he wasn't sure.

He kept on jabbering because he was nervous and trying to think of a way to let him down gently about *not* coming to the Jacobs family Christmas at Fabyan Place. While driving north on Route 21, wracking his brain on what to do with his passenger, a lightbulb switched on in Sonny's head, and he snapped his fingers:

"Weequahic Diner, Elizabeth and Hawthorne," he said aloud and then turned to JC. "Look, before we get to where we're going, let's get a bit of food to tide us over." He had suggested this already but repeated it for emphasis and because he was looking to fill the gap of any awkward silences. Sonny didn't know how he could have forgotten the place. Being a Jewish diner, of course, it would be open on Christmas. And all the waitresses were buxom blondies, right up Sonny's alley. And they had great garlic dills.

As soon as he could, he turned off the road, drove under the overpass, and did a U-turn back on Route 21 headed south toward the diner.

Sonny didn't know what was more surprising, the fact that they had already found three places open or that they had been refused entry in all three. He turned toward JC with an apologetic look and was about to speak when JC opened up: "That's okay, Sonny. I been up North before, and this don't surprise me. Thanks for taking the time this morning." JC had noticed some initial reticence on Sonny's part but didn't want to bring it up. He enjoyed his company and just liked being in the presence of his son's estranged friend. He was wise, and he understood Sonny's chatter and babble was due to nervousness, and while he wasn't quite sure why, he had an idea.

FIVE

SONNY OVERSEAS

Just before shipping out to the war, Sonny and some of his men had enjoyed a night out in Philly, giving themselves a proper hangover for the morning. Handing him another beer, his buddy from North Jersey—Franny, also in the Quartermaster Corps—had asked Sonny where he thought they'd end up: Europe or the Pacific. Sonny had looked at him slightly slack-jawed. They were both trained in understanding bits of rudimentary French and German and reading road signs, taught to them so they could understand the idiosyncrasies of British English versus American English; the difference in the gauges of the British, French, Belgium, and German national railroad tracks; and the details of each country's logistics and communications.

"I don't know, Franny. Where do you think we're headed to? If you hadda guess, what would you say?" Their destination was clear to everyone but Franny.

Franny had his heart set on the tropics ever since he

entered the service; he always imagined himself with a hula girl on a South Pacific island. And no matter what they studied in supply school, he imagined the white sandy beaches and warm ocean breezes. He got particularly excited when they were first shown photographs of the beaches up and down France's northern coast. The whole class knew of his obsession and continually wound him up. "Franny, you know they speak French in most of those islands out there—study hard!" And he did study diligently. And his study of French did become useful down the line—just not in the tropics.

❧❧❧

So, with his Quartermaster training coming to an end, in late 1943, Sonny was assigned to his first posting "across the pond" to help with setting up the massive operation that was geared toward invading Europe by Allied troops and supplying them as quickly as possible so that they could rapidly defeat the Nazis.

❧❧❧

One peculiar thing began to unfold for Sonny that he only peripherally noticed during his training: the lack of Negroes training alongside him and the other White enlistees. There were Negroes on the bases where he received his military instruction, but it finally dawned on him that they were there in support roles only. They were doing almost civilian, menial labor. There were none training alongside him to fight, and certainly none in leadership roles. The only ones he saw mostly acted as cooks, servers, waiters at the officers' tables, and busboys. If there was heavy lifting to be done or cleaning of building interiors, it was the job of the Negroes, though dressed in Army clothing. He saw no Negro officers either. And it finally (albeit slowly) dawned on him that he didn't see any Negro managers at the brewery either, which didn't really strike him until he actually witnessed the severe segregation of Negroes and Whites in the Army. Moreover, no one had ever classified what he was seeing; Sonny didn't know what to call it. He didn't comprehend at the time that the Army had instituted "Jim Crow Segregation."

When the US entered World War II, Jim Crow segregation, a pejorative term originally derived from Negro minstrel performers, used to describe institutionalized laws proscribing poor treatment of Negroes throughout the South, had permeated every aspect of American society, mainly in the lower states, including the military. Sonny never knew it existed and certainly didn't have a term to describe it. When Negroes volunteered for duty or were drafted, they were assigned to segregated divisions and usually given only support roles, such as that of cook or mess attendant, or they were assigned grave-digging duty, unlike the more logistical and operational work assigned to White soldiers. The Quartermaster Corps' most menial tasks were done by Negroes, and there was a separate grub line for any Negro servicemen, a rule that also applied to the very few Negro officers he finally saw, if they were not served in a separate canteen altogether. The segregation was as total as it was institutionalized. Negroes protested the Army's treatment quite vociferously, which in a way bordered on being court-martial worthy. They were not successful, and Negro segregation in the armed forces remained official throughout the duration. And while Sonny pondered it from time to time, it did not immediately impact him at that point.

༄ ༄ ༄

Once in England, in the Quartermasters, Sonny became quite proficient at his job. He rose through the Corps' ranks and became the first of the soldiers trained to take significant responsibility for the supplies used by the fighting troops pre- and post-invasion. Though as far as a promotion was concerned, for every step forward, he moved two steps back. He'd already been a lieutenant twice since he had enlisted since his superiors found his photographic memory priceless. But, as everyone knew, he had an eye for a well-turned ankle. And unfortunately, those ankles tended to belong to the wrong women.

"Sonny," began Franny, who was shipping to England with him and who had become somewhat encouraged when he learned before embarking that England was an island, asked him, "why can't you just keep your fly zipped shut? It baffles everyone that you are relentlessly drawn to the girlfriends and or wives of superior officers. Chasing skirts ain't a problem. It is whose skirts you're chasing."

"Franny, aside from the fact that you should mind

your own business, where'd you learn 'relentlessly'?
Ten-cent word for you. I doubt you've used more than a
three-syllable word in your entire life."

"What, did I use the wrong tense?"

"Huh?! Where do you come up with this stuff? Wrong
tense? And also, mind your own business."

"A teacher used to say that to me—wrong tense—all
the time."

"Great. A teacher. Did she also 'teach' to mind your
own business?"

❧❧❧

When he wasn't chasing "birds," as they were called
in England, Sonny was a good sort and stayed with his
men, mostly Negroes from the unit who acted as stevedores, and managed the handling of the smaller crates as
well as the towering cranes that were needed to unload the
ships. Sonny also helped the troops with the actual grunt
work of loading and unloading, which was unusual for a
White NCO.

After they arrived in Liverpool, England, what
followed was three straight days of unloading the ships
and supervising turning the rail track over to the British
sappers and US engineers. At the end of the third day of
nonstop work, they celebrated.

"Boys, in the nearby town—somebody said Bammer
Bridge or Bamber Bridge—there is a bar called the Ye Old
Hob Inn. I'll meet you there: First round's on me," Sonny
said to cheers. Then he added, too quietly to be heard over

their glee, "And if my commanding officer had not found out I was chasing his English counterpart's lady, chewed me out about the necessity of better diplomatic relations, and wanted to see me in his office tomorrow morning for a dressing down, I'd be nowhere near buying any of you guys any drinks. I'd be out with Major Thistledown's lady."

As he approached the pub alone, his men having gone on ahead, he was surprised to see a professionally printed sign that read, "NEGRO TROOPS ONLY."

Sonny saw the sign and said, "This must be a joke," and proceeded inside to meet his men.

He was met with "Sorry, mate. Invite-only party" as he pushed the door open. Sonny was held firmly back by a stout "chucker-out" as the British called them, employed by the public house to make sure nothing untoward happened between the Negro and White soldiers.

"But I see my boys inside," Sonny protested.

"Look, mate, until you start being my boss, no entry. Take a walk." He was tall and burly but missing his leg below one knee, which had undoubtedly kept him out of the military.

Luckily, one of the soldiers from his team was departing arm in arm with a local British girl, and he told the doorman to let Sonny inside. She was a cute, curvy blond who, because of wartime austerity the last few years, was clearly out of practice with both makeup and perfume, tonight having applied a little too much of each.

"Sergeant Jacobs is okay. Let him in," the soldier vouched. "I'll go in with him."

The soldier brought Sonny, as well as the disappointed young lady he was escorting outside the pub, back inside in order to make sure he found the table where the rest of their unit was seated. The men cheered when they saw him as well as the soldier they thought had departed. As Sonny sat down, a pint of tepid beer was placed at the small table in front of him.

"Sergeant Sonny, for you. Warm, but still good."

He took his first drink, and as he looked around the pub, he realized that he was, in fact, the only White serviceman. Indeed, the clientele was all Negro except for the bartenders and several waitresses as well as some White British civilians spread through the house.

"Guys, am I the only White Yank here? I thought the sign outside was a joke."

"Look, Sergeant, we ain't allowed in no White tavern, so we just returning the kindness in Ye Old Hob Inn. We just *happen* to be able to get away with it in this country!" said one of the men to gales of laughter.

Sonny was in the middle of something he never saw in the US and had never experienced until this moment. Dozens of Negroes who, in this case, were also soldiers, congregating in one place, one massive pub, and him in the middle of it. And for the first time in his life, he was the true visible minority and beginning to see what segregation actually was. It made him uncomfortable.

"Tell us a story, Sergeant!" several of his men called out.

Sonny demurred. "You'll have better ones than me. G'head."

As the beers sank in, the men started spinning what at first he thought were yarns, but in fact, they were in earnest. He listened as the seasoned soldiers already stationed there for months regaled him with anecdotes and narratives about life in the UK, which made him feel a little strange—like he was a part of the hierarchy of life that forbade normality to these fellow Negro soldiers. Still, he suddenly realized why one of his fellow sergeants, whom he had bumped into on his way to the pub, told him in a very severe tone, as another Negro soldier passed by them with an English girl, that the one thing he noticed is that the English do not draw any color line and therefore must be pretty ignorant.

"I can't see how a White girl could associate with a Negro," he had said loud enough for the mixed couple to hear him, and Sonny had given him a noncommittal look. The other soldier had seemed indignant that there was "co-mingling" of the races going on in England.

In fact, what Sonny didn't know was that the official rules of segregation applied just as strictly in the United Kingdom as they did in the southern USA. If a Negro soldier saw a White soldier approaching, he quickly had to get himself across to the other side of the road. Many ranking officers in the US Army demanded that pubs be segregated. They tried to do it with Ye Olde Hob Inn, trying to make it White only, but the Negroes resisted, filling it up once duty was over before Whites could enter.

Stories were flying about. One guy cried, "Iram. Iram Lawrence. Tell the sergeant about the thing you read in that multi-color magazine."

Iram, a lanky man with a beaming grin—he looked like he was smiling even when he frowned—began speaking in a dulcet southern United States dialect. As with most of the southern Negroes Sonny had encountered, sometimes he used double negatives in his grammar and incorrect contractions and sometimes singular verbs when plural was called for. But it was always melodious and passionate.

"Some of these people are nuts—some love us, and some are like good old 'cracka' boys from the South. The wife of a local minister, I think they call him a 'veeker' or a 'vikker,' wrote an article that says, and I quote, 'Cross the street if you saw a brother approach; move away if one sits next to you in the cinema; shops should serve them as quickly as possible and make it clear they should not return.' And, 'On no account must colored troops be invited into the homes of white women.'"

"I don't believe it!" Sonny cried.

Iram took out a folded article from an uncommon rotogravure Sunday magazine and handed it to Sonny, who read it over the pub's din with widening eyes.

Iram finished: "Lady was run out of town on a rail." The group all laughed.

"They didn't go as far as burn a cross in front of their house, but they left town and ain't been seen since."

More laughs.

A Negro born and raised in the northern US spoke up, emboldened by the grape and grain. "Unfortunately, the Army is not doing it simply to be mean to us. Most

US soldiers actually believe we are inferior and should be treated that way."

Sonny stayed mute.

Yet another soldier, Tony Powell, pulled out a folded letter from his shirt breast pocket. It was a letter he'd ripped off the wall in the waiting area of the unit's commanding officer's office while waiting with several other Negroes; they were there because they had prevented a fire in a warehouse from spreading to the ordnance. They had to destroy some walls to extinguish the flames, and they thought they had been summoned there to be reprimanded, but in fact, they were being congratulated by the major for risking their lives. He read it on a bulletin board covered with other memos, one on top of the other, and had ripped the sheet down and stuffed it in his pocket before he and the waiting group were called inside to see his commanding officer four ranks above them—a man only typically seen when addressing groups of soldiers numbering in the hundreds. It was a memo written by a senior British officer saying that British soldiers and civilians should not fraternize with "Negroes" because they were "of a simple mental outlook" and lacking "the White man's ability to think and act to a plan."

Sonny read it gravely and said, "This doesn't help the war effort." He looked at Powell. "Who has seen this crap?"

Everyone reached into their shirt pocket and held up a carbon copy of the letter's contents, typed by a friendly Negro clerk for distribution.

"This is awful and embarrassing," Sonny said to himself.

The message contained in that memo did not represent a universally held belief in Great Britain. The British Colonial Office condemned the general's memo as "puerile and prejudiced," but the British War Office did nothing to challenge the US forces' official attitude. They did not want to offend the "helping hand" that Americans provided in fighting the Nazis. But plenty of ordinary Britons did.

Nearly all Britons regarded the institutional racism of the US forces as absurd. A study of popular attitudes found considerable admiration for Negroes among most dock workers and felt that the idea spread by the US Army that they were "stupid and dull" just did not hold up.

In Gloucestershire, an American journalist said that "Negroes were welcomed with open arms on a footing of complete equality" by the English. In many quarters, these northern Negro GIs and a growing number of southern Negro GIs were already unwilling to tolerate the treatment they got from their White counterparts in the Army.

So, it wasn't surprising then that tensions between Negroes and their White American peers could spill into outright violence. Sometimes this was simply because Negroes were pushed around, and other times it was about sexual jealousy—Negro soldiers were charming curiosities, quite popular among young English ladies.

SIX

THE NEWARK SEARCH, CONTINUED

The Weequahic Diner on Elizabeth and Hawthorne, while a good idea, did not work out. As they got closer and tried to pull into the parking lot surrounding the eatery, both Sonny and JC could see it was jam-packed with cars from people who obviously had the same idea. There was a long line of over a dozen people, families standing in the cold waiting to get a Christmas breakfast, and it appeared that the inside was so filled with patrons and the condensation on the interior of the window so thick that Sonny got the impression that arms and legs would be sticking out the windows if they were open. To be honest, Sonny was somewhat relieved as he drove past the entrance searching for yet another place to bring JC. Two of the buxom waitresses he remembered on the drive over had been targets of his amorous endeavors before the war, and thinking about them, and with his recent, more mature shift in attitude about women in general (and, indeed, about a lot of things since his capture), made him ashamed. He quickly put it out of his mind as he focused his full attention on the task at hand. It would not be easy to find a place to bring JC.

The next tavern, an East European Slavic bar, was more of the same, unusually closed on Christmas Day, but the owner had no place to go after his wife came home way too early from last-minute shopping and caught him with their neighbor's wife in their marital bed. He slept in the back of the tavern on Christmas Eve. When Sonny and JC walked in, the bartender, cranky already, threw a glass mug partially filled with beer at them. Ironically, the immigrant owners of most of the taverns they visited that day never knew any type of intolerance before they came to the US—least of all based on how patrons looked or dressed. Their children had fought hard in the war and probably would have been more sympathetic toward the strange duo entering their establishment if they knew of the damage Sonny and JC's son had done to the Germans.

The partially filled glass missed them but hit near the top of the door, shattered, and some beer streamed onto them, along with some shards of glass as they hurried out.

Newark was still separated into ethnic enclaves, pretty much as it had been for the last several decades. They were not the thriving communities they once were, but the owners and patrons of these bars were the ancestors of the boys who fought in the first great war. One would have figured they would be more compassionate, given that they had experienced their own share of prejudice in the country of their birth.

It was back to the automobile, where the snow had started to accumulate again on the windshield. Still warm, the car immediately started. Sonny looked again at his companion with apologetic eyes, though JC understood and was glad someone was there with him.

SEVEN

CURIOUS ENGLAND

The men in Ye Old Hob Inn became more intoxicated and their conversation more animated: "I ain't ever leaving this country if I can help it," said Hector.

"How do you mean?" Sonny asked.

"I mean just that. It is a whole different world over here. It is the world turned upside down," he said emphatically, saying the last two words louder than the rest. "First, we make more money than White English people here. As a matter of fact, we make more money than everybody here. And the people here, the English, are nice to us because they are nice people, not because they are scared. They treat us with respect. They don't know enough to hate us."

Black Tommy spoke up. "A man tipped his hat to me the other day!" and they all laughed because they had seen similar acts of respect.

Ballrooms and dance halls in England had been closed due to lack of business after the start of the war in 1939 but opened again when American troops and their excess cash began pouring into the country. At the same time, there was an extreme pent-up desire to show dance moves on the floor among the troops, especially the Jitterbug by the Negroes, a craze that was taking the US by storm.

The US government had levied an inordinately high excise tax against "dancing clubs" in America due to pressure from music composers and band owners because royalties were not being paid for recorded music, and the hall owners could not at all afford big bands to remain open. But the only thing holding back these venues in England was lack of disposable cash, and the Yanks had this in excess. Working-class girls in search of entertainment and company in England, who had never danced before, made up a large part of the attendees—along with American soldiers, of course.

Jimmy Gaston from Jersey City interjected, "You know the Jitterbug? Me and some of the boys started doing it in here last week to a Dorsey record they had. We got a buggin', and the English loved it. We took the place over, and they wouldn't let us stop. We musta' danced two hours straight before we collapsed, and the girls and some of the boys got out and begged us to show them how to do it. They went nuts, and we didn't have to buy ourselves beer the whole night. And they don't have a lotta cash. Most people loved it, though a few we met outside when we finally left asked if we were doing 'rude' American dancin' inside." More laughter.

The men, including those Sonny did not know who had joined the group, began telling him their own experiences. He felt like he was in an exclusive club where secrets he would have never heard were now being shared with him.

"I have never seen White people treat me like the English do here. The almighty shoe is on the other foot in this country. We got money in our pocket, we got jobs, but most of all, we got respect. More respect than even from our own White US soldiers, particularly the good ole boys from the South."

Some began chiming in: "Got any gum, chum?"—a phrase that kids on the street called out to them. "They are calling us the 'friendly invasion.' Local kids love us. It just takes some kindness…and gum and chocolate," he said to universal chuckles among the group.

"They are even running errands for us like picking up fish and chips from local shops and taking notes to our sweethearts when we can't leave base." The laughter rose among those listening. "And the attention we get is great."

Gaston spoke up again, "Most of the young kids have never seen oranges, apples, and ice cream, and they get it now from us when we can sneak it off the base." The soldiers genuinely cared about the children who lived around their bases and would do things like smuggle them under their coats to movies shown on the base (many of the younger ones had never seen one).

Segregation was not the order of the day among UK citizens, but while it had the support of the government (to keep favor with the Americans) and some un-enlightened citizens, for the most part, it did not work.

"Then why the sign out front?" Sonny asked.

The soldiers looked at each other, and Bobby Harrison, drafted out of college and therefore called "college man," spoke up. Because he had been a burly, athletic man during induction, he was assigned by a bigoted, prejudiced corporal to be a stevedore to take advantage of his brawn rather than his brain. He should have been placed in officer training. He shared in a subdued voice with Sonny a story of a "battle" that took place over a year ago at Bamber Bridge.

"Sergeant, we had a dust-up a while back. Mostly Negro soldiers hot under the collar because of the riots in Detroit back then. Our brothers were protesting dangerous working conditions for sure, but it was mostly a hot summer, and people were pissed off that Negroes were up in White neighborhoods—and the Negroes weren't none too thrilled either. Lots of violence. It just bled over here to Bamber Bridge, a continent away. Just right here. A couple of, shall we say, 'opinionated' MPs tried to arrest some local boys from a Quartermaster truck regiment for walking arm in arm with some local White girls."

"Why?" Sonny asked. "What were they doing?"

Three of the Negroes at this table delayed the swig they were about to take to glance sideways at Sonny. *Was he kidding?* they mused to themselves.

"Negroes were walking arm…in…arm…with some local White girls," the first man repeated. "Things started to get out of hand, I would say, and quite by coincidence, more ofay MPs arrived with machine guns and joined in the altercation, and in response, some of our Negro soldiers raided the local base's armory to arm themselves with rifles and handguns. They did this because rumors started that Negroes were being shot randomly by White military police. Exchanges of fire took place until the early hours of the morning. This has been happening a lot around here. One Negro soldier was killed, and several MPs and regular soldiers were injured.

He took a break in the story, and everyone within earshot in the crowded pub stayed silent.

Another deep swig, and Harrison carried on. "The court-martial convicted dozens, but they got off light because they proved that the MPs were pretty narrow-minded. Coulda been put up against a wall and shot this close to the invasion. Only time I ever seen they blamed Whites for a riot started by Negroes!"

Sonny listened in silence—it was strange to see the sheer boldness of them telling stories about things that would normally be considered mutinous among soldiers. And in the men's eyes, Sonny saw despair as well as fear. He only now realized that he had never heard Negro men speak with such candid confidence, but then, he had never mingled with such a large group of Negro men, sharing food and beer and socializing in an environment where Negroes felt comfortable to speak their minds. Ever. Perhaps they always did, just not typically in front of a White man. It was a different world for him.

༽ ༽ ༽

Sonny's next functional move was to Bristol, across the River Severn's wide mouth from Wales, another part of the United Kingdom. He was being moved to make sure that the goods coming into that port were staged correctly in anticipation of being sent to the very south of England to support the coming invasion. At this point, Sonny had to be on alert 24/7 because while he didn't know when the invasion would occur, he knew it was coming; the rumor mill reported that it would be in May (indeed, the well-publicized "Big Three" meeting of Churchill, Stalin, and Roosevelt indicated it would happen in the spring of 1944), and the deadline was closing in.

༽ ༽ ༽

Sonny was paired with Sergeant Paddy Bucek, a Canadian on loan from their own Quartermaster Corps as some of the supplies were designated for the Canuck soldiers taking part in the invasion. Though the same rank, Sonny took the senior, since the infrastructure of logistics was headed by the All-American-looking Bucek, a stocky soldier with the ubiquitous military crew-cut and beefy hands who was clever with the technical aspects of logistics and Canadian military needs. The two got along well.

After a few weeks, Bucek pointed out after a long day, "Sonny, I think that is it. This side of the depot for Yank forces. This far, far smaller pile over here for the Canadians. Hard work."

"I never thought we'd find all your ammunition," Sonny said. "Wouldn't it have been far easier just to use American weapons?"

"We were in the war a bit longer than you, and you weren't sending us anything! Besides, we needed rifles to train, and they had to come from England."

"Yeah, I got it. It just seems bizarre that we're sending cases of rounds to England, made in the US, for Canadian guns manufactured in England. Seems like a waste of effort."

The supplies being accepted, sorted, and organized to go to the right points in their proper sequence, Sonny and Paddy saw the infantry troops begin to disembark south to prepare to invade.

Once most of the White soldiers had departed, Bristol's nature changed dramatically as it seemed overnight the city was stripped of the soldiers who had been so much a part of its daily life. Most of the military police had left too, and the only GIs in the city were servicemen from the Quartermaster Corps who were still taking goods off incoming vessels and getting them onto the trains moving south.

With most of the MPs gone, discipline among the US troops in the city began to deteriorate, which was when some racial tensions began to heat up. There were many fistfights between Negro and White soldiers in pubs where the segregation rules were not enforced, though such altercations were commonplace among all troops, and not just due to racial divisions.

❧❧❧

The racial tension came to a head in July 1944, similar to Bamber Bridge a few weeks after the invasion, when White paratroopers, not scheduled to be dropped in France until well after the invasion began, were billeted at the same inferior accommodations as were the Negro soldiers. These US paratroopers, many of them White Southerners, were quite disrespectful to their fellow Negro soldiers, chasing them through the streets and challenging them if they saw them walking or talking with White English women.

❧❧❧

Sonny arrived in Bristol in the early morning and went directly to the port area to evaluate the flow of goods, and his keen eye picked up a few blockages, which he immediately fixed. That afternoon he also had the opportunity to cast his eye over the British operation loading trains bringing supplies to the south for shipment to Normandy, and he saved the British hours if not days in transporting goods. Sonny's time learning how to send beer across the US was paying off.

Grateful for his help, the British, assigned a sergeant-major, Dilip Chandra from the British Raj in England for an exchange program to learn more efficient logistics, to find better lodgings for Sonny than the hastily built barracks near the harbor. Chandra, stationed in the UK for a year now, was originally from Bombay, though he had a refined English accent, and he escorted Sonny and another Quartermaster sergeant from Maryland, Sam Cooper, crew-cut and quite fit but not terribly bright.

Taking them to the nicest part of town, Chandra explained, "This is Park Street. Though it took a pounding by the Luftwaffe early in the war, and then again this past May just before we invaded, there's been nothing since, and I dare say their attacks are over. Jerry has his hands full in Normandy."

Chandra continued, "Quite nice with lots of shops, restaurants if you grow tired of your own canteen food and need liquid refreshment from pubs, which I know are important to you Americans. Just like home! I can arrange daily transport between here and the harbor."

Sonny was impressed by the architecture, layout, and cleanliness, but didn't share that fact. "Interesting town. I like the way you have the houses stepped going up the street. What is that tall building? It's massive!"

Sonny was throwing Chandra a bone. It was only two hundred feet tall. Puny by New York City or even Newark standards, but he could see Chandra was proud of it.

Chandra told him it was the Wills Memorial Building and then asked, "This part of town a good place to be 'bunked' as you Yanks say? How does this compare to your hometown? Where was it from whence you hailed? New-Ark?"

"Noork," Sonny pronounced it. "And yes, nearly identical," he lied. "What do you think, Coops?"

"Much nicer than Baltimore," and he meant it.

Honesty was one positive quality of his, but unfortunately it was mostly because his mouth seemed to be attached directly to his cerebral cortex.

"I heard about this section of town from some of the officers, and they recommended it. No niggers allowed. White troops only," he said with surly triumph, and Dilip and Sonny nervously glanced at one another. Cooper apparently did not notice Chandra's skin color, and if he did he was oblivious. Sonny was too embarrassed to admonish Cooper, and as they had just met, he didn't know how he'd react. At the same time, Chandra did not want to take a chance and upset American sensibilities and official policy of supporting segregation if Sonny was a racist as well.

Chandra cleared his throat and explained, "Well yes, your 'White' troops as you call them appeared to complain that your Negroes were allowed to 'roam' all over Bristol. So they slapped in place some rules that made it difficult for them to go about town, anywhere. They could not even come here to spend their money to buy gifts for back home or imbibe in the lovely local pubs. 'White' MPs saw to that. And your Negroes were seething. In fact, a few days before you arrived there was a sort of 'mutiny' when your Negroes working on the docks refused to report for duty, and they just sat tight in their barracks. They just refused to do their duty, and that created a problem. Three of your Liberty Ships were in the middle of being unloaded and another seven were waiting out in the harbor, waiting to dock and unload."

"Jesus, what happened?" Sonny exclaimed. His brow was furrowed, and he was showing real concern.

"Shoulda lined them up against a wall," Cooper said, matter-of-factly.

Chandra continued, "After a brief investigation, your officers cleverly and quite rightly took the dock workers' position as they realized otherwise the boats would remain unloaded, but to be honest, the Negroes *were* being 'abused' as it were, and mostly by your own paratroopers. They also blamed the MPs, transferred several to different cities, and calmed the Negroes' 'agitation,' let's call it. At least for the moment. Though the harassing has continued, somewhat lower-key but still unabated. It could percolate again. And the Negroes are still denied several areas of the town, including here.

"You know what," Sonny said, "let's find something closer to the port."

࿔ ࿔ ࿔

Sonny arranged for Cooper to be sent to another part of the harbor, and he found someone else to room with. Paddy Bucek was a perfect fit. One evening in mid-July he burst into the flat that he'd acquired for them both a few blocks from the harbor. As Bucek ran through the door he abruptly stopped short when he saw Sonny sitting on his bunk reading *Stars and Stripes*.

"What are you doing here?" Bucek asked him.

"Enjoying a quiet dinner with a lovely lady," Sonny sarcastically replied.

"Seriously, what are you doing here?"

"Confined to quarters," he said, then added, "What's the rush?"

"Not sure, but I think a mutiny is underway."

"Where?"

"Park Street."

"And…?"

"Grab your sidearm and helmet. We gotta get there. I have a jeep outside," Bucek said as he grabbed his own helmet and sidearm.

"Confined, remember?"

"It's our Negro stevedores. They finally getting pissed off again…"

"Tell me on the way," Sonny said as he leapt from his bed, got his helmet out from under the bed, and strapped on his sidearm.

As they ran down the steps from their top floor room, Bucek cried out, "They refused orders to report like they did last week and remained in their barracks, and they demanded better accommodations and insisted the paratroopers from the 101st stop harassing them. Then, they piled out of their barracks and started marching toward Park Street."

In a jeep speeding toward that location eight miles away down narrow English roads, Paddy eyed Sonny with a bemused look on his face and said, "Confined to Quarters?"

Sonny screamed over the wind rushing by in the speeding jeep. "Well, I had a free evening and I kind of approached a young lady who, unbeknownst to me, happened to be the eldest daughter of a high-ranking member of the local constabulary, who also happened to enjoy intense but friendly evening card games with Major Campbell. I think she thought I got a bit too 'handsy.' For the life of me, I cannot remember her name."

"Our major? Major Christopher Campbell?" Bucek asked.

"The same," Sonny replied.

"Sonny…," Paddy started.

"Yeah?"

"You've been here two nights. How do you get in trouble in two days?"

"A rare talent?"

Bucek remained silent, smiling to himself during the drive until they reached Park Street. The jeep was still rolling to a stop as Sonny jumped out. He unsnapped his service weapon but did not unholster it. There they discovered an unfortunate aftermath.

Sonny grabbed an MP running by and asked what had happened.

"Negroes acting up," and the MP continued on.

Sonny saw Harrison, one of the soldiers from the pub Ye Old Hob Inn near Liverpool, who had a cut over his eye. He was staunching the blood with a small tablecloth a civilian bystander had given him. Sonny stopped him and asked, "Bobby, what's up? What happened?"

Startled at first that a White NCO addressed him by his first name, and then recognizing him, he said, "Sonny, near as I can make out, two MPs, southern boys, stopped some brothers walking down the street with some White girls. The brothers had a few and weren't hearing from it, so they pulled knives after they were called 'nigger' enough times. One of them stabbed an MP and he was shot dead by the other. It got messy after that and it only started to calm down after they shut down the street at each end and shot our remaining boys in the legs. They're corralling them back to the barracks now. They were even shooting guys standing by the side of the road not taking part."

Sonny let Harrison quickly join the line of Negro servicemen, who were sadly murmuring sedition while returning to the barracks, before something happened to him as well.

The incident and the men being shot in the legs left a deep impression on Sonny. He thought the stabbing of the MP was not justified, but he had never seen Americans so abusive and savage toward his fellow countrymen in this aftermath. Indiscriminate shooting, even if it was in the legs. The MPs would never do that to White soldiers, he thought. The Negroes they shot were shot because they were Negroes, not because they were taking part.

It was well known that the murmuring inciting the soldiers to further violence was, in fact, a lit fuse on a powder keg that could explode if the cause of the tension was not extinguished, so Sonny entered the barracks to reason with his men to completely stand down. Sonny could be extraordinarily persuasive when he wanted to, and in explaining simple math, he excelled.

"Look, fellas, we're at war. You are committing the equivalent of mutiny. The penalty for mutiny is death by firing squad. No questions asked."

"They wouldn't do that to us. Who would unload their fucking boats for them?" asked a disgruntled soldier.

"You think you're the only guys that can unload boats? They hanged a White soldier a few months back at Cornhill Prison for killing an officer. You think they'd hesitate to keep discipline by not doing the same to you?"

The name Cornhill jolted them because quite a few drunk and disorderly Negro prisoners in their unit had recently been released from there, and the stories from the inside were not good. Severe abuse and little food. And though the Negro soldiers had "had enough," the mutiny ended that same night promptly, with the soldiers agreeing to return to duty the next day.

❧ ❧ ❧

Since arriving in England, Sonny was realizing that the things that were happening and the scenes he had witnessed were gradually chipping away at a thick layer of ignorance that was so much a part of him that he hadn't even realized his initial beliefs were "wrong-thinking." He starkly discovered something that he never realized before: Segregation, discrimination, bigotry, and the so-called "Jim Crow Laws"—a term that was only with difficulty piercing the mist of his intellect and that had fully permeated the southern part of the US—was, in fact, an invented phenomenon; it was artificial, and it had to be imposed. And it pervaded the North as well, especially Newark, but in a quiet, insidious way.

He also recognized something he felt was disconcerting: that the true believers of Negro inferiority believed it as part of an almost religious doctrine. It was a firmly held belief. And since it was passed down to them from their society, friends, and parents, generation to generation, they considered believing it a perfectly normal way of life. And they would believe it as strongly as most Americans clung to the concept of freedom. The belief was indoctrinated into them from the time they could first breathe.

ॐ ॐ ॐ

It was clear that Sonny had notable expertise in shipping coordination as well as leading soldiers, and soon, his more recent transgressions against superior officers' women were forgotten. And his eagle eye and conscientiousness provided him another promotion back up to master sergeant just after the invasion on June 6, 1944, and right before he shipped off for France.

When Sonny arrived in the very South of England before heading farther south to jump to France, he came into work the first day, and his keen eye immediately picked up a problem everyone seemed to have missed in a caravan of around thirty trucks (or lorries as the Brits called them) that was preparing to leave for Salisbury Plains.

"What's this?" Sonny asked no one in particular, looking at a clipboard he'd grabbed off a transport about to leave. He scanned the paperwork, jumped into the back of the truck with the shipment, and immediately jumped out again and commanded the driver to turn off the engine. To everyone's annoyance, especially to the men who had just loaded the convoy from nearby trains and were due to come off an eighteen-hour day, he stopped the entire convoy of thirty trucks. He called over the captain supervising the move.

"Captain, what does this say?" Sonny asked, pointing to a line item on the list. Sonny had been a senior officer himself, so he had an air of authority, and though he had only sergeant stripes, the captain paid attention.

"One-fifty-five millimeter shells for the artillery training on the Salisbury Plains. What's it to you?" the captain asked, gaining his personal confidence and footing against a seemingly insubordinate underling. Sonny crooked his finger to the captain and, getting his attention, pointed to the back of the truck, then pulled back the canvas curtain. The captain looked inside, then back at the clipboard, and then turned away from Sonny and screamed, "Lieutenant Dannick, get over here. Did you supervise this convoy?" The lieutenant focused on the captain, then the clipboard, then the back of the first truck and immediately discerned that it should have been 155mm shells transported, as that was what was needed for training the artillery—it should decidedly not be fifty-five-gallon drums of petrol. A lowly staff corporal misread the papers that said 155 shells. Shipping the fifty-five-gallon drums of petrol already loaded instead of crates of 155mm shells would not only have been quite dangerous, but it would also have delayed artillery training for precious weeks.

The sheepish captain stepped over to Sonny after finding all the trucks were loaded incorrectly, thanked him for his diligence, reminded himself to praise Sonny's immediate superiors in his chain of command, and got to work chewing out the men supervising the loading. He delayed the shipment and had the wrong cargo removed from the trucks and the crates of shells loaded—and the shift coming off of hours and hours of work never made the same mistake again.

EIGHT

SONNY ON THE MAINLAND

From January to June 1944, nine million tons of supplies arrived in England along with 1.4 million troops, give or take, and Sonny oversaw a good deal of the next nine million tons of supplies starting in July. Now the challenge was to get the supplies to the soldiers who needed them.

Though most everything was in order, Sonny roamed the supply staging ground in England, with wooden crates stacked yards high, verifying that everything was where it was meant to be, and he came across the items to be sent over by boat in the weeks after the invasion. The smell of fresh cut wood permeated the depot, from pine used for shipping crates to neatly stacked oak that would be needed to replace railroad ties on the continent. He was with a subordinate holding a clipboard to make sure everything was in its proper position in line—and each page was marked "Top Secret" in red with a rubber stamp at the top.

"Lessee, boots, chewing gum, k-rations, grosses of condoms—to be distributed at fifty per man for the last

item. All this stuff needs to be in the soldiers' hands beginning week two, and it is right where it is supposed to be,"
Sonny exclaimed.

"Sir, can I ask a question?" the corporal ventured.

"I don't know, can you?" Sonny replied.

"No, sir—may I?"

"Ask away."

"Fifty condoms per man?" the corporal asked, seemingly impressed. He was only five feet one inch tall and he
never had a way with the ladies.

"You think maybe the soldiers are being a tad ambitious?" Sonny shot back.

Sonny called the armed private who was trailing
them front and center and reached into his pocket to pull
out one of the several condom boxes he always kept "for
an emergency."

"Watch this." Sonny opened the small tin holding
three, rolled out one, and put it over the tip of the soldier's
rifle.

Sonny said, "There is nothing better for it. Keeps
mud from blocking the barrel. But to be honest, the men
are being a tad ambitious, but they're motivated to keep
their guns clean as they may need this supply for other
activities."

"Sir, how long did it take to get all this shit shipped
in?" asked the corporal.

Sonny looked at him with a slightly furrowed brow.

"Sorry, sir. I mean supplies."

"Coupla a months, but it would'a never got here

unless we improvised," answered Sonny. "We had to ship in over a thousand locomotives and twenty thousand freight cars and reinforce hundreds of miles of tracks. For every guy on the front line, there are six of us. So who is more important, do you think?"

"Six of us what, sir?"

"Six to one. Quartermaster soldiers to fighting soldiers on the front lines."

"I had no idea." After a short pause, he added, "Sir, can I ask you another question?"

"I don't know, can you?"

"May I, sir?" he spoke with a slight lisp.

"Shoot."

"It's quite personal."

"Ask!" Sonny was getting exasperated.

"Why are you still a sergeant, and you have all this responsibility?"

"Well, I'll tell you," replied Sonny after a bit of a think. "It would appear that I have pissed off a superior officer or three during our time over here."

The corporal smiled. He knew that Sonny's reputation for having an eye for the ladies preceded him.

"Well, how does that get you busted?" the corporal inquired.

"Well, it does if you catch the eye of your commanding officer's sweetheart." He added after a pause, "And he finds out about it."

"Oh."

"Twice."

"Oh, okay. That'll do it."

"Three times. Okay, five times. With different officers' ladies, of course. As well as with English officers' sweethearts. But sadly, none of my commanders could live without me, so rather than throw me in the stockade to be punished, I was demoted and kept close at hand."

Tiring of the conversation, Sonny finished his spot inspection, signed the lading order, thereby releasing it, tipped abbreviated salutes to the armed guards patrolling the inside of the warehouse who were storing the soon-to-be moved supplies, and returned to his barracks for a much-needed sleep. He was shipping out tomorrow across the Channel to France. Apparently, there was another logistics challenge there that needed a "Sonny" solution, and his major had asked for Sonny precisely because of his expertise. So, after spending time up in the northwest and west regions of England, Sonny crossed the English Channel the next day to France in a supply ship. His time in England had come to an end.

ॐॐॐ

Once in France, Sonny discovered that the Allies' understanding of the French rail system was all for naught. And it was his own side that managed to engineer that waste of time. Allied bombing was so efficient at blasting away at the local rail systems that very little of the network remained. Between Allied bombing and German "destruction upon leaving" or as they called it, "scorched earth," there was little left.

He immediately assessed the situation and conferred with fellow logistic experts of all ranks of the American, British, and French armies. The situation was challenging. They looked at the problem from many angles, thinking about initially rebuilding the rail system, but their colleagues in the Air Force had been fairly methodical and thorough in guaranteeing its destruction. A significant battle still being fought in northern France, the battle of Falaise, where the Germans were about to break east toward Germany and escape, was coming to an end, and they needed a solution fast. The Allies chasing them would need supplies, and this challenge was still not solved.

Two weeks before that battle ended, when indeed a large part of the German Army escaped through a gap in the lines toward their own country, it was a young man skilled in quickly and efficiently distributing Ballantine beer throughout the northeastern United States because of a scarcity of refrigerated transport for kegs that needed to be delivered chilled who came up with the idea of how to get the Allied armies their supplies while they chased the Germans back home. He ran the idea up the line, and his superiors loved it. Simple, elegant, and it could be put together with what they already had at hand. And it became known as the famed Red Ball Express. Sonny explained it to one of the innumerable Quartermaster generals who were anxious to take credit for the brainstorm:

"We put together a series of continuous trains of two-and-a-half and three-ton trucks, a convoy system of about forty thousand vehicles supplying Allied forces moving eastward toward Germany. We move goods via any vehicle we can get our hands on to deliver all the ammo and supplies and food the soldiers required. We have no need for the rail system, which would take months to rebuild in any case." They were all impressed but it was so elegant and simple they couldn't figure out a way to steal the glory.

Sonny became a bit of a celebrity among the higher-ups because of this innovation and was considered once again for another promotion, this time to captain, since he had served as lieutenant twice before—as he told the touring brass who, from time to time, wanted to get a look at the colossal consolidation center he organized.

He didn't share with them that seventy-five percent of the convoy crews were Negroes. Though this task was considered critical to the war effort, the Negroes were not deemed to have the courage, intelligence, or bravery to fight in combat, let alone next to White soldiers, so their contribution was rather diminished by everyone. The Red Ball Express was a resounding success, and once it was working on autopilot for lack of a better word, Sonny with a sense of pride went on to all the supply concentration points throughout France fixing bottlenecks.

భాఖ

In mid-December, Sonny's troubleshooting journeys took him back to La Queue-les-Yvelines, one of the main consolidation points for Red Ball supplies. The express had been shut down weeks already, but there were necessities he discovered that needed to get immediately to the front. He found a substantial mountain of crates destined for the front blocking several points of egress to the supply acres itself. Nearly all the rest of the crates in the area were there for local troop consumption. These destined for up the line were radios and warmer trench coats.

"What the fuck are these supplies doing here? Why were they sent here? Why are they blocking these areas? What bonehead is responsible for this?" Sonny cried to no one in particular.

Though only a sergeant by official rank, he had a commanding voice, and several corporals and other supply sergeants ran to deal with his requests, not being used to an enlisted man screaming questions.

Those converging upon him first were led by a very slight and chubby corporal warmly dressed and holding the ubiquitous clipboard, and he said,

"It was the last shipment to arrive back in the third week of November, sir. Red Ball had finished, and supplies were already going through Le Havre and Antwerp. Nobody had authorization to move 'em."

Sonny gave him quick instructions after eyeballing the stack of crates. He saw a pool of about fifty idle two-and-a-half-ton trucks near the acres of supplies and gave some very brisk orders.

"Requisition twenty of those trucks with forty drivers, the guys standing in front of those fires. We gotta get them to Belgium as soon as possible. Make the calls up the line to make sure fuel is available. If you can't confirm in the next two hours, grab another two trucks and fill them with drums of petrol. What are you standing there for? Move!"

As the convoy was being assembled, Sonny saw a familiar face.

"Jefferson?!"

A fit, bald Negro with a pile of papers in one hand and a pencil in the other walked toward him.

"Sonny! I thought I recognized those screams. What are you doing here?"

The men embraced, stepped back, and took a look at each other, beaming. Though, before the hug, Sonny glanced around to make sure no one saw him clutching a Negro.

"Corporal! Impressive!" Sonny cheered him.

"Master sergeant! More impressive!" Jefferson volleyed back.

"Don't be. I've been busted from lieutenant. Twice. What are you doing here?"

"Same question!"

"Been here in France since a few days after the invasion. Goods had to get through, and someone had to keep them moving through. Somebody had to provide bullets to kill the bad guys."

"Agreed. I was all over England moving stuff through. Easy as moving barrels of beer!"

They both laughed, and Jefferson continued, "Why here now? Am I going to be working for you again? Shit..."

"Things are more sorted up north, and the rail lines are in better shape from Antwerp, so we can start running things directly to the front lines via boxcar from there starting now. We just have an initial batch of cold-weather gear and some ammo to get honchoed to Belgium, and we're going to revive a little 'Red Ball Express' of our own using the old route."

"That ended a month ago," Jefferson pointed out.

"Yeah, got that. Critical shipment of some radios, ammo, and some warm clothes. It's getting a bit chilly at the front," Sonny said.

"Take me with you. Please," Jefferson entreated.

"What? The war is almost over."

"Exactly. I want to get closer to the fighting before this whole thing is over. Maybe get a chance to take some of the bastards out," Jefferson growled.

"Mike, not to take away from your obvious bravery, but we're not fighting teamsters." They both smiled. "I hear these Nazis are pretty brutal."

"Yeah, I know," Jefferson said with a mixture of sadness and anger. "I got here right after D-Day and saw our boys piled up in stacks. I also heard the Nazis were particularly brutal to anyone they captured, especially Negroes, shooting them right away. The fighting is a coupla hundred miles away. If I'm close to where they're shooting, they might let me pick up a gun."

"Mikey, I'm sure knocking off prisoners is going both ways," Sonny said with a pained grimace. He had heard some stories.

"I'm sure, but please, Sonny…please take me with you." Jefferson's eyes showed a great deal of expression.

They were pleading at this point. His eyes became almost wild because he knew with no eyebrows his face needed to show it.

Sonny thought about it ever so briefly.

"Mikey, I'm coming back in less than a week, and I have been ordered to manage shipments going directly to Antwerp from England, and I could use your help there. If you go on this trip with me, you'll be coming right back 'cause I'm coming back tomorrow night. I'll put you on one of the first boats and get you to a depot in Belgium right away. I have an old friend running the place there, a guy named Corcoran, and I'll see that he puts a rifle in your hands and lets you pick off a couple of Heinis."

"Okay, Sonny, I'm going to hold you to that. See you in a week. I'll be here."

❧ ❧ ❧

Sonny hopped into the cab in the deuce and a half at the lead of the twenty-truck convoy in the very final Red Ball Express. The truck hadn't been used in a couple of weeks and the smell of horsehair upholstery permeated the interior of the cockpit, not an unpleasant aroma to him. It reminded him of the smell in the cabs of the Ballantine delivery trucks when he had to drive them around the brewery yard to make room. He was joined by two Negro drivers as they got underway. Sonny commented to them once they were traveling at speed,

"You know, the Germans gotta be wondering where we're getting all this stuff from and would probably be shocked senseless if they knew how much there really was. Christ, I know I am. I don't know why we're sending this—this whole mess will be finished in the next coupla weeks." Sonny said it to no one in particular, but his driving companions took note because they liked the idea that the war would be over soon. Sonny, like everyone else, wanted to return home, maybe even in time for December 25.

In an effusive mood, he bragged to the men in the cab a bit. "The Red Ball was one of the most successful things I ever worked on, at least according to the military," Sonny immodestly explained, "if I do say so myself."

࿎࿎࿎

Just after midnight on December 16 in the early morning hours, Sonny had arrived into Gouvy, conveniently right near the middle of the main Boigny-Bastogne rail line. The last link in the Allied supply chain was the town, and he was looking forward to a warm meal and a safe and comfortable place to sleep.

When he arrived, he connected with the one NCO still awake, an old friend from basic training: fellow sergeant Rich "Corc" Corcoran.

"Corc! People still think you're a college boy?"

"Hey, Sonny, what are you doing here? Coming for some winter R&R? Frankly, you ain't getting nothing here but rest. No babes, little booze, and plenty cold. You shoulda stayed down south. At least it's not as cold." Corc enjoyed telling folks he hailed from Princeton, New Jersey, and was thus treated with reverence by all as a "college boy"—it was merely where he had lived, and though intelligent, he had never set foot on the university's campus. He made the depot work run like a Swiss watch and was well regarded as a hard worker and competent non-com. They walked along the length of the depot, with crunching snow underneath and the delightful smell of burning wood permeating the area. After their greetings, Corc spoke up.

"Christ, Sonny, why are you bringing more ammo up to us? We got plenty of ammo. What we need are warmer clothes," Corc cried out over the revving engines of the trucks, the drivers hoping to keep the cabs warm.

Sonny yelled back, "Full winter gear and uniforms are not expected till probably January at the earliest. I did bring some in this shipment. I don't know why you need the ammo either. Some colonel demanded it, but the Germans are beaten already, and if they do fight us, it won't be until March. We have a football game coming up day after tomorrow to blow off some steam. You interested in playing?"

"Can't. Gotta leave tomorrow since I'm accompanying a major shipment by boat to Antwerp. Shoulda gone directly from England, but with the Red Ball being stopped last month, we got tons of equipment and supplies that gotta be restacked in boats and sent up to the line that way.

They stepped into the rail station waiting room, which had been commandeered as the NCO barracks, which also had a fireplace and was the source of the delightful wood-burning smell. Sonny and Corc spent the evening catching up and swapping stories about where the easiest local women could be found as well as drinking plenty and generating a potent hangover for the morning.

The depot was only protected by a straggly group of soldiers—many Negroes who were being poorly treated by Allied rank and file, while many of the "real" White combat soldiers were in the rear enjoying movies and warm meals. These Negro guards were warmly clothed from dwindling winter stocks, but they had little else. Even constructing warming fires outside were forbidden this close to the front, so they ate their tinned rations, warmed by keeping them between their thighs for body heat. Really miserable.

 తఁ తఁ తఁ

That same early morning, while Sonny and Corc were still reminiscing, at 5:30 a.m., Operation *Wacht am Rhine*, or the German Ardennes campaign, was launched by the enemy with horrific force. It was just miles away from the soldiers who were guarding and dispensing supplies from the Gouvy depot and from the newly arrived mini-convoy of Quartermaster soldiers, Sonny among them.

NINE

THE BATTLE

The Allies, of course, knew the Rhine River at one point was the border between two long-term adversaries, France and the Fatherland; so, for the Germans, it was appropriate to call the attack the "Watch on the Rhine," chosen to give the impression that it was a strictly defensive plan—should word of the assault ever leak to the Allies.

The German attack was colloquially referred to among the Allies as the Battle of the Bulge, named for the colossal insertion or "bulge" the enemy forces made into the Western Front. For the last several months, they had been surreptitiously amassing three hundred thousand troops for a sneak attack with the intention of taking the Allies' main supply port in Antwerp—with the hope of disrupting all Western movement toward Germany and giving them a pounding that would confuse them and get them to sue for peace.

Hitler's generals thought it was mad, particularly

given that the Russians, a much more significant threat, were eating up the miles toward Germany and Berlin—and they didn't think the Western Allies would be that easily cowed. But Hitler had planned it months before during early summer just after the Normandy invasion and correctly predicted that the Allies would need Antwerp as a supply junction if they were ever to make it that far in their campaign. It was a prescient move on Hitler's part, though the Allies were not as easily shaken as he would have liked.

∂∂∂

In between gulps of beer, Sonny and Corc heard something—something that went through the air above Sonny and Corc at incredible velocity, followed a few seconds later by the report of an explosion.

"What was that?" Sonny asked Corc.

"We're shelling the Germans," came the reply.

"No, it sounds like it is going the other way."

Immediately, one sounded like it was coming directly toward them.

They looked at each other. "Incoming? *Incoming!*" they both screamed.

They dove for the deck and covered their heads, and the shell hit the nearby tree line, felling four trees. Because they were designated as "supply" and so protected behind the combat lines, no one had bothered to dig any foxholes, and they were dangerously exposed—not only to the elements but to any enemy who happened to be nearby. Many of the White Quartermaster soldiers were billeted in the nearby town with warm beds and showers. The company of mostly Negro soldiers was left to guard the depot, housed in tents that barely sheltered against the cold. They hadn't bothered to dig fox holes either, but they were armed.

The Germans pounded the area with mortar and artillery barrages but had yet to hit the depot directly as the terrain did not leave adequate spotters for their gunnery. Some of their tanks and infantry sorties were pushing toward the supplies; some intelligence of the riches held in the depot had reached them from the capture of some terrified, poorly trained Quartermaster soldiers days before, and though their senior German officers were more interested in petrol than clothing and food, the lower echelons, though motivated by victory for the Führer and Fatherland, particularly desired warm undergarments and full stomachs as much as advancing on the Allies.

The Germans continued to plow their way through on their way toward Antwerp, the source of supplies for the advancing Allied armies and an incredibly rich collection of stores in depots that could significantly enhance the Germans' aggression in and around Gouvy—right where Sonny's Quartermaster supply depot was located. Shipments there from Antwerp were stored in an orderly fashion for distribution: spare weapons, all manner of ammunition, high explosives, K-rations, D-rations, self-heating soup cans (in a variety of flavors, including tomato, oxtail, pea, and mock turtle) as well as initial installments of warm winter coats, helmet liners, grosses of wool caps and socks, and millions of cigarettes. Things the Germans troops desperately wanted.

❧❧❧

The outskirts of the forty-acre depot and many of the items in the rear were small arms ammo as well as larger shells for the 105 and 155 howitzers—two items coveted by the Germans because they had the same-caliber guns. German shelling sparked bedlam, with men running back and forth, finding positions to defend the place and keeping out of the way of the incoming.

Corc ran up to Sonny. "Corc, what do you hear?"

"Sonny, I got through to command. We've been ordered to hold fast, as long as we can. Can we do this with Negro soldiers?"

"Look at them, Rich." He pointed toward the troops returning fire. "These guys are energized. They've been well trained, though none of them have picked up a rifle since basic training. Ferocious fighters, given the chance.... Look, they're already taking the initiative dispensing ammo and food. They're scared, but they're good." More bullets flew overhead, and Corc and Sonny hit the ground and leopard-crawled behind some crates.

The Germans carpeted the area with mortar fire, but their rounds were falling curiously short of the supplies. Corc furrowed his brow and said out loud, "Why are they doing that?"

"They need this stuff," Sonny said. "That could play

to our advantage." As a result, the Germans received far more resistance than they anticipated and were dealt far more casualties than they'd expected.

Sonny pointed toward the rear of the depot. "That is what they're here for. The fifty-five-gallon drums and Jerry cans filled with petrol. It seems like a lot, and I don't know how big their assault is, but I'll bet they need it to get to Antwerp. They've got expert troops trying to pick us off, and they're being careful not to hit the gas or the shells. We gotta get ready to blow it all."

Sonny and Corc, with about a dozen other men, were piling the cans up, one on top of the other, to facilitate blowing them to smithereens before the Germans got them.

While they were constructing them into a small mountain, Corc asked between heavy breaths, "Sonny, why are they called Jerry cans?"

"Huh?" Sonny wasn't sure he'd heard him correctly.

"Sonny, why are these cans called Jerry cans?"

"You're kidding, right?" Sonny was sweating profusely, though the temperature was below zero. "We're getting flattened by gunfire and mortar, and you want to know where the name Jerry can came from?"

"I kinda really do. We're likely not going to get out of here alive, and it is something I could never figure out. Did we steal the idea from the Germans?"

"Well, yeah, kinda," he said, reaching for and passing the cans as briskly as he could.

"We used large fifty-five-gallon drums to transport

gas in bulk, which is too heavy, and if punctured, was 'goodnight, nurse.' The German cans are easy to make from pressed steel and hard to puncture. Very safe," he said, grunting and passing. "They designed the cans. Did you miss that day in basic training?"

"But why 'Jerry'?" Corc pressed.

"Honest to God—seriously—we're about to get shot or blown to kingdom come, particularly if a bullet or mortar shell hits anything here." He motioned toward the cans they were moving. "They'll never find our bodies. Concentrate. Is it that important?"

"Yeah—we're not likely to get out of here alive," Corc repeated.

"You said that already. Understood. Thanks for the reminder. Well, you know the Brits call the Germans 'Jerrys,' right?"

"Yes, could never figure that out," mused Corc. "Why?"

"You know what a chamber pot is, right?"

"Yes," Corc replied. "We used them when billeted in the UK—nobody in town except the commissioned officers had indoor plumbing. We had to go downstairs and out the backyard to an outhouse. We had chamber pots under the bed to take a piss in the middle of the night if needed."

"Did you have a tall one or a short one?" Dirt was kicked up in front of them from incoming bullets, and rather than moving their position, they worked more quickly.

"A tall one," responded Corc. "These guys are awful shots," he added as he continued shifting supplies.

"They're really not," Sonny told him. "They don't want to take a chance of hitting the gas, but they wouldn't mind stopping us at what we're doing."

"Okay. So, a tall chamber pot...," Corc murmured.

"You think if you turned it upside down, it would look like a German helmet?"

More small arms fire zinged past their heads as if for a brief moment their enemies had forgotten that the mountain of cans they were building was no longer directly behind them.

"So, yeah, upside down they look like army helmets, but not necessarily German ones," Sonny continued.

"So what?"

"Well, the Brits thought the German helmets looked like chamber pots, and they call the pots 'Jeroboams,' or 'Jerrys' for short. That's why the Brits call them Jerrys."

"Ahh...." Corc was satisfied.

Just then, three soldiers next to Corc and Sonny fell nearly simultaneously with bullets in their back and neck, each because they had stepped into the open area just adjacent to the gas mountain. The remaining troops hit the dirt and crawled as quickly as possible behind nearby wooden crates holding rations, which were now being splintered apart by rapid German gunfire.

There was return fire by men in the depot because one of the German shooters inadvertently used a tracer bullet, and that area along the tree line received hundreds of rounds in return, which promptly silenced them.

Despite the incoming weapons fire, the Germans were taking a gentle approach to capturing the depot—they called in the snipers they could find within their ranks and tried to pick the defending soldiers off with gunfire—doing their best to capture the storage area, mainly for the petrol. The Negroes and all Quartermaster soldiers defending the depot did not have the same restrictions, and they had behind them all the ammo, grenades, and warm clothes in the world. They fired at the Germans with abandon and pushed them back on several occasions over the first day and part of the next. But their resistance was waning; though the Quartermaster Corps were fighting with intensity, the German fighters' experience, much of it honed on the Eastern Front against the Russians, soon began to show.

৵৵৵

"Sonny, the captain was shot through the eye running across the compound. You're in charge now," yelled Corc during a slight lull in the battle. Sonny became their de facto leader, though he only marginally outranked everyone else there.

"Shit," Sonny replied, not really wanting the responsibility, but he had the presence of mind to make some reasonable decisions calmly. He tried to maintain a semblance of order because of his senior experience and the fact that he was confident and comfortable with the fighting skills of the Negroes.

When he took command and realized how close the Germans actually were, Sonny decided to initiate the rapid-setting fire to the existing stocks of ammo, fuel, clothing, and food before heading west, back toward the safety (or so they thought) of more superior Allied troop positions. He gave orders to make preparations. When the troops at the depot got wind that this was probably going to happen, their attacks on the Germans become more ferocious.

Corc ran back from giving the prep order to destroy the dump and screamed over the din to Sonny, "Christ, I don't think we can cover the forward infantries' backs."

"Let's continue to prep the demolition. Distribute grenades as we might not get everything before we leave. Though for now, let's start with the food and follow with the winter gear. Leave the ordnance and gas for last," Sonny screamed back.

"Why?"

"You want to be nearby when the gas and ammo blows?"

"Good point."

The depot was once again reliving the bedlam of the initial battle, with soldiers running about, putting crates of small arms ammo in jeeps and trucks heading away from the oncoming Germans, distributing rations (but not clothing) among many of the soldiers running toward the incoming fire, Negroes and Whites mixed and both equally scared.

Corc ran back up to him with some more information after executing some of Sonny's commands.

"Sonny, we're almost surrounded. We think the main force bypassed us on their way to Bastogne, but they left some bastard snipers to pick us off one by one. You're right, they want the gas. You think that's why they haven't flattened us yet?"

"Of course. They want what we got, and they ain't gonna get it," Sonny answered confidently.

Corc then added, "I heard the Germans also broke through into St. Vith, and there was nothing between them and us, so that's it. We're fucked, except there's one road open due west and we might be able to slip through their lines. Let's go!"

"Think we should verify we should blow the dump?" Sonny asked.

"Tried to. Can't. Phone lines were cut," Corc replied. A bullet grazed his helmet and knocked it off, but not before spinning on his head. He picked it up and placed it back on his head, and Sonny replied after smiling at the way his helmet spun before hitting the ground.

"Radio?"

"We gave them away, and the others are still in their crates—no batteries—coming in the next convoy."

"Then let's light it up and get the hell outta here," Sonny said.

They heard incredibly rapid gunfire extremely close, but Corc wasn't sure if the rounds were incoming or return. He asked Sonny.

"Corc, you really didn't pay attention during basic, did you? It's German fire. They got better powder so their guns can fire faster. Shithead."

"I forgot," he said, self-conscious.

The men, and there were about fifty left, set fire to the depot's periphery, then grabbed rifles, sidearms, and again as much ammo as they could carry, and headed for the road in a deuce and a half. They were a little less than three hundred yards away from the fires when they found their escape blocked. Three three-ton trucks blocked the road—all turned over, one burning—making the road impassable. They ran back to the railway dispatch center and tried to tamp the hell out of the fires set only moments ago with whatever they could grab—snow, earth, tarpaulin. They were highly motivated as the fire was spreading to the ordnance and petrol near the far edge, and unless it was put out reasonably promptly (as there were no hoses or water for the fire pumps—the lines were frozen solid), the depot would be on the map for an entirely different reason. Before it blew them, the depot, the Germans, and most of Gouvy to kingdom come, the Americans needed to come up with another solution.

The soldiers were scared but disciplined. If and whenever they happened to get a moment to contemplate what was happening, they became afraid. Very afraid. But they still did their job.

Sonny realized that the Nazis hated the Jews, and since Germans were well-known racial lunatics, he reasoned Negroes fell into the category of "hated races." Though for the first time in his life, Sonny faced an armed enemy known to be racial bigots who would probably throw American Indians into that mix if anyone figured out his race, and it petrified him. Very suddenly, he no longer dismissed his own jokes and comments as "fun" and understood more clearly what it must have been like for his Negro comrades.

Sonny gathered the men and ordered, "Take up defensive positions and try to hold the Germans back from the supplies as long as we can—maybe relief is on the way."

Sadly, Sonny would soon find that it was not the case.

Some of the men uncovered a 105mm howitzer at the back of the yard with several cases of shells, and they let out a muted cheer. Sonny called out, "Okay, let's fire across the perimeter, about one mile, all air bursts. Who has spotter experience?"

He looked at their blank faces. Some had received the training, but none wanted to venture beyond the tree line and the depot's relative safety.

Sonny had previously come across two complete walkie-talkies and put them on the front seat of the one undamaged deuce-and-a-half truck for safekeeping. He retrieved them and gave one to a trusted man remaining with the makeshift gun crew, jumped behind the wheel of a smaller truck, and went forward to reconnoiter and spot the shell-falls. He drove as fast and as close to the front lines as he could. A quarter of a mile away from camp, however, while trying to avoid explosions from incoming German shelling on the road ahead, he swerved his truck to avoid the explosions from the projectiles falling from the sky, and the vehicle careened down a snow-covered embankment.

"Shit. This is a bit uncomfortable," he said jocosely because he thought he had dodged the danger. But he had not. The truck was about to hit a tree when another blast went off just near the cab of his vehicle, and he jerked the wheel to the left as the back of the truck barrelled into that tree. He flew over the steering wheel and through the windscreen and landed forty feet away in a giant pillow of fresh snow. He relaxed as he fell, and though he'd hit the ground hard, he didn't realize he was in shock and a level of comfort fell over him as he thought he was no longer part of the stress of the battle itself. The impact of the accident would soon render him unconscious, and his thoughts briefly flashed on his captain's girl, Ethel, a svelte and attractive brunette, whose eye (and much more) he had grabbed back in England. He thought of being back home with his family on Fabyan Place on Christmas last year. He could smell the needles of the trees in the wood and thought of the Christmas tree in the parlor last holiday season. And he thought of the young ladies in his neighborhood in Newark he had left anxious with his departure for the war. And then his mind went blank.

TEN

CAPTURE

It was snowing heavily now near Gouvy. Sonny had no idea how long he'd been unconscious, and though his arms were numb with cold, he thought it had only been moments.

He woke up flat on his back with his head tilted forward, pillowed by a rock. He hadn't hit it hard when he fell, and he was stretched out in cold, powdery snow. He could hear his breath, though his hearing was muffled. He was staring at his naked toes and wriggled them to confirm ownership, struggling to remember how he got this way. He could hear voices and metal clanking, but the air was still for some reason as if his ears were covered by bolsters of down—until, that is, the sky was momentarily pierced by a loud explosion. He looked around but his neck hurt as he turned his head. Sonny tried gazing down—he could not feel one leg, and there was a garnet red stain very slowly spreading through the snow where his limb was supposed to be. Fortunately, his leg was still there—just a superficial scrape. He could see both his warm boots about thirty feet away, comically still standing upright beside each other as if supporting an invisible person. He briskly got up, ran over, and put on his boots. The rest of his body was still quite warm as he was wearing the best Army-issue winter clothing the military could provide. An advantage of being the Quartermaster Corps in the richest army in the world is that you got the first choice of everything, and the entire corps took advantage of that. Incredibly, his warm, wool socks were still sitting in his boots.

It gradually came back to him why he had been supine in the woods—the Germans had attacked the Allies at the least likely time through the least likely area of Belgium.

The sound of the explosion was the last thing Sonny heard a split second before a rapid and powerful rush of air had thrust him out of the truck, though he had no idea it was a concussive blast that hurled him back into the snow as his truck hit a tree. His wristwatch and compass strapped to his arm had flung off during the accident, he lost his bearings and had no idea which direction was east or west.

As he came to, he tried to orient himself. As it was lighter now with a heavy overcast, he walked toward what he thought was a setting, blanketed sun. In fact, the sun was so low in the sky, he thought for sure that it was still morning—and he had walked erroneously eastward.

A trick of the air currents allowed him to hear German voices as if they were closer than they actually were—he crouched and continued toward what he thought was sunset. A western route, he thought, would be safe as long as the Germans had not passed his position. He came across an enemy tank with flames jumping through its open hatches.

How had the Germans come so far into Belgium territory? Just behind the tank, he saw a young soldier—a boy, actually, in a Waffen SS uniform carrying an MP 35 submachine gun—and froze still. The boy had been crouched, relieving himself behind the burning vehicle. They saw each other at the same moment, and Sonny became stone-still when he saw the gun muzzle quickly turn, and pointed inches from Sonny's head as it went off.

The bullet grazed his skull, and he ran around the backside of the tank, but the youngster soldier ran around the other way and pointed the gun at his face once again, shouting "*Halt! Hände hoch.*" He poked Sonny's chest with the muzzle of his rifle. Hard.

"Okay, okay. I got it. You got me."

"*Leere Taschen.* Empty pockets!" The German supplemented his commands with English to make sure he was understood.

"For what?" asked Sonny.

He was punched in the gut with the rifle butt as another German soldier joined them, but the first kid kept his finger on the trigger. His gun veered to one side and went off, and the bullet hit a tree. German soldiers now joining them ducked lower at the sound of the gunshot, and the German soldiers accompanying other prisoners started to scream at the young soldier who had captured Sonny.

Though he was captured and had blood flowing from his head, Sonny got off easy. It appeared that the child soldier had already shot two other Americans who were lying dead near the tank. More soldiers and prisoners joined the quickly growing group. They went through his now empty pockets, but after a moment, Sonny collapsed with blood pouring from his skull. He was forced to stand back up.

Experiencing this, though, Sonny preferred to look at the positive aspects of his imminent incarceration. He mused, *This could be much worse. I could be wounded or dead. Mommy and Daddy told me that during the Great War, the Germans were accused of committing atrocities, and none of it was true. All the Allied countries were trying to boost enlistment. Same shit is happening again. I doubt the SS are as brutal as everyone says they are. They're just trying to get us to fight harder.*

It turned out that just the opposite would occur in this war. The captured soldiers refused to believe in the rumors until they had proof, and unfortunately, they got it. Most significantly, the Americans got their first inkling when they fought against Hitler's Waffen, or armed, SS.

Sonny was immediately gathered with other captured soldiers into a German mustering point on the edge of a clearing near the tree line. They all had been stripped of anything of value, and their most valuable possessions at that time were their heavy gloves, warm coats, wool caps under their helmets, and boots. The prisoners all began to genuinely feel sorry for themselves and quite a bit fearful.

Oddly, while the American prisoners could see hatred

in the German eyes, they were relieved when they started marching toward another location, led by their conquerors. Those marching believed now that they would not immediately be shot upon capture.

However, a few yards inside the tree line, just outside of their sight, another commotion and shooting took place that involved their comrades not present in line.

Sonny asked in an undertone to his fellow prisoners, "Is this all of us? Some guys must have got away."

"Who we missing?" a soldier quietly blurted out to no one in particular.

"Where are Charlie, Zeke, Snack, and Black Sammy?" Sonny said. "I don't see them anywhere. In fact, I don't see any of our Negro soldiers."

No answer from his friends. Only shouts of German guards could be heard.

Sonny at one point was pleased to see Corc in the line, the last American he saw before he was injured and captured. When the guards' backs were momentarily turned and walked farther away, he sidled up the column to be just behind him.

"Corc, thank God you're okay. What's the latest?"

"Aside from being captured, not much. Sonny, where you been?"

"Otherwise occupied."

"Seriously?"

"I think I wrecked a deuce and a half and got knocked out trying to spot for the 105. Corc, you seen any of our Negroes? I can't find a one."

Corc was afraid to respond because he noticed a German coming closer and listening. He had a knowing look, giving the impression that he likely spoke English.

When the soldier turned his head and walked away up the line, Corc whispered to Sonny, "I think they were shot right away—they're still shooting them. They're just in the woods." He nodded in the direction of the tree line and the sound of sporadic gunfire just out of sight. "They first made them strip to their underwear and then made them hand over their outer clothes. I saw them shoot half a dozen while they were shivering, and they walked the rest into the woods when they saw we were watching. I think that shooting we just heard was to finish them off."

"I don't believe it," Sonny replied, his face now a mask of anger and rage combined with helpless fear, something he had not experienced before "What types of animals are these guys? We're all just prisoners, for Christ's sake."

An officer who had been billeted in town was brought to join the group, and he was being escorted to the front of the line. He overheard the tail end of the conversation and was stopped a moment while his guard lit a cigarette. Standing near Sonny he said in a low tone: "I saw it coming over here. They stripped them and shot them. Just before I was captured, I heard on the radio reports that SS bastards also captured and shot a dozen Negroes from the 333rd FAB. A few miles east of here." He received a hard shove with the bayonet of the German escorting him, which pierced his shoulder and caused him to let out a scream. Most of the men knew the 333rd had a rare combat field artillery regiment of Negroes, a one-off. When Sonny heard this story, he was horrified but strangely simultaneously flooded with personal relief. "I'm glad I didn't bring Jefferson along on this trip," he said to himself.

かかか

Sonny and the group he had been captured with were mustered with a still larger group of prisoners—a few of whom he had previously seen running through the depot in retreat to the west. A few were from his own group, though it took a few moments for him to realize once again that none of them were the unit's Negroes. If he could have strolled over a few yards beyond the tree line, he would have seen the twisted corpses, their faces almost blue-white from the cold as the blood drained from their bodies.

He was lined up with a group of friends, some he recognized from basic training, and to keep up morale, he tried to crack some jokes to make light of the situation, to some encouraging laughter.

"These guys are so serious—they get that way from all the sauerkraut they eat, and probably that's why we named them 'krauts.' Yeah, that's why their faces look like they're shitting all the time."

Corc, standing next to Sonny, had the misfortune of blurting out a guffaw at the joke as a young guard happened to look directly at him. The soldier walked up to him, turned his rifle around, and caved in the front top of his skull with such force that Sonny, standing nearby, was splattered with blood. Corc fell like a rag doll, and Sonny was absolutely aghast. He was filled with almost uncontrollable rage and he started to lunge toward the offending guard, but a gun was immediately leveled at his face and he stopped dead still. One American prisoner who saw this started running to the tree line—he made it five yards before he was shot in the back, and the German soldiers, all warmly dressed, some with prisoner overcoats on top of their own and all heavily armed, started prodding the remaining men directly east using the ends of their bayonetted weapons. And they had no qualms about pushing quite diligently.

As the guards moved forward among the captured troops, the guys in the back could converse in whispers.

"Christ, these guys are playing for keeps," Sonny said in a very loud whisper.

"Shut the fuck up—you want to get us all killed?" a nameless soldier said.

And Sonny took the advice as promptly as it was given.

He was grouped at the end with some other stray soldiers who were found hiding in the woods. By now, he had lost his boots and his heavy coat—an enemy soldier had taken them quite eagerly since they looked brand new (which they were).

They began marching in slushy snow toward an unknown destination, and Sonny was nearly barefoot but for his socks and the thin boots he had taken off a corpse after his own were confiscated. Serious stragglers at the end of the line were given one admonishment, and if they failed to promptly comply and march more quickly, either because of pain or fatigue, they were immediately shot, which kept motivation high among those remaining toward the front of the column. These soldiers were capable of great cruelty, and Sonny, fully comprehending what happened to his Negro colleagues, thought about what they might do with half-breeds such as himself if they discovered his origins.

The conditions were so cold, and they were so ill-clad for the weather, that many soldiers died with each mile they walked, either by shooting or exposure.

ELEVEN

DEEP REGRET

Dot walked in the front door at Fabyan Place at about 5:30 in the afternoon after work. She saw her dad's winter coat on a hook inside the front door—it was unusual for him to be home so early in the day. He was working on constructing a small office building in midtown New York City, and by the time he quit, he got a subway to Penn Station in New York, and then managed to catch a train to Penn Station in Newark—followed by the subsequent three-mile walk home. He usually didn't make it through the door until long after 7 p.m.

Worried, Dot went into the front parlor, where she found Mom and Dad sitting on the couch together. The perennial scent of the carefully decorated Christmas tree provided an incongruous backdrop to the moment, as did the smell of the savory pot roast and macaroni coming from the kitchen. Angus Sr. had his right hand around his wife's shoulders and was gently stroking her left forearm with his other hand. Mom was sitting there, silent, head down with her eyes closed. She busily worked her rosary beads, her lips moving with the recitation of the prayers.

As Dot walked in, she started to blurt out "Wha—"

She didn't finish the question as her dad had heard her coming in and pulled his hand away from his wife's forearm long enough to put his index finger to his lips. Dot, still wearing her winter coat, sat across from them in the comfy chair, which gave its familiar creak, and just stared at her parents. Her mom opened her eyes briefly at the noise and her dad said softly, "Sonny is missing in action."

They all sat silently for a moment. Mary Jacobs acknowledged her daughter's presence with a glance and a nod and then closed her eyes once again, rubbing her beads, praying for Sonny.

Eileen walked in the front door moments afterward in her WAVE uniform. She was delivering dispatches to New York City, and since the train to her base in Connecticut didn't leave till ten that evening, she decided to stop in to see family in Newark. She'd figured she'd be able to board a train at Penn Station in Newark by 9 p.m. and make it to New York in time to catch her train back to her base.

Eileen saw her mom silently weeping on the couch and was about to ask what was going on when Dot quietly said, "Sonny is MIA." She spelled out the letters.

"Sonny changed his name to Mee-A?"

"No, scatterbrain. He is missing in action."

Eileen abruptly left the parlor and started crying but stopped when she was diverted by the front doorbell. She disappeared and returned, holding a yellow envelope.

"This is for Mom," she said and handed it to Dad. Mary cried a bit harder as she thought it could be more bad news.

Her father opened the envelope and read the printed words.

WESTERN UNION
MRS MARY JACOBS 50 FABYAN PL

SECRETARY OF WAR DESIRES ME TO EXPRESS HIS DEEP REGRET THAT YOUR SON MSTR SERGEANT ANGUS F JACOBS JR HAS BEEN REPORTED MISSING IN ACTION SINCE TWENTY DECEMBER IN LUXEMBOURG IF FURTHER DETAILS OR OTHER INFORMATION ARE RECEIVED YOU WILL BE PROMPTLY NOTIFIED = DUNLOP ACTING THE ADJUTANT GENERAL

❧ ❧ ❧

Her dad read it, then handed it back to Eileen. After scanning the words, she passed the note to Dot, then looked up. "How did you know, Mommy?"

"They called a few hours ago to tell me the telegram was coming, but they couldn't tell me much. I called Daddy's foreman, and he came right home," her mom said.

Mary stood up and headed toward her bedroom. "Let's get dressed and go to church."

They all promptly rose and prepared to head to church to pray for Sonny's safe return, but none of them, including his mother, ever thought they'd see him again.

TWELVE

ROAD EAST TO CAPTIVITY

The SS Hitler Youth soldiers, Sonny's captors, represented the "future" of Hitler's Germany.

The SS was initially set up as a paramilitary group acting as Hitler's personal bodyguard detail in 1924. Eventually, the organization grew so large that an entire army group was ultimately established with over 285,000 personnel: the Armed or Waffen SS.

The Hitler Youth, on the other hand, was set up in the same fashion as the Boy Scouts in America or Britain, and members were inculcated with Nazi doctrine from a very early age, taught of the purity of the Aryan or German race and the inherent inferiority of all other races, especially the Jews.

This philosophy was indoctrinated to the point where it (and Hitler) overtook their lives, and when they had reached the right age, only the most fanatical Hitler Youth, extremists to this cause, were recruited by the Waffen SS. These were the soldiers on the front line of the attack that

December. This fanaticism gave them ingrained cruelty toward any enemy.

సౌసౌసౌ

The men were being roughly marched toward the east by the Germans, poked with bayonets and told to keep their hands on the back of their heads, fingers locked. An officer up the line resented the roughness and talked back to the soldier poking him. He was then forced to show his dog tag. It had an "H" on it, and so the officer was taken out of the line, told to walk toward the trees, and was promptly shot in the back of the head. One less prisoner for the Germans to guard. News filtered back through the prisoner lines: "Hey, all Jews—lose your dog tags. You've got an 'H' on them. They're shooting Jews." Immediately, a dozen of the silverish, tin rectangles that had their owners' religion embossed on them were dropped and buried by a dozen boots. It identified their faith with one letter: "C" for Catholic, "P" for Protestant, and "H" for Hebrew.

The Jews then realized a new problem. One called out: "Everybody else lose your tags too. Otherwise, they'll identify us easily by default." Another dozen or so were dropped and stomped on.

The Germans were rounding up certain prisoners as they moved along the line, taking non-Whites such as Hispanics and looking for those who had the "H" on their tags, but they found only one or two of the latter who had not gotten the word. They pulled Bobby Shaw out of the line and shot him immediately. His fellow prisoners didn't know why because his name was not obviously Jewish, until a close friend said he had an "H" embossed on his tag. They made short work of these prisoners, shooting them as they had shot the Negroes, who were quite easily identified. Some were taken once again beyond the tree line by the more clever SS and dispatched so as not to make the remaining prisoners too skittish.

Sonny was finally shoved into yet another group of hundreds of American soldiers who had been billeted in the hamlet of Gouvy the evening before. He wondered if the Germans had captured the entire American Army. The captured soldiers spoke in low tones, the fingers of both hands entwined behind their heads.

"Sonny, where you been?" asked a lieutenant who had been helping to set up the 105mm in the depot.

"Not exactly sure—I went to spot and somehow got knocked out."

"How were you going to spot?"

"I had a working radio with me."

"You did this for two days?"

"Guy, shit. I dunno. I just came out of it. I don't know how long I was out, but a day or so would explain my soaking wet clothes. I heard all our Negroes were shot on capture," he added. "Did you hear that?" Sonny asked, hoping the earlier reports were wrong.

"Yeah, dead," the lieutenant replied with an incensed look.

"Dead? All of them? Did any of them go down fighting?" Sonny responded with anger rising again.

"A few, and they fought like wet cats. But nearly all got overwhelmed at one point and then were shot while they were surrendering—all the Negroes. German bastards."

"*Jesus*," and he felt sick to his stomach. He looked as if he was about to cry.

"Yeah. Shut up. Guard."

A menacing-looking German teenager with SS runes on his collar and a mean look came closer as he heard them talking.

The captives next came under the custody of another group of German soldiers charged with escorting them further back in the lines and to their eventual destination. Though still in the SS, these were older men seemingly not fit for active combat, though deemed able-bodied enough to look after prisoners—a duty that humiliated them. They were determined to take their shame out on their prisoners, and this they did as cruelly as their caprice allowed.

At this point, any warm clothing that they had managed to hide from their first set of captors was confiscated by the second, and the prisoners stood shivering with hardly enough of anything to keep them warm.

"*Jetzt Stiefel Ausziehen*. Off boots now!" cried out one of the guards, armed to the teeth.

"What am I going to wear?" Sonny asked. "These socks aren't going to cut it." For this, he received a smack on his temple from a rifle butt.

"Okay, okay," Sonny complied, keeping his mouth shut.

Fortunately, he still had on the heavy wool socks, and while they were soaked by the snow, they did provide some minimal protection. But every time he found replacement clothing, he somehow lost it.

A German guard with many pairs of American boots under his arm pointed to a dead American in the deepening snow with clearly substandard boots.

"Sie haben eine minute."

Sonny had no problem understanding "one minute," and with some difficulty for the second time that day, he pulled the boots off the unfortunate soldier lying in the snow and put them on his own feet. They were cold, quite wet, and a bit small, but they were better than just his socks.

As an afterthought, the soldier pointed at the inner lining of Sonny's coat that he had managed to hold onto—until now.

"Mantel! Schnell!"

Sonny didn't have to be told twice—he removed it quickly. His temple still throbbed.

Again, the same guard pointed to a dead American in the snow who had a short threadbare coat. Out of what the SS trooper undoubtedly considered kindness, he allowed Sonny the chance to steal it off the lifeless body for himself.

ॐ ॐ ॐ

Then it began: their long trek into incarceration, their cold hands still clasped behind their heads. Having seen an unfortunate pattern emerge, Sonny took off his warm gloves, which, being covered in white canvas as camouflage, had so far avoided detection. He jammed them into his pockets—having them on display behind his head would have guaranteed their confiscation.

Their initial stop on this windy, snowy day was a rail station at the nearby Troisvierges, only a few miles away. Sonny already had his education on prisoner etiquette. He dared not speak even if addressed after the first incident at his capture except with a confused look, a seeming desire to understand, and complete silence to not appear insubordinate.

Stragglers were continually bayonetted if they did not walk quickly. Some pokes by the guards were hard enough through the layers of clothing they wore—even for those in long johns or something thicker—that they drew blood.

If "Shit, cut it out!" was screamed by a jabbed recipient, the next jab penetrated deeper.

"*Schweigen!*" the soldier screamed, which the Americans quickly figured out meant "Silence!"

Yelps of protest were either met with a smack on the side of the head with a rifle butt or a deeper parry with a blade, the goal being to get them as quickly as possible to the next destination—a train station with transport to carry them into captivity.

They thought some relief would be available on the train; however, they were soon disabused of that idea. Upon arrival, the prisoners were forced to climb into a boxcar, stripped of any remaining personal items the

Germans could find while being counted and marked on a clipboard by a German corporal, and then forced to climb into surroundings that, though it cut out the wind, were decidedly colder than the outside air temperature. As the prisoners piled in, though, and were pushed into uncomfortable postures as they did, for a very short while, their combined body warmth kept them all reasonably comfortable. That is, until the awkward standing, the need to relieve oneself, the inability to move, or the hunger, a new companion, made this part of the trip full of indignities that would continue for many days.

One guy, always in the rear of the front group and not fully appreciating the knowledge the others had learned from their shared experience so far, asked, "Where are the benches for us to sit on?"

Several cast a glance in his direction, wondering if he was joking. When they realized he wasn't, they felt bad for him.

"Are we supposed to stand? I hope it is a short trip."

There were men crammed into the boxcar quite thickly—it was called a forty-and-eight car, French-designed and thus designated for forty people seated or eight standing horses. In their case, the Germans stuffed one hundred men into each car. They were packed in this cattle car, well, like worse than cattle. And if a few others standing by them happened to collapse from exhaustion or pain, they remained nearly fixed in place as if in a rugby scrum, their position marked by an indentation made by a slightly shorter group of soldiers in the middle.

There was one five-gallon bucket in a corner of the car on top of a pile of old straw for relieving themselves, but if they could not make the bucket, they freely urinated where they were standing, though with reluctance and to the reprobation of those nearby.

"Where are they taking us?"

"I think I know," Sonny cried in mock seriousness.

A number of men in the car looked at him with eager anticipation as he was the ranking man in the car. Those who knew Sonny recognized his ill-timed sarcasm. Some laughed and some were annoyed by the false hope he gave them for a moment.

"Will you stop that?" cried another sergeant, Dave Adams, in the car with Sonny.

"They're probably going to take us and shoot us," said another very young solider in a frightened voice.

"They're *not* going to shoot us!" Sonny cried out. "They wouldn't be spending the fuel or using manpower to guard us. Adams, keep that guy quiet. We don't need panic. Men, you *know* they already shot our Negroes when they captured us. Don't be numbskulls. We'll be okay. They wouldn't be guarding us otherwise," Sonny added.

The tedious conversation continued until the men became tired of it, with some people in the cars mentally breaking away, contemplating snippets of the chat to ruminate on over and over, which either set their mind at ease or gave them more fear.

The journey continued for hours and then more hours—and then those hours stretched into days.

Sleep—if any came at all—was the only respite, but many could not because of the screaming nightmares of their comrades, the scraping of grinding teeth, the snoring, and the never-ending moans of pain. If they knew that this journey would eventually be over four hundred miles and would last over seventy-two hours, with only a few stops to relieve their captors and only coincidentally themselves, many would have died of despair earlier than they did.

On the morning of the second day, in sunlit but still bitterly cold weather, they arrived at a location deep inside Germany no one had seen before. The doors slid open and cold air and the smell of manure from a nearby farm, mixed with the scent of evergreens, wafted into their faces as they jumped to the ground.

Sonny pointed out to the men in low tones as some painfully climbed to the frozen earth, "The Germans have removed most station signs in an attempt to confuse us and anybody nearby. Start looking for any signs of where we are." The Germans forgot one at the back of a broken bench at trackside, and one of the men told Sonny, "It looks like we're in a town called Marsberg at a stop called Bahnhof-Bredelar."

The soldiers could hear the troops walking closer to their boxcar, coming down the line. Screaming German soldiers yelled "*Raus*" and "*Mach schnell*" and continued to prod them, this time admonishing silence again. They looked at each other standing on the siding, and for the first time could see that their uniforms were largely soiled with sweat, excrement, and urine, and this caused most punctures that drew blood to become infected.

The prisoners could see their breath as the doors of the train car opened. In fact, the exhalations of over one hundred men streamed moisture down the inside of the train car in rivulets. A further shove came from the inside when the car was unloading slowly, and the more cramped prisoners finally started pouring out of the train cars and were quickly positioned two abreast by the guards. The men shivered where they stood. The guards too were cold, but they were led into a train station nearby that had smoke pouring from the chimney on the roof while fresh sentries came and took their place.

The men fell out of the smell of human filth in the rolling stock, and those with more control relieved themselves on the siding short of the station. There were far too few guards for the number of prisoners.

Another soldier pointed out, "Sonny, hardly any guards. Some of the stronger guys could probably take them."

"Great, and then what, genius?" Sonny asked. "The Germans realize most of us are physically useless, especially with empty bellies. It would be suicide to try anything at this point, so far inside Germany. We gotta be three, four days east of where we were captured."

Still, some attempted a run for the tree line, no longer able to withstand the claustrophobic and filthy conditions of the boxcars, but whether they were diminished or fit, none of them could outrun the German bullet. The cooler heads watched in horror and could do nothing, but they were certain they knew why these men chose suicide.

Unfortunately, to the detriment of their still living comrades, the Germans dragooned 'volunteers.' An English-speaking guard said "Grab the bodies," and the fallen soldiers were dragged back to the train siding and shoved into the boxcar, where they had been alive only moments earlier.

At the same time, several altercations among the remaining captives broke out.

"You shit on my trousers."

"Not me—you were closer to him." A shoving fight started but quickly ended as still another prisoner was shot, for no other reason than for the fact that the Germans were annoyed and distracted by the altercation and feared it might be an attempt at a diversion, possibly as part of an escape attempt (not that the prisoners had anywhere to go). Sonny coveted the freshly shot soldier's warm-looking boots, but a more quick-witted soldier pounced and had them off and on his own feet in a flash.

The hundreds of soldiers stood outside for a time— some bent down to grab what nearby pristine snow they could find to quench whatever they thought the white powder would satisfy. In a moment, there was an order cried in German, and back into the fetid and filthy box-cars they climbed—as quickly as possible so as not to be among the ones jammed against the sidewalls of the box-car and to have some warmth in the middle of the pack. Some soldiers screamed bloody murder over the thought of getting into the cars again—they couldn't stand the conditions. They stayed outside, and soon after, the doors slammed shut, and the latches locked. Those in the rolling stock heard rifle shots, one for each protester, and then no more complaining. The door once again opened, and the occupants closest were directed to jump down and collect their deceased comrades. There had been much grumbling from local officials about cadavers strewn near the station verge in the past days.

After another twenty-four hours of the same misery: no food, water, or sitting down, and revolting toilet facilities. They arrived at what they assumed must be their final destination, and the men, for the last time, fell and then crept out of the reeking boxcars. In Sonny's car there were at least eight dead—including the three shot the day before—and they were beginning to reek. They were added to the dozens already deceased in the other cars on the rest of the train.

"Take them out gently," Sonny called to the soldiers who were lifting out their perished comrades.

"Why? They're dead," called one of the soldiers as he jumped down from the boxcar.

"Because you would want the same for yourself if it was you instead of them."

Everyone kept silent.

"I doubt they'll let us take care of them where we're going," the soldier said, looking at a horse-drawn wagon nearby with bodies already piled onto it as if they were cordwood.

Sonny replied, "Grab their dog tags if they still have them and hand 'em over. If no tags, then check their pockets for orders or letters they managed to hold onto and then give them to me." Then, as an afterthought, he added, "Anybody who needs different clothes, now is the time." And the eight soldiers from their boxcar were left nearly naked along the side of the tracks on the horse-drawn wagon.

Here, the Germans had once again removed the station identification, but one of the prisoners saw a name on a broken-up sign on the end of the station platform flung off the back end: Mühlberg. For most, this would be where they would end the war. And for many, this was where their lives would end.

THIRTEEN

STALAG IV-B

The prisoners arrived at their final stop during what appeared to be very late in the evening, given the lack of sunlight. In the cattle cars, they had lost nearly all sense of time. They could, however, tell it was evening because of the heavily overcast dark sky and because the arrival station (such as it was) and the road heading south were well-lit, which was unusual, given that the Allies controlled the skies.

They were going to enter Stalag IV-B, located the northeast of the town of Mühlberg in the Prussian Province of Saxony, just east of the Elbe River and about thirty miles north of Dresden—a city where prisoner work details were sent from time to time. It was not terribly far from Berlin, which surprisingly ended up being a morale booster as the prisoners heard Allied aircraft far in the distance regularly bombarding the city. It was deep inside German territory, and therefore the idea of escape was considered impossible.

It was about a five-mile walk to the camp—more cold, slush, and mud for the soldiers to plod through. Eventually, with some relief and a little happiness, they could sense the journey was coming to an end, but they would experience little of either—unless being off their feet was enough to satisfy any of them. They arrived at the camp entrance, a modern-looking squarish arch with two rows of some serious barbed wire in three layers (the top row being electrified) stretching out for hundreds of yards in either direction. The wire fences were placed in rows that were twenty feet apart and patrolled continuously by guards with Alsatian shepherd dogs. Towers were placed along the camp's perimeter every several hundred feet, manned with soldiers with machine guns and powerful search lamps. At the top of the square, arched entrance was a type of watchtower also with armed guards, and in the middle of the arch was an incongruous art-deco clock. Just below it, in raised letters, it read: "M. Stammlager IV-B," for "Team Main Camp IV-B Stalag," M. Stammlager being the abbreviation for "camp" in German, and IV-B, the number designation.

The incoming prisoners would learn that the camp was home to Danish, Polish, French, British, Australian, and Russian prisoners already, and now, they'd be adding 7,500 incoming Americans captured all over Europe, bringing the number of prisoners to almost 35,000—in a camp meant for far less than a third that number.

Upon entering the camp, the incoming prisoners were first told to strip in a room that felt colder than outside and deloused by receiving a shower in lukewarm water. Their skin turned an unhealthy, light shade of blue as they jumped up and down, shadowboxed, and swung their arms to keep warm and circulate their blood while their clothing (along with any previously undiscovered contraband they carried) was put into individual mesh metal baskets. The prisoners were then poked and pierced by guards, who dared not touch them, and sprayed with a fine mist of a pesticide called Zyklon B (empty tins were piled high outside the shower anterooms). Had the prisoners been aware of the other most common use for that particular product in concentration camps further east, they would have rioted, but the pesticide in this case was used only to kill the insidious lice already in their clothing.

After dressing once again in their still-dirty but lice-free clothing, they were assigned to barracks, some even filthier than the boxcars, which had been recently occupied by Russian POWs who had all manner of hygiene denied to them. These barracks came with an awful smell combined with large numbers of lice so big as to seem almost edible. And some of the men were so hungry they braved the bitter taste to get something into their bellies.

When the incoming soldiers had time to mentally absorb their environs, they realized everything about the camp and their surroundings was abysmal, *especially* the barracks. Sonny and some of the other Yanks were placed in barracks with veteran prisoners captured in North Africa over two years earlier. He grabbed the bunk on top with a thin, straw mattress and a current occupant since they were forced to share now, two men topside, one below. Sonny was able to place his feet beneath his bunkmate's legs, and they shared a thin blanket (everyone was doing everything they could to keep mutually warm), and soon his feet began to thaw for the first time in over a week. At first, it felt quite comfortable, but only for a moment. The warmth allowed Sonny's blood to more freely circulate— and feel the full force of the frostbite that had previously attacked him through his wet socks and boots.

The prisoners were hungry for news from the outside, and the information exchange began almost immediately. In the lower bunk was an already sickly American who seemed to have one foot in the grave. He was weak and infirm with a gentle wheeze, and he could not lift himself up off the bunk. He was wearing a thin though warm US Army Air Force uniform, which Sonny could see as his meager blanket only went halfway up his chest. The name Cunningham was nearly worn off the breast pocket but still could be made out. Sonny thought he was sleeping until the ailing man felt Sonny's lingering gaze and asked, "What are you looking at?"

"You Cunningham?"

"Yep."

"You a flyboy?"

"I was."

"Cunningham, don't they have special camps for Army Air Force POWs? What are you doing here?" Sonny asked.

"The name is Mike. Our planes were brought down

early on over Tunis, but I reckon mine was the very last. Any survivors of the early crashes or bailouts were taken back to Germany to their so-called 'Luft Stalags,' and I got stuck with the stupid ground soldiers."

The other prisoners in the barracks had heard this story a million times, but because the guy was feeling poorly, no one bothered to admonish him.

"By the time they sorted me out, I was here and feeling pretty bad. They didn't want to move me, and I've been stuck with these guys ever since."

His breathing was slightly labored, and he didn't lift his body at all while he spoke. He was clearly weak but had a strong voice.

Unfortunately, nobody had any news on the outcome of the German sneak attack up in the Ardennes, but the thousands of prisoners here and the fresh ones coming in every day precipitated low morale among the men. After Sonny shared the Allies' successes since the invasion in June, finishing his news with the debacle of the Bulge, it was time for Mike to carry on and fill them in about their new home.

"Well, the most worst off of the prisoners, and those treated the most dreadfully, are the Russians. Don't get me wrong, the Germans have a pretty loose attachment to the Geneva Convention, and we're not living the life of Riley here, but they have nothing with Russia and treat them as they like, which isn't good. They place the Russians only slightly above Jews, which really isn't much. The rest of us are treated with varying degrees of courtesy or cruelty, depending on our usefulness. The Danes are treated the best here in this dump, apparently, because Denmark, one of the first countries to throw in the towel with the Nazis, has a serious quid pro quo with Germany over food. Mistreatment of prisoners would turn off the Danish food supply to the Reich. That said, I've heard that Denmark has an active and courageous resistance movement against their occupying Germans, and their defiance *and* food production capacity is paying off. They don't particularly love the Jews in Denmark either, but according to them, they're still Danish, and they look after them—mostly hiding them from the Hun."

"Where are you getting this information from?" Sonny asked.

"The English. They seem to know everything. They got the best deal here. They've been here the longest, and most of us are pretty sure they got a working radio or two in their midst. And they're constantly making the Germans look stupid. They manipulate the Heinies by maintaining order among all the prisoners here, except the Russians who are unmanageable, by hoarding, utilizing, and dispensing the goods they received via their Red Cross packages. Things have been getting worse for the Germans the last year or so, and they haven't started stealing the contents of our Red Cross parcels yet because they are afraid what'll happen to their boys in our POW camps."

Sonny asked, "And what do they think of us?"

"Yanks are pretty much universally hated by the

Germans. They think we're far less hygienic, but they give us nothing to clean ourselves with. They want us to keep shaved, but they give us one razor per two hundred guys. They think we show utter disrespect to them in general, which is true, but they, for some bizarre reason, are offended more by any insubordination we show toward our own officers. They think we have a lackadaisical approach toward anything approaching discipline, and our constant escape attempts, when individuals can get the energy, make this more than a 'standard guard job' for them".

"One successful escape, and the Nazis would hang the offending German who let it happen as quickly as they would shoot the Yank trying to bust out. Plus, they know our industrial capacity is supplying everybody, including the Russians. Word got out that a Russki convoy was captured during a German push, and they were all Fords. With full tanks of gas. We got treated pretty badly for a few weeks after that news got around. The fucking Germans are still using horses to mostly transport their stuff 'cause they're running out of fuel."

Sonny asked him if he knew what type of truck the Russians had, just to make conversation. No answer, so he asked again, then looked over and realized that Cunningham was fast asleep. Sonny climbed up on the top bunk and did the same.

᠈᠙᠈᠙᠈᠙

The next day, beginning with prisoner muster and roll call in the morning and ending with the single ceiling light bulb for the entire cabin being turned off in the evening, the routine was mind-numbingly identical: prisoner reconciliation at 0600, 1100, and again at 1500 hours with a final one at 1900 hours. If there was no Allied air activity, the compound lights remained on for this last count.

This monotony continued for what seemed like forever, and they thought it could not get worse, but they were also constantly disabused of 'this could not get worse' notion. Some were given work details to collect wood from the forest for fuel for heater stoves, only to discover that after hours of working, they were given no wood at all for their own heaters—it was all designated for the guards.

Sonny was walking around the yard with a veteran prisoner, hungry as usual, but it was a sunny day, and they wanted to take advantage of the meager warmth offered by the sunlight. He saw a group of a dozen Americans being gathered under guard and led out of the front gate toward the town.

Sonny asked a veteran of the camp, "Where are they going?"

John Devane, captured in North Africa early in the war for the Yanks, a tall and cheerful guy who had a good sense of humor and helped keep up morale, told him, "Mule labor. Once a week, they're sent to the train station to lift heavy wooden crates of food—mostly small, miserable vegetables—off a train and onto a horse cart. Only there are no horses there. The *prisoners* are the horses. A month ago, one of the guys tried to grab a potato through one of the boxes. He was successful, and he wolfed it down on the spot. Problem was, he grabbed a second one, and a guard saw him and shot him dead. Fucking awful, sending hungry people to collect food."

"You're joking," Sonny replied.

"I wish I was. Since we heard that, we've been doing everything we can do to make the guards' lives miserable. Sometimes some men go back in the barracks to disrupt the count during muster and the prisoner counting. Other times, they return to barracks to which they're not assigned, only to have their numbers counted twice by the Germans to increase and disrupt their work. This makes our own lives more miserable because we have to stand outside for the recounting, but it pleases us because it puts fear the fear of God in the hearts of the Germans. After all, they know an escape, even an unsuccessful one, would be taken out on them as well as the poor slob trying to escape. So, it's worth it. Otherwise, our lives are unendingly boring."

Devane continued, "As time has gone on, there are only a few things that persuade us to get up in the morning, aside from an innate will to live. I've been here for over two years, and our motivations keep on changing. Now, it is the belief that the war is ending soon—we hear the Russians are getting closer every day."

"How do you know that?"

"We're pretty sure the Tommies have a radio, they tell us."

"Pretty sure?" Sonny had heard this already.

"Almost. They just know too much."

"What else?"

"You may have noticed the sound of Allied bombers way north of the camps?"

"Is that what it is? I thought it was a storm that never reached us."

"USAAF and RAF. Nearly daily."

"Great. You mentioned another reason?"

"Red Cross parcels. And any other mail. The oldsters started getting mail middle of last year but only about three times since. And the parcels—every registered prisoner is supposed to get one every two weeks, but they've been coming every month and a half. Seriously pilfered."

"Anything else?"

"Aside from that, our only other relief came when a newly placed German cook was rotated into the camp, and not knowing any better, inadvertently provided more food for the Russians. Nearly started a riot. He was fired the next day, and we were told he was sent to the front to cook there. That was good entertainment."

❧❧❧

Sonny was introduced to the food regimen on his first full day in the camp—the cruel, monotonous, depressing food regimen. Bobby O'Mara, the other flyboy in his barracks who had been provisionally looking after the wretched Cunningham, took him to the food line outside to show him the ropes. The men were handed small, tin bowls just before reaching a large cauldron holding what passed as their food, and no one was allowed back in the barracks until all were collected after eating. Careful counts were kept.

"Why were you given two bowls?" asked Sonny as they held their food.

"Mikey has got to eat, and the boys scooping this shit know I'm getting his food for him," Bobby replied.

Sonny gave a nod. O'Mara continued, "The morning 'food,' such as it is, is always a very thin gruel with something resembling the taste of peppermint. Warm water and whatever was thrown in when the guy handling the food was 'thinking' of peppermint."

Sonny chuckled.

"Lunch, the same, and dinner, the same, but sometimes with an odd turnip or rotten potato refused by the German guards' cook thrown in. If the ladler likes you, he'll scoop from the bottom."

"This is why all you guys are so thin?"

O'Mara gave him a sideways glance. "Give it a week or so. There is a brief time that doesn't last long when you newcomers all look like you're in the best physical condition of your lives, weight-wise, compared to us. But after two weeks of this shit, you'll shed the pounds very fast."

This turned out to be true. As their hunger became more significant, they very quickly got to a point where their body started consuming its own body fat, and in the absence of any calorie replenishment, they became very thin very quickly, and after a week or two, they started to look as emaciated as those who had been there a lot longer.

கைகைகை

One morning Cunningham weakly called up to Sonny in the bunk above, "You hear the moaning during the dreams last night, Sonny?"

"Yep," Sonny replied, laconically. He was reading a well-worn book by Jane Austen for the umpteenth time. He didn't know the title as the cover had fallen off, and in the barracks it was only referred to as "the Austen book."

"How many did you count?" Mike said.

Sonny looked up at the ceiling and pondered and replied, "Four, I reckon. Food, food, home, food and fishing...for food. Five." The most frequent dreams the prisoners had were of family or food (or sometimes the unspeakable horrors they had seen before capture, which precipitated abbreviated sleep and terrible screaming, rousing all within earshot from their slumber), and then the present reality upon awakening would hurt even more.

"Wait, six. Another was losing comrades during capture. First fighting they saw. Lots of crying," Sonny admitted.

"Yeah, I got that too. This place stinks," Sonny observed, turning back to his book.

கைகைகை

Though he had the skill of a captain, and was about to be promoted to that rank after setting up Red Ball, having been broken twice from lieutenant, Sonny's last official rank was sergeant. He was also considered the head of the camp's Catholics when they were without a chaplain, which was frequently. Some called him the pope. After muster and roll-call the next morning, a friendly ranking captain from another barracks came up to him and said,

"Chaplain passed last night."

"Shit...*so*?" Sonny replied.

"You're point on education and Sunday services again. Get ready," the captain replied.

"Shit," Sonny said again. When there was no chaplain available and the Americans organized church services and sometimes even when they didn't have a chaplain, the secularly faithful would fill in as surrogates, and this always fell to Sonny. They did this to practice their faith, of course, and surreptitiously remove suspicion of any Jewish affiliation their captors had of a handful of soldiers in their midst. When they were captured in the Ardennes after ditching their dog tags, they were savvy enough to concoct false surnames. With the names Fenster and Korngold and Silverstein and Feinberg (a lawyer before the war) being a bit too obvious, they were now Windows, Grainy, Stone and Goodmount. Many had also created and practiced a false history in advance of coming near the front lines. Sonny was 'education point' as he knew all the prayers in both English and Latin.

O'Mara explained, "When we first arrived two years ago, we all knew the Nazis' aversion to all things Jewish. But we all thought it applied to European Jews. Never to Yanks, and we were protected by the Geneva Convention. But a few weeks after arriving, we all went through what we thought were standard interviews for information to let our families know we were safe. It never went beyond 'name, rank, and serial number' but a few, proud of their religion, spilled the beans. The Jews all disappeared in a few days, and our commanding officers' protests were ignored. That was a few years back, but we never forgot. That's why we gotta teach the new Jews how to be Christian in case the Germans pull the same shit again."

And so it was that the Jews among them in a few weeks' time were taught decades' worth of Christian practices and services, along with such details as the Our Father prayer (one version for Catholics, one for Protestants). A smattering of Latin prayers was even added to the Jews' repertoires for good measure. Though most of the German guards were Catholic, the prisoners still had to prepare the Jews among them who had identified themselves as Protestant to answer queries correctly.

So, being raised as a Catholic, Sonny naturally took an active part in all these activities as well as leading Sunday services as if he were a true priest. Since Germans might question the ethnic origins of his last name, Jacobs, he thought it important to eliminate any suspicions as to his possible religious roots.

"C'mon, Sonny. You were a priest in civilian life, weren't you?"

"Hardly likely. But I was an altar boy. My mom was a lunatic about going to church, even when it wasn't Sunday, so I memorized the entire fucking mass, having listened to it several thousand times." And it was true. When there was not a chaplain among the captured, or the Germans deigned not to send in an RC priest from other camps, Sonny conducted the services on his own. He was conscientious about it, though not terribly pious, and could pull services off even in front of the Germans because the ritual was in Latin and had remained the same for centuries. It was merely rote memorization, bolstered within him by his firm belief that God would save him in some way.

One of the men noticed him collecting bits of matches used to light the stove during a rare time when there was fuel. It piqued interest.

"Sonny, don't tell me you're eating them."

"Nope. Gonna use the end of the burnt matchsticks as beads to count off the prayers during a recitation of the rosary."

"Recitation of the rosa-what? What the fuck is that?"

"You'll see tonight after lights out." Everyone in the barracks participated, not only the Catholics. It was something to do, and even though it was tedious, it took the men's collective minds off their never-ending hunger. With a pile of over sixty bits in the palm of his hand, which he carefully stored in one of his pockets, he could lay them on the floor in front of him to lead prayers in the five decades of the rosary, dutifully saying the ten "Hail Marys," with the obligatory "Glory Be" and the "Our Father" nestled in between.

While the Nazis officially abhorred Jews, they were not terribly fond of Catholics either (few knew Hitler was Catholic and continued to pay his tithe to the church monthly until nearly the end of the war). But to those Germans who could reconcile their faith in a celestial God alongside their present temporal one, they treated those religious prisoners with a general understanding and even (if they weren't being watched) compassion. They certainly treated other Catholics with some consideration. Rejecting that upbringing was difficult even among agnostics or non-believers; so, there were many who continued to remain sympathetic to the Christian prisoners.

❦❦❦

Soon after he began the services, and it was somehow discovered by the Germans that he was leading the barracks in evening rosary, he started to gain the favorable attention of one of the guards, a wounded regular Army soldier by the name of Marcus Trager. Trager stopped Sonny once in the yard and said in rudimentary English, "Sergeant, thank you for doing *Sonntagsmesse*. I *katholisch* and cannot go many times. And I hear you do *der Rosen-kranz*...or rosary for the men at night. Commendable!" And Sonny was treated quite benevolently by Trager from that point on.

O'Mara at one point asked, "Sonny, what is it with Trager [one of the few guards not given a pejorative nick-name] and yourself?"

"What do you mean?"

"You're picked every week to go on the wood scavenging hunts outside the gates for twigs for the stoves, and he obviously lets you keep some for the barracks. You're the only one not searched. And how do you get kitchen mess duty every week? Each potato you bring back is gold!"

"I think he is a lonely Catholic. Nazis are not too fond of them, and he'd be berated if it was known he was going to church. But he can do it guarding us. I think he treats me well because he thinks I'm a priest."

"Who woulda thunk religion would pay off! Hey, if he comes to you for confession, tell him his penance is more food for all."

It was true: Among the reasons Trager liked Sonny so much was that his services made Trager feel very nostalgic about the religion in which he was raised.

Both O'Mara and Sonny laughed at the "pay-off" of religious illusion, and while it was generally well known that Sonny ran the church services (no communion) as he did that outside, Sonny was surprised to learn that it was common knowledge that he led the men in prayer every evening. He suspected now that there was a mole among the prisoners, but Sonny shared that with no one because he wasn't a hundred percent sure whom he could trust.

ᔔᔔᔔ

The prisoners didn't know that Trager's dad had died when he was a week old, and his mom quickly remarried someone who could have been classified as an undesirable at that time, with whom his mom had a son: Trager's stepbrother. Both his stepfather and stepbrother, whom he adored, packed up and left when things happened to become challenging for them to live in Germany. Marcus' mom gave him no explanation for why they were deserted except to reinforce with people and friends their Christian heritage and that Marcus was not sired by her first husband, who was rumored to be a Jew. In fact, they moved to another city and changed their name to make it even more difficult for people to discover their lineage.

ॐॐॐ

Trager's kindness was counterbalanced on the German guard ledger by a particularly virulent and sadistic creature who everyone nicknamed Schwartz, though his real name was Kratzer. *Sturmbannführer* Kratzer. He was an Aryan blond, made somewhat more evil-looking by a black eyepatch, and he was more than a literal thorn in all the prisoners' collective sides.

Sonny saw him strutting about the yard at one point, seemingly looking for trouble, with a private in rank equivalent, or a *Schütze*, and a straining Alsatian dog at the end of a taut leash.

"Who is that asshole?" he asked O'Mara, who had become his companion when he wasn't looking after Airman Cunningham.

"Mr. Perfectly Fit and Impeccably Dressed? Kratzer. No one knows his first name. His nickname is Schwartzie."

"Why is he called that?"

"No one knows, but the name does get under his skin. About a year ago we had a new Heinie guard assigned to the camp, and when he first saw him in the yard, he yelled out, "Schwartzie!" A friend from his back home, no doubt.

Kratzer screamed at him, and that was the last time we saw the guy. He was only here a day. He seemed like he had the potential to be—and this was confirmed by one of the friendlier guards—shipped off to the Russian front."

"Nice guy, that Kratzer."

"Well, that's not all. One day he was dressing down a lone soldier, a Canadian, for not saluting him while passing, and the Canuck made the mistake of calling him Schwartzie."

"He get pissed off?"

"Yeah. He beat the guy to death with a rifle butt he grabbed from another solder in front of a hundred other prisoners. And after we were all pretty sure he was dead—by the way, while we were held at bay by gunpoint by other guards—he shot the guy in his bloody head. Nobody intervened. Even the other regular Army German soldiers seem scared of him."

Kratzer looked like his uniform was cleaned daily, and his jackboots and leather holster for his Walther P38 were shined to a high polish. He had SS runes on one lapel and four silver pips of a *Sturmbannführer* on the other. No one who got close enough to see his smile ever survived, but he usually wore it before he did something incredibly evil. Though it was nearly impossible, everyone did their best to avoid him because his gaze could mean pain or death if he was so moved.

But what no one would ever know about Kratzer was that he had applied unsuccessfully for the SS on several occasions. Finally, after Stalingrad, when things started to go badly for the Germans, he found an SS doctor doing physical exams for military transfer. The doctor was inebriated, having just learned his own son was missing in action. Times being what they were, the SS were desperate for recruits. When Kratzer showed up without his eyepatch (though he needed it due to a prior injury), he was brought on as an SS prison guard almost immediately. He had diminished vision and was advised to wear an eyepatch to keep sunlight out of that eye as much as possible. But for the physical examination, he had placed it out of sight in his pocket. He passed the exam. He immediately became a guard and never saw active service.

People merely thought the eyepatch was due to a war wound, and because of that injury "during battle," he was an honored member of the guard group at Stalag IV-B.

FOURTEEN

FABYAN BACCHANALIA

A regular pastime for all the soldiers was to talk about food—an almost self-emolliating torture in and of itself, but it was the only thing that seemed to alleviate their lack of it.

Sonny's story, a POW favorite, was always the same—the tale unfolded just before the Christmas holiday on Fabyan Place in Newark. He recounted the tale of his grandparents Giovanna and Ferdinand getting a ride over from Queens from somebody in the borough's large Croatian community. The family then began the "prep," making their way to fruit and vegetable grocers, butchers, and general grocery supply stores to buy the meats, peppers, onions, and a Christmas bird. Uncles, along with friends and neighbors, brought preferred delicacies—cauliflower, string beans, spinach, and flour—among other things to begin the process. The meal prep started the day before, and Sonny described in exact detail everything that had happened. As his memory became focused on the food and food alone, his retention surprised even him. He was, as were they all now, slaves to their bellies, and his memory trumped everyone else's in the barracks.

Whenever he had a quorum of an audience (meaning at least two other prisoners), he would begin. "During the winter holiday months, food served at the various Iroquois reservations throughout New York State were heavy on soups and potatoes, and that was the case even in my hometown of Newark and in my own house. There'd be fresh fish bouillabaisses with additions thrown in caught from the nearby Passaic River. The river was a coupla blocks from my home."

"Wait a second, Sonny. You lived in the middle of a city *and* you had a river going through it?"

"Yep. And it was great for swimming and fishing. And we got whatever fresh produce they could acquire from local farms."

"It sounds amazing" was the consensus of the various murmurs Sonny heard.

"It was, and after I get home, I'll never take that for granted again. All this was in addition to pan bread mixed with berries saved from the summer harvest up in Canada and brought down by my uncles."

"How many?" they asked, trying to picture the scene.

"Three or four. The number varied. But you could tell they were all one hundred percent Indian. Darkish skin, thick hair, and weird accents. Put them in skins and stick feathers in their hair, and they'd pass as the real thing in any Hollywood movie."

Sonny's comrades smiled at the thought of movie actors visiting him in his home.

"During the Great Depression, most of my relatives and many of the Indians survived out of necessity on hunted muskrat and beaver."

"Both rodents," someone pointed out for lack of a better term.

Sonny continued with, "Both ended up becoming a family staple at nearly all holiday tables. When I was young, my oldest sister and I fought over the muskrat brains, a delicacy back then."

"I'd kill for a plate of muskrat brains right now," chimed in a more ambitious and hungrier comrade.

Sonny described many of these meals he learned to cook as a child and could prepare in his sleep.

"The hams for the Indian portion were from pigs raised on farms close to our home in Newark."

"Wait, Sonny—I thought you told me you lived in a city," one of the guys reminded him.

"I do."

"Then how are there farms nearby?"

"There just are. We lived near a huge park, and there were farms just alongside the outskirts...and they prepared the pigs beautifully. When we cooked them, they were just dripping with fat. It seemed everyone in the house was cooking since the night before."

"What else besides ham?"

"Lots of standard dishes—mashed potatoes prepared with pork grease." Half the soldiers closed their eyes, lay back down in their bunks, and let out an almost silent hum. Others, who still could, drooled a bit.

"In addition to the ham haunches, we had perfectly carved pork chops cooked with leeks and smothered with a strong herbal tea mixed with maple sugar *and* maple syrup for sweetness."

"Heaven... Delicious...," came the chorus from the men.

"My Indian uncles prepared a meat meal called flat-tailed rat."

Eyes opened up, and the drooling momentarily stopped.

"Wait. What, rat? Really rat?"

One of the men chimed in, "I could eat a whole rat live, right this minute. Skin and all. Was it really rat, Sonny?"

"Shaetzle, you'd eat practically anything," Sonny interjected and then said, "That is what I thought the first time—but it turned out to be beaver."

"Beaver?! What does that taste like?"

"Like the best sirloin you have ever tasted in your entire life. We had a double oven in the kitchen. In one was a turkey, and in the other the pork—chops on the sides of both. But my uncles had to improvise with a few covered Dutch ovens hanging from some makeshift three-legged stands over a couple of flames in the backyard. The aroma of the cooking meat, the veggies in the pot, and the burning of wood beneath them filled the yard. And it is generally freezing on that day, but they still go outside and smoke their ciggies..."

"I would kill for a ciggy. Anyone got any?"

"Krauts haven't turned any over from our packages in weeks. Bastards."

"What else, Sonny?"

"Whatever vegetables preserved from the recent Canadian harvest were also part of the mix—certainly dried corn on the cob, carrots, and squash would be part of the meal. And to top it off, boiled cornbread—Mohawk style. It was simple. Made with cornflour mixed with boiling water until it had the consistency of clay, then formed into flat, egg-sized patties and finally fried in a pan of cooking oil and turned until they were brown on each side. It was delicious and easy to prepare. Served hot with butter dripping from it—you had to be careful if you ate too many 'cause you'd fill your stomach and leave no room for the rest of the meal."

Sonny's fellow prisoners imagined the food and reacted accordingly.

This story became the staple entertainment among the men. Not only because of its painfully delicious details, but because Sonny was well-schooled in his American Indian history, and everyone "knew" Indians by watching Western movies in the theaters. The prisoners had just never met one before.

Sonny educated them about the tribes, how the Mohawks were just one of six tribes of the Iroquois nation—"just like states in the United States." He explained that *Haudenosaunee* was the actual name the Iroquois gave themselves and that they had been responsible for setting up the first honest-to-goodness government in North America.

His comrades felt as though they were back in school again, learning pieces of history they had never known about. And it had an emotional impact because they now grasped that what they gleaned in the cinema was not reality.

"So, my dad and sisters were born on an Indian reservation in Canada. I was born in the kitchen under the Hell Gate Bridge."

Ignoring Sonny's history and focusing on that of Sonny's dad and sisters, one soldier asked, "In tepees?" No doubt he remembered the term from the movies.

"No, stupid. In our family home. Nice, big homes too. Indoor plumbing," he said sarcastically.

"Where'd they get the money? Selling white man scalps?" another asked to loud laughter.

"No, idiot. Haven't you ever heard that Indians were ironworkers in construction? Nearly all of New York City's big buildings like the Empire State, Chrysler, Woolworth, the Hell Gate Bridge—right near where I was born—and most buildings constructed during the early part of the 1900s in New York were built in part by North American Indians."

"Near the Hell Gate Bridge? Outside? Or in a tepee?" More laughter, but it rolled off Sonny's back. He'd heard jokes like this since he was a schoolboy, and it rarely got more imaginative than the last comment.

Sonny enjoyed telling them his cultural history and

all about his holiday celebrations with family. Wouldn't shut up about it actually, and because his stories were so precise and articulate, he was asked to repeat them over and over again as if it were an evening radio broadcast. After what seemed by the ten millionth time, Sonny's stories became convincing—far more compelling to his audience than even to himself, and guys started inviting themselves to his family festivities at Christmas. Sonny could hardly refuse. All they could think about was their collective hunger and spending Christmas Day on Fabyan Place. Their own families became secondary, Sonny's picture was so vibrant and alive.

In fact, as time went on, and even as the weather became warmer, Sonny's fellow prisoners had only to invoke the name "Fabyan Place" to persuade Sonny to retell the Christmas story from the beginning. He had a gift for reciting a perfectly pictured narrative. His tales were so elaborate and offered such local color, his fellow prisoners could see and imagine the smells of the food on the table and the holiday decorations in his house. They could almost see through the living room windows and spot the tree inside with the bunting. They could feel the warmth of the kitchen aromas and savor the tastes and textures on their tongues. Once again, those who could, salivated.

"Sonny, tell us about your sisters again on Fabyan Place."

Sonny gave him a sideways glance. He wasn't sure whether he was feeding their prurient desires or their nostalgic ones at that point until one said, "Sonny, I gotta tell you, you're a damn good storyteller. When I close my eyes, I think I'm someplace other than this shithole."

Those listening murmured agreement, and Sonny continued, "I told you about my sisters, Dot and Eileen..."

"Eileen is the cute one, right?"

"Yes, but my sister Dot was a classic beauty. Guys would line up to date her."

"I'll bet!" The soldier's shout was followed up with some catcalls.

"Knock it off, or you get nothing," Sonny warned, and silence ensued.

"I told you about Dot and Eileen, but I had a stepsister of sorts, Martha. She was slim, beautiful, and had amazing, gorgeous blond hair. That was different. Everyone in my family had black hair, so she stood out. And what a cook. Her fritule was to die for."

The men imagined Sonny's previously described warm kitchen, his family working diligently to prepare a feast, and they all longed for food along with comfortable, dull domesticity.

"I barely remembered her mom. Martha was my cousin, but her mom died when Martha was five, and my mom promised that she'd look after her. So, she became a sort of stepsister."

"Sonny, I want you to introduce me to her—I'm from upstate, and after this mess, I'll come down to Newark to meet her."

"Too late, Andy. Married with a young son."

Murmurs of disappointment followed.

"Maybe the guy got knocked on the head in the war—there'll be a lot of war widows when we get home—with a lot of ready-made families. Or maybe Martha's husband will turn out to be a jerk."

"Not a chance. He's a funny guy who loves my Indian uncles. He can slug it out with them beer for beer, and *they* love him for it," Sonny continued. "Irish. I've heard the Irish have been known to like the grape and grain. Right, Bob?"

O'Mara smiled in response.

"In any case, Martha and Walter have a little boy now named Gary. So, outta luck, Andy."

"I almost forget what beer tastes like."

"Christ, forget the women and get back to the food, for crying out loud."

Sonny went on. "Tough shit. Hands off my cousin." After a pause, he continued, "One thing we served at Christmas was pigeon."

"Pigeons? What do you mean, pigeons? You mean the flying rats that swarm on the streets of the city?" exclaimed one guy from Manhattan.

"Yep," replied Sonny.

The rat gourmand from before chimed in, "I could eat a pigeon whole right now. Feathers, bones, beak, and all. Uncooked."

More hums of agreement came from those listening.

One of the prisoners captured long ago in North Africa contributed, "It'd probably be your last meal. There was a time when there were a lot of pigeons in the compound, and we could trap them for food when the Krauts weren't looking—until the boids apparently got wise and avoided the camp completely. One guy did what you want to do." The North African soldier directed his comments at the hopeful raw-bird eater. "But rather than bring it back for the group, he stuffed a smaller one down his throat after wrenching its neck. He choked on the beak."

"You from Queens?" Sonny asked him.

"Yeah, Astoria. What's it to ya?"

"That is what my Uncle Freddie from Astoria who brought the pigeons calls them. *Boids.* He used to race them, and when they got a little "long in the tooth," he'd break their necks, pluck, debone, cook them, and then bring them to my home in a tray by the dozen. Tasted amazing."

Sonny continued. "Now, the Croatians during the Christmas season traditionally prepared lamb, roast pig, turkey…"

"Wait—did you cook a whole other pig and turkey?"

"We had a huge kitchen and oven and another small oven outside to supplement the Dutch one my uncles made. Over sixty people attended—they all had to get a bit of everything."

"You live in a mansion?"

"No, regular-size home, but the front and back porch and even the backyard would be stuffed with people even when it was freezing cold outside. Sometimes it seemed like arms and legs were sticking out of windows."

"What else?"

"My grandmother also made a dish known as Sarma, a lump of minced meat wrapped in cabbage, stuffed with peppers and onions, served with salads with chopped tomatoes from that summer's jarred Victory Garden output. We also had all types of freshly baked loaves of bread from a local commercial baker, still warm when we picked them up Christmas morning, and all of the Croatian desserts were made by my grandma, such as fritule, a pastry that looks like a doughnut, and strudel, which my grandmother learned how to make in Austria. We topped it off with walnut and poppyseed cakes, made by my mom."

"What was there to drink?" came one of the many questions from men whose imaginations were now racing quickly.

ትትት

Sonny continued with details of the libations, not realizing his verbosity would set in motion a chain of events that would place him in peril and at the same time make him very popular with nearly all the soldiers in the barracks.

He repeated the story it seemed ad infinitum at the request of his comrades. It allowed them to escape reality for a moment during the hundreds of recitations, and many could repeat the story by rote, pointing out each deviation from his original version. In order to cheer up his fellow captives, he would also sometimes recite with his near photographic memory what supplies he was responsible for, the overall input from America into the Allied war effort, and what goods came into Normandy already and what was scheduled for Antwerp.

As they were wont to do, the Germans had spies installed in most barracks to inform and perhaps tip the captors off to any escape plans. It was not surprising what some additional scraps of food could do—not enough to make potential spies put on noticeable weight but just enough to stave off starvation. The moles mainly consisted of German speakers who could facilitate communication between themselves and the guards. The Germans realized Sonny's war duties from his expositional stories, and they wanted to plumb his mind to gather as much additional information as they could and also verify if it was true. For obvious and various reasons, they would ultimately go to great lengths to pry this intelligence from him.

The knowledge Sonny possessed put him in great danger—both from the Germans who wanted it and from his comrades, who would hold him accountable if he shared it.

FIFTEEN

JOHN

Allied prisoners came into the camps in dribs and drabs following Sonny's initial incarceration throughout January and February.

About fifty Yanks and nearly half as many British prisoners were brought in one afternoon in late January from the Italian theater of war. The current inmates were advised the day before to make room, but for how many men in total, they were not told. Still, they did their best to prepare a welcome with whatever spare items they had previously hoarded: warm, dry clothing; extra rations; and cigarettes supplied via Geneva Convention-mandated Red Cross packages. Residents of each of the American barracks were commanded to clear enough space for at least five new prisoners each, an easy task for Sonny because the lower bunk just the day before had been vacated by Mike Cunningham, who quietly died in his sleep the night before. No reason could be detected for his death other than camp conditions and extreme malnutrition, and as a result, Sonny managed to acquire a relatively clean blanket from the camp guards, which he took for himself, and put his old one on the now free bunk below him.

That evening, five men were shoved into the barracks. It was JC's son, John, who walked to the back and saw Sonny sitting up and pointing to the free bed. John plopped down on it, exhausted. John closed his eyes but was too tired to sleep—though he could chat. He looked at Sonny briefly, closed his eyes again, and exhaled deeply.

There was something different about John but also familiar. Sonny's confused, tired, and hungry mind tried to make sense of it but couldn't, so he let it go for a while, knowing at some point his mind would resolve it.

"How long you been a prisoner?" John asked him.

"A month. You?"

"The same."

"The Ardennes?" Sonny inquired.

"Italy."

"Bullshit—our troops never made it as far as Italy."

"This isn't the only theater fighting the Germans, asshole." John gave back as good as he got.

"101st?"

"92nd."

"Quartermaster?" Sonny asked.

"Nope," John said with a mild look of disgust. "A *real* soldier—infantry."

Sonny ignored the insult and appeared unimpressed—while suppressing his extreme jealousy. Though he disliked the danger, he enjoyed the exhilaration of what little fighting he had taken part in that December, except, of course, for the bit about being captured.

"Where you from?" John inquired.

"New Jersey. Yourself?"

John thought it better to not necessarily share his deeper origins, just sticking to from whence he came in the US.

"Originally New Orleans and then later in Georgia, which is where I enlisted," John explained.

"A southern boy."

John disliked being referred to as boy, but he was too tired to argue and didn't quite know the nature of the person in the bunk above.

"Yeah," John muttered. "Is there anything to eat?"

Sonny had been given a distribution of dry crackers to share with one of the incoming soldiers who would take the free space. Though he greedily and surreptitiously ate one of the packets moments after he received them, Sonny was able to turn over several to John, which *he* then ate quite voraciously. It was the first food he had that day. In a moment, he was forced to eat more slowly as his body had a difficult time producing the saliva needed to consume the dry food. He looked at Sonny in acknowledgment, then turned on his side and fell fast asleep.

෨෨෨

The following day, the new prisoners in the barracks had difficulty waking, having missed quite a bit of sleep already, but the early muster and counting were mandatory and something they would have to get used to.

Afterward, the men greedily surrounded the caldrons brought near the barracks with the weak mint tea. Sonny had managed to save one last package of dry crackers, which he split with John.

"Is this what they normally serve here?" John asked.

"Yep, though not the crackers—that was given to me to share with you as you're a newcomer."

"This is it?!"

"Well, today is good because it actually has lots of mint in it. Sometimes there is only a leaf or two."

"I'm guessing it is why you guys are so thin."

"Nope, it's mostly because of all the exercise we get."

John looked at him sideways and let out a laugh.

The two soon became well acquainted, sharing their military experiences during their first few days together, which turned out to be radically different: John fighting, Sonny in support. But they each had interesting and unique involvement in the war. John was impressed to hear of the apparent overwhelming material superiority the Allies possessed, mostly because at times it had been denied to him in Italy.

After a while, they slipped into talking about family. Sonny greedily shared everything about his own family, his Christmas meals (John would hear about that more and more in the coming weeks and months), and once he felt comfortable with this newcomer, Sonny's aboriginal ancestors, provoking interest from John more than anything.

Sonny asked him about the South, suspecting his roots but not wanting to jump right in.

John told him, "We had German POWs there. They were shipped down from Canada on the sly before Pearl. We were doing the Canadians and the English a favor. And they were treated a whole hell of a lot better than we are here."

Once, before their energy gave out and while they could still walk the length of the perimeter of the interior of their compound, they traded bits and pieces about their home and family, and John came to fully trust Sonny.

At one point, John expanded on a previous story and said, "The German prisoners we held in Georgia were treated much better than some Americans citizens, to tell you the truth."

"How is that possible? Who treated Germans better than Americans?"

"Southerners."

"And how did people down South get away with treating these bastard Germans better than Americans?"

"Well, we weren't at war yet, but we saw it coming. But really, they treated the Germans better than the Negroes." John wished he could take it back as soon as he said it. He had let the cat out of the bag; he could hide his race from most people who weren't from the South. He looked like a white man, but he had some subtle Negro features.

At one point, still trying to resolve the incongruities of John's racial ambiguity and different accent, Sonny asked where John was born. John hesitated but trusted Sonny enough to admit, "Not too far from here, actually."

Sonny was startled but didn't press. Instead, he stared at the gravel-covered earth mixed with mud that caked on their shoes, and after a few moments, asked, "But you're a Negro, aren't you? How is that possible?"

There was a long pause before John spoke. "So…?" He said it not harshly but with some trepidation of discovery in his voice. He was taken aback by Sonny's bluntness because he had been so sensitive up to that point.

Sonny's guess wasn't a stretch—in fact, John, upon reflection, looked a lot like Mike Jefferson, and though they were not related, John had the same handsome features except he was light-skinned and had a full head of very dark brown hair and penetrating, deep, jade green eyes.

John went on to say that there was tremendous racial prejudice and unreasonable hatred for Negroes by Whites; however, the best argument that Sonny could construct was that John could, for lack of a better phrase, pass for a White man. He told him this, and John was somewhat insulted. He began to explain his origins more in-depth, and Sonny stopped him and said,

"John, most people think you're White anyway, so what's the problem? Why don't you just do that all the time and take a load off your backside?"

"Sonny, to be honest, I could never figure out the reaction of most White people toward Negroes. And I want people to know I'm Negro back home. Just not here." They looked at one another, walking side by side, and both let out a chuckle. John thought a moment before offering one of his more compelling arguments. "Sonny, suppose the skin of every Negro in America were suddenly to turn white. What would happen to all the notions about Negroes, the icons on which are built race prejudice and race hatred? What would become of their presumed shiftlessness, their cowardice, their dishonesty, their stupidity, their body odor? Would they not merge with the shiftlessness, the cowardice, the dishonesty, the stupidity, and the body odor of the Whites? Would they not then be subject to individual judgment in matters of abilities, energies, honesty, and cleanliness as are Whites? How else could they be judged?"

It was now Sonny's turn to be taken aback because he could not overcome John's compelling logic. John was clearly proud of his Negro heritage and never hid it in America, even though it would have been relatively easy for him to do so in the North, much the same way he could do with the Germans, but he knew that it would not result in a black eye or a ferocious dust-up with the guards. They would instead shoot him just as soon as look at him. So, he begged Sonny to keep it to himself. Sonny said he would, and John's dilemma began to sink in. He never had to experience anything remotely similar, being an invisible minority himself. But he was beginning to bring himself to understand what it could be like.

Sonny told him, "It matters less to me than to lots of others, and you do want to stay clear of the idiots in Barracks 9. It seems they attract each other like flies on shit. There are some serious Southerners in that hut that would sooner turn you in to gain favor from one of the guards—or a piece of bread or a piece of wood for the stove."

John appreciated the warning and continued, "In the US, I really don't care because I'm proud to be a Negro and dislike looking like a White man. The only ones who do care are some idiots, and most of those are in the South. But the Germans, they do care. Please tell no one, Sonny."

"Stop asking me. I forgot already." But Sonny was surprised to hear that John disliked looking White.

To the Germans who had rarely encountered Negroes except in posters showing cartoon caricatures printed by the racially bigoted German press, John had no noticeably racially ambiguous appearance to them. He could "pass," and pass he did, as a Southern Mediterranean, such as a Sicilian or Greek, more normal in Germany. To an American from the deep South, though, he was usually easily identified.

ॐ ॐ ॐ

Soon, all the newcomers to the camp had started to experience severe stomach distress accompanied by dry heaves and severe aches all over their bodies. John was especially hard hit. This made no difference to the Germans, who made them do work in any case, and around this time, Sonny was sent on a wood-collection trip just on the outside of the wire. As they collected the sticks and wrapped them in collections of fags, Sonny looked down, and it prompted a memory from his youth on the reservation in Canada. A particular plant called plantain was growing all over the forest floor. With it, he could produce a tea used as an Indian remedy for severe upset stomach.

He glanced around to see whether or not the Germans were looking, then reached down and pulled several clumps of the plants out by the roots and stuffed them in his pants pocket. He took it back to the barracks and, using a makeshift boiler, made a new type of tea to supplement their already inadequate rations. No one in the barracks could stand the idea of yet another type of brew, given the swill they suffered through for "breakfast." The awful smell of Sonny's new batch didn't help matters, but the prisoners had noticed a certain air of heightened health after a few days in both John and Sonny, who were benefiting from a mixture of plantain tea. Soon, the entire barracks, though weak and hungry, tried it. Afterward, they had a new look on life—in fact, a somewhat mildly ebullient view as the concoction was distributed to all. In addition to its supplemental use as a topical antibacterial application for their more serious cuts and scratches, it had an anti-inflammatory effect on their entire internal system. With his remedies and food stories, Sonny's reputation reached a new level of esteem with his fellow prisoners.

With what little hot water he could produce, Sonny made another weak but equally awful-tasting tea from pine needles that he'd collected in his last journey into the woods. He remembered his uncles made it every Christmas and served it after everyone overate. It tasted awful, but it soothed many an upset, overfed stomach at Christmastime, and in IV-B, it would soothe an empty and cramped stomach just as well. Fortunately, the new plant was also commonplace in the woods around Mühlberg. While it made the drinker retch, it was a remedy for the constant runs of dysentery from which quite a few of the prisoners suffered. It had a remarkably restorative effect on their empty bellies, and while they were still weak and hungry, Sonny's mixtures made the prisoners feel healthier and better able to withstand imprisonment.

☙ ☙ ☙

Time went on, and Sonny treated John just like any other White soldier, though he knew he was a Negro. That rarely happened to John with people who knew him to be Negro, and he was sincerely grateful to Sonny for not treating him differently. But while John was looking for acceptance, Sonny was only looking for survival. Sonny held a tenuous grasp on life by celebrating the holiday at Fabyan Place in his mind and with his fellow prisoners. This was not enough, though, for John.

☙ ☙ ☙

John was so weary of *not* being accepted throughout his life that he thought he might want to move to his grandfather's birthplace, Senegal in Africa, where he felt he could gain acceptance among others of his race. At one point, when he began to trust Sonny and knew he considered himself a "half-breed" as well, he told him this during one of their chats about origins and race.

"At least I wouldn't have to deal with all the shit I've put up with here for most of my life. First from the French in the Rhineland where I spent my first years, then from the Germans who came back in, then from the Americans in Louisiana, then Georgia and now here again. I think when this whole thing is over, I'll move to Senegal."

Sonny asked him where it was, and when he described the location, Sonny thought to himself, *Why would he want to live in a place where people live mostly naked in tribes and carry spears?* He quickly forgot the name of the country because he never heard of it before and was unlikely to hear of it again. Sonny's view of the world, particularly Africa, was informed via films such as *Tarzan*. He did listen to some of John's stories, however, and so was getting a new education on the subject.

When the two could talk undisturbed by others, in one of their long chats about race, John continued about the bigotry he'd faced when his race was sussed. "It got to the point where, when I was a teenager, I finally asked my dad to start teaching me Wolof, the language of Senegal he knew, so that I could begin the process of moving there, though I already spoke French, which is widely used in both Senegal and the Rhineland."

"Wait, where did you learn French? I thought you said you were born not far from here," Sonny pointed out.

"Well, closer to here than Georgia is. And I was,

but that's another long story. My dad was born in New Orleans."

"Huh?! Then how did he learn Wolof?"

"His parents were born in Senegal, and they spoke it to him growing up."

"Then how were you born near here again?" Sonny's confusion raised the pitch of his voice.

"He was in the French Army and was posted in Germany."

"How was a guy born in the US in the French Army? Wait—you know...? Hold on, tell me later. My head is starting to hurt."

"It's another long story, but let me get to the point of this one. One time, my dad sat me down, lit up a cigarette, and began to explain to me that while he liked some bits of his parents' home country, there were large swaths of it he did not." As he told the tale, John himself was transported in his mind to another time and place. He could smell his dad's Gitanes cigarette and see the ash getting closer to his yellow fingernails. He inhaled the scents of the food in the market near their home in New Orleans and heard the noise on the street.

"My dad told me that in his younger days, an opportunity dropped into his lap because of the French Army. Because Senegal was a French colony, during the Great War, they signed up natives by the thousands, and they received what was to them a king's ransom of a bounty: a salary and room and board. The French Army even went to the US looking for those that moved away. They were so desperate for troops, and my grandparents—my dad's parents—were easy to find in Louisiana."

John continued, thinking tangentially of the food in the market. "The recruitment made him aware of the opportunity, but he knew he couldn't join the French without jeopardizing his American citizenship, so he ended up joining the American Army to go and fight with the French in Europe. It was the best thing he ever did, he told me—aside from the training and the food and the shelter. They paid him enough so he could send money back to his folks who had hit on hard times as servants when their employers could no longer afford them. Before that, my old man had never been on a train or even a boat. He saw things he'd never seen before while going from New Orleans to Arizona for training and then by train to get a ship from New York City, and there, he went on to see multi-story buildings, fully paved roads, and people enjoying different cultures and stores and such. All new to him.

For various reasons, when he got to France, he got better training than he'd ever received with the Americans and was assigned to be with the Frenchies where, for the most part, you could be whatever color of the rainbow you wanted. As long as you spoke French, they would accept you. And my dad picked up a reasonable amount of a 'type' of French in New Orleans, where lots spoke it, and his parents spoke it as they came from a French colony. True, there were exceptions among the 'upper classes' as we would say, but for the most part, people were very welcoming, and he didn't have to worry."

John went on. "My dad also told me what it was like to be Negro in Europe. 'Be aware, son,' my dad said, 'that prejudice against you because of color exists everywhere. If people find out about you, just seek out and find the special friends. The people who see through this bull-shit—you're no better or worse than these people. The people that treat you poorly the way they do are really scared, scared of themselves, scared of the world around them, and scared that at some point, almost, there but for the grace of God go themselves.'

"My dad told me, 'John, there are always going to be voices out there, trying to put people they don't like down. Because of their religion, their height, if they're smart, and even because of their color like me.'

"'Like us, Dad?' I told him. 'No,' Dad corrected. 'Like me, but you got one up on me, cuz you look White.' I tried to say otherwise, but my dad just went on. 'Don't interrupt. Use it, boy. Use it to make the voices smaller—the voices which speak wrong. You're not gonna do it overnight, but you can start. And you can bring others along with you. Things are never going to change, else.'"

At the time, John was pretty sure his dad had never before spoken to him about any topic for such length and with such emotion or detail. John could listen to just about anyone without interruption, and though he had listened intently to his father's words, his mind was spinning with questions to ask.

When his dad had finished, John looked at him and understood his message and what he had been through.

He understood the upheaval going on within Germany where John was born (and, indeed, would read about it later from the US) and the populist socialist wave going through the country in the Rhineland. He was, in fact, glad that his dad had taken him to America to be raised. There were too many things going on in that part of the world that he didn't like. The supposed friends he had in Mainz treated him differently, and not in a good way once they learned his dad was a Negro. He was yelled at and berated on the street, and he could not fathom why. His dad became increasingly irritable, snappish, and angry, and John could not attribute it to anything in particular. A journey to another place, any place would be a change, and, he hoped, a welcome one. In America, when they finally got settled, at least in some parts, he was surrounded by other Negroes who thought like himself, and at least he felt better, and his dad became more complacent. It was only when he hit specific geographies in America did he once again become "uncomfortable," a feeling he thought he certainly did not deserve.

All John decided at that point was that what he really wanted was acceptance—if not necessarily by a large group then at least by a few individuals. His self-esteem was not that he needed it, but he could see that there were people whom he felt were far less worthy than him who received unbridled acceptance.

He said what he was thinking. "Sonny, what I want is acceptance."

It was unusual for Sonny to have a conversation

with someone speaking of aspirational and very personal things—unheard of, really, in Sonny's orbit, where people existed, lived life, and died. Mostly, other soldiers he met talked about recent service, but Sonny was intrigued. So, he went with the flow. And when John found a special friend, he coveted and took care of him—looked after him like the brother he once had and still wished he did.

"Johnny, I wished you had been through England with me. It wasn't at all bad for Negroes, in fact downright accommodating. The Limeys in fact preferred Negro soldiers over White ones. They said the Negro American soliders were the ones who 'brought the White Americans over.' And the Negroes responded in kind. A lot of the Whites never saw that response even from Whites. The Negroes were incredibly polite and generous with their supplies and rations. Many of the Whites, not all of them mind you, gave off the impression that they were the only ones fighting the war, and the English hated that."

John put England on the list of places to immigrate to rather than his grandparents' home country.

᠊ᡣᡠᡦ ᡣᡠᡦ ᡣᡠᡦ

John was born in the Rhineland, part of a demarcation piece of land between France and Germany, ceded to the French right after the Great War. His mom, Anna, had previously given birth to a young boy before her husband was beaten to death in the city of Mainz. Anna wasn't quite sure how she would survive so far away from her extended family, let alone raise a boy without a father, but not long afterward, she fell into the arms of an occupying French soldier with whom both she and her spouse had become friendly with before the husband was killed. Ultimately, they had a child together: John.

As a young boy, he thought it was perfectly normal to have a Negro father and a White mother and couldn't understand it when people treated him unkindly with *prejudice*—the label for treatment he couldn't and almost didn't want to understand. Yet experience prejudice he did when he proudly told people his race.

This happened with Whites everywhere: Whites in the Rhineland who knew the race of his dad, Whites throughout the world when they discovered his race, Whites who hated Negroes who could discern his race without him telling them, and now, by his White German captors because the US was their most powerful enemy in Europe. Throughout his life, John faced bigotry and prejudice, and he just wanted to be another person not judged by his appearance, but even some Negroes mocked his features and his white skin.

What happened to John when he moved to the US had a profound impact on his life. John knew physically he was somewhat racially obscure, and though he was proud of his Negro race, he let people assume he was White if he knew they had a tendency toward violence toward Negroes. In fact, only those with a very sharp eye or who had lived among Negroes in the South could tell that he carried some of the tell-tale markers of his ancestry.

ॐॐॐ

As he told Sonny in detail, long before America entered the war and before he had enlisted, John saw something that at once amazed and sickened him. He saw German prisoners treated better than he was, and in turn, the Germans were appalled at how the Negroes were treated by the Americans.

He was dismayed and felt as though this was the height of the prejudice that he experienced while living in the US. Sonny would do his best to hold John's secret, and in any case, it would be one of the last times they could have a private conversation away from other soldiers in the camp. It began to get far, far colder, and men just stayed in the huts to keep warm, which cut down on the number of intimate conversations anyone could have.

And while the importance of the story wasn't lost on Sonny since it didn't impact him directly nor had he seen it happen up to that point, his mind already raced to other questions he considered important.

Sonny realized he only knew what made up John the person, and he selfishly wanted to learn more about Italy. He was intrigued that as a Negro he had fought in combat for the American Army.

"You were in combat? In Italy? Tell me about it," Sonny requested.

In addition to being curious, Sonny was jealous.

SIXTEEN

BRITS

At the end of what seemed like hours of talking as they walked aimlessly throughout the camp, Sonny exclaimed, "I am *so* jealous you got to see some action."

"Sonny, don't be an idiot. Everyone else in my unit got to 'see' some action. And none are around to talk about it 'cept me. How do you feel about those odds?"

"Fair point. I guess if you get through to the other side safely, it's great. I didn't face any action until the Ardennes, and it was exhilarating, though a lot of my friends didn't make it through, come to think of it. Let me tell you about the stuff we did get done, though. And I suppose, while it wasn't as dangerous as what you were doing, it still helped the war effort."

The chat so engrossed them that, without realizing it, they had inadvertently wandered into the campgrounds of another nationality. This was forbidden by the Germans. John was a newcomer and did not realize that this was banned, so Sonny would be the one considered responsible for committing this serious and punishable mistake.

They were confident they would be beaten or worse when a guard in a watchtower screamed at them both as they fell to the ground to lower their profile, and the German guards were only just around the corner. As the Germans began running in the early dusk in their direction, a nearby barracks door opened briefly near where they had fallen, and several massive arms grabbed them both by the shoulders and dragged them inside.

They were pulled into another world—exceedingly warm, clean barracks, the likes of which Sonny had not seen since entering the camp, with soldiers in proper (though worn) uniforms, looking up from playing cards they had just a moment before been contemplating while enjoying cigarettes, at least one pipe, and drinking what appeared to be tea.

The pair was quickly shoved under a bunk, and the soldiers doing the rescuing resumed their cardplaying. The Germans shoved open the door, looked about, and saw the usual place setting within the hut, which was more like a cabin.

"Bugger off, mates. Every time you open the door, the temperature drops ten degrees. We'll remember that next time we get our Red Cross packages."

The guards poked around but only half-heartedly—the Brits were generous with sharing their supplies and information from the outside world as bribes, and they departed promptly.

৵৵৵

Once captured, the British, including those who had recently been snared in the Ardennes campaign, had it much better than the Yanks. Their improved conditions were not seen as shameful by the other prisoners since the British, being expert scroungers, would regularly give the Yanks food and fuel, but of all the prisoners, the Brits were clearly the most comfortable.

The Brits, God bless them, unbelievably had several radios. How they ever got parts was beyond comprehension, but the items were explained as contraptions built from commonly stolen items.

Once explained to them, Sonny finally grasped it and said, "It's a Rube Goldberg." A Brit who had lived in America before the war said, "Exactly."

One radio had been built while most of them were recent POWs in Italy, and many of the parts had been collected along the way. On top of that, those particular Brits were lucky enough to all be sent to the same camp. Other radios were built from scrounged parts bartered for with the contents of their Red Cross packages with risk-taking Germans who were not as convinced of their side's invulnerability and thus had supplied some critical components.

Most of the goods they received they got from the Danes, with whom they had developed a tight relationship over the last several years, and as miserably as the Russians were treated and tortured during their time incarcerated, the Danes were the equivalent of a protected species within the camp.

Sonny looked around in disbelief, and his first question after the guards left was: "Where are you getting all this stuff—are you taking it from our Red Cross packages?"

"That's not a terribly grateful attitude to take, mate," said Cliff Stichbury who appeared to be the ranking soldier, only because he was still wearing an officer's cap. "All you Yanks have a bit of an arrogant edge to you, do you know that?"

"Sorry," Sonny offered but then asked, "Why save us?"

"We dragged you in because your mate here is a good fellow. He once knocked a Jerry on the head who was particularly troublesome to some of our lads," replied the officer.

"What? Here in the camp?"

"No, in the luxury cattle ride up from Italy." The officer nodded at John. "He climbed on the top of the car in the middle of the night while the train was going through a tunnel, knocked him on the head, and dumped him over the side, with no one the wiser. It was a hundred miles before Jerry even figured out one of them was missing and guessed, we assume, he must have deserted as no prisoners escaped. We likely wouldn't have dragged you in except for your mate here."

Sonny's jaw fell slightly open.

He looked at John, who said nothing and barely even nodded—but the look he gave acknowledged consent.

Sonny tried to lift the awkwardness, at least for him,

of the moment: "What do I have to do to become a Danish prisoner?"

"Well, old man, the Danes are a nationality," the officer said, stating the obvious, assuming Sonny was an ignorant Yank, though Sonny had known about the Danes already. Before he could enlighten the soldier of this fact, the Brit went on.

"It turns out they have been spared harsh treatment because Jerry uses that country as a breadbasket—if their prisoners are mistreated, no food for them. So, they take care of them, feed them German rations, give them fuel for their stoves. We generally don't like them as they could share a bit more, but why ruin the 'gravy train' as you Yanks call it. And in fact, we received word back from London that their underground is quite active ruining German lives—but Jerry dare not mistreat the prisoners as their population needs the food. They do not particularly love their own Jewish population, but they are still *Danish* Jews, and Denmark has been able to hide all their Jews from being shipped off to God knows where."

Sonny and John enjoyed the subsequent several hours bonding with each other and the Brits, swapping stories, accepting little bits of food, and sleeping in a clean, warm environment for the first time in what seemed like forever.

Sonny shared with the Brits his experiences about his recent stay in their home country, and they, in return, had dozens of questions about food, pubs, how people were faring, how the cities were where he stayed, the damage done by German bombing, etc. Sonny told them about the friendliness of the Brits he had encountered, particularly toward Negro troops. People in England appeared color-blind. Sonny told the stories that he hadn't gotten around to telling John during their walk, but he didn't want to let go of his secret, so he thought this would be the best way to explain to him while sharing it with British troops.

"Frankly, mate, we can't figure out why you Yanks treat your own Negro boys like rubbish. Good people down to a man, including your mate, John, here."

Sonny was silent, hoping *he* didn't let the cat out of the bag about John's race.

"Johnny, here, can pass as a White, though he is Negro, and he doesn't bother. He'd give us the shirt off his back, he would. You're lucky to have him as a friend."

☙☙☙

They left the British barracks early in the morning, having had no sleep. Their pockets were filled with food and cigarettes the Brits could spare for the Yanks in John and Sonny's barracks. It was pre-dawn and difficult to see anything at that time in the morning save for the searchlights that cut like knives across the parade ground and the outside barrack walls; the end of the light beams took different shapes depending on how they traveled—the shape of circles of the lamps on the ground outside and moving rectangles on the inside walls. They had to make it back to their own barracks in time for muster and roll call.

Not wishing to alert anyone with loud talking, Sonny

spoke in a low voice to John as they walked. "All the awful guards and officers got nicknames. Screamer, Stinky, and a particularly sadistic one called Schwartzie. He stands out, not necessarily for his sadism but for his quickness in killing a prisoner for the smallest of infractions. I saw him once shoot a prisoner because he tripped and fell into the guy in front of him when lining up for counting. We all give this Schwartzie guard a wide berth."

However, once they entered the large parade ground in front of the barracks, while briskly going back to their "home," Sonny and John were spotted almost immediately by two guards, one of them, unfortunately, the bastard *Schwartz*, ranking asshole in the camp.

He had two soldiers walking just in front of him, holding back two anxiety-ridden Alsatian shepherd dogs who began barking like mad when they saw John and Sonny, looking for all intents as if they wished to make a meal out of them.

Schwartzie pointed at the two out-of-place men, then yelled a command to both the dogs and the restraining soldiers, who obliged him. The canines were let go from the leashes attached to their collars, and they ran swiftly toward their intended prey. Once released, Sonny felt they would be ripped to shreds, and he tried to imagine if the teeth would hurt.

Sonny and John froze in their tracks. All of a sudden, John screamed out something in German, and Sonny looked at him with surprise.

The dogs stretched their bodies out with their long

strides and rushed past them on either side, making a sharp turn behind the corner of the building near the Russian barracks, then skidding and pitching up dirt as they rounded the bend and barked loudly. Moments later, their yelps ended rather abruptly, replaced with high-pitched screeches.

The two German guards who had been holding back the dogs looked at each other and ran double-time into the Russian camp, ignoring John and Sonny. Schwartzie joined them at a fast pace. Both Sonny and John scurried toward their own barracks, entirely overlooked by an ever-growing number of German guards running toward the Russian encampment.

Sonny was out of breath when they reached their own squalid shelter and asked, "How the hell did you do that? Where did you learn German?"

"I picked up some German while I was captive in Italy."

"Yeah, and I picked up Russian while I was working in England. What did you say?"

John at first demurred. "The German, I learned, I had no choice over because I was sent to school in the Rhineland."

Then, looking at Sonny's pleading face, he relented. "I just said, 'Go to Russians.' I'm just glad the dogs know the difference between Russians and Yanks. I suspect they use the national labels a lot here."

It never dawned on Sonny or John that even the most intelligent dogs would be hard-pressed to determine an individual's ethnicity, but it was the command they were given and the smell of the Russians that drove them toward the attack.

Once among the Russians, and sadly, because of their intelligence and ability to understand instructions, the shepherds were grabbed by a dozen hands each—two tightly holding their muzzles shut—and were skinned with improvised shivs and eaten raw quite promptly. It took the first two German guards, with help from Kratzer and another dozen soldiers, hours to evacuate the Russian barracks and find the most likely final resting place offered to their hounds. Their pelts were discovered an hour later in huts far away from where the dogs were captured, beneath a meager pile of straw, and their bones were hidden in an unused potbelly stove, there having been no fuel in months. The bones were already broken apart and the marrow sucked out of the center. Butchering and consumption had taken less than ten minutes.

The offenders found with canine blood on their face and under their nails did not live long enough to fully digest their meal, though it was the best they had eaten in what seemed like forever. And truth be told, in their hearts, they would have honored John for what he did.

SEVENTEEN

JOHN BEFORE IV-B

Though John faced bigotry where he was born in the Rhineland, that much-disputed stretch of geography between France and Germany, he was too young to know or understand the discrimination his dad felt. In school, where his ambiguous racial features made him a curiosity rather than a comrade, he had such a likable personality he became quite popular—many showed him what he called *richtige freundschaft*, or "right friendship." However, after a while, the children who shared stories about their amiable friend and his "coal-black" father with their families soon began ignoring him while at the same time staring at him intently on a constant basis to try and discern the badness their parents could see.

When John and his dad fled the Rhineland during the Nazi ascension to power, they faced bigotry almost immediately when they sailed across the Atlantic to the US from Marseilles. Though they had second-class tickets, and his dad explained that different tickets cost more, they were still relegated to the back of the dining areas as well as a substandard berth on the boat.

He experienced similar treatment while walking down the gangplank when they arrived in New York, and though he didn't know why at the time, he knew his dad was deeply unhappy about something.

"Papa, what's wrong?"

"Well, this first area is full, and they aren't taking any more passengers leaving the boat. We have to walk a bit further down."

But John could see the debarkation area was hardly populated. He couldn't read the sign above that read "Whites Only—No Colored," though, and the Negroes were herded into a line and sent off to a receiving area one hundred yards from the main one where all the Whites were converging and entering the country. And while John could not read English at the time, though the language would flow smoothly into him as his life in America progressed, everywhere he and his father traveled, he was able to make out the word "colored"—though, at the time, he didn't know what it meant.

John spent his formative years with his dad growing up in New Orleans, but his father discovered after a while, with his own parents gone and many of his friends dispersed, that the pricey city had far less to offer him and his young son than he had expected. So, they moved to Georgia in the 1930s to a town near Ft. Smith in Lumpkin County, far less expensive than Louisiana, to where some of the Chalmet distant cousins had been transplanted while he was in Europe.

After hostilities began between England and Germany and though the US was not yet in the war, America secretly agreed to keep some German prisoners for the UK because of the severe English housing shortage, and the Canadians couldn't do it as they needed their manpower to support Britain. To keep it low-key, they shipped some of them to an obscure Army base in the middle of rural Georgia to help alleviate this British and Canadian stress point. Not long after arriving in Georgia, John was able to put the fluent German he learned in Europe to good use by doing interpreting work for work-release German POWs who were being held by the Americans. He tagged along for fifty cents a day—a fortune to a young Negro in Georgia, and indeed, for any young man—with a group of ten work-release German POWs and their guards.

Once, after a hard day's work in the fields, of course picking cotton, he went with the Germans and their armed US Army guards to a roadside diner. They pulled up to a local well-known greasy spoon on a lonely road across from a field of cotton that John had passed dozens of times but never entered: a lone building along a dusty road. Inside were some locals eating typical local food. As the guards and prisoners hopped out of the back of the military truck, they beheld, parked out front, a new 1940 Cadillac 75 Convertible Coupe, gleaming and maroon in color with a white canvas top. They all stopped and admired the fine automobile while John described in English all the different features of the vehicle to the Germans. The large diner windows were open wide, and the fans inside on the ceiling were spinning like mad to cool the place down, and it was blowing the fragrant smells of grilled food out the front: Some grilled meats, some fish. It was a hot day. Everyone in the establishment could hear John speaking German, and he held the door while everyone entered. Incongruously, there was a middle-aged, astonishingly well-dressed, and attractive woman sitting solo in one of the booths, likely the Cadillac owner, finishing off a peach cobbler with what looked like vanilla ice cream on top. The guards and the prisoners filed in first and sat in some booths, followed by John.

"Outta here, boy," the man behind the counter yelled loudly. The Germans who could speak a tiny bit of English stood up and began to leave, thinking the man was talking to them. The US guards motioned them down.

"Outta here boy. *Now!*" he screamed again, and John knew it was directed at him, but he refused to move. The man reached below and pulled a sawed-off shotgun out from behind the counter. The US guards took their weapons off their shoulders in preparation but didn't point them at the diner owner, and those sitting at the front at the counter with their back to the entry moved to the far ends.

"Last time, boy, get outta here, or you're gonna have a hole in you." One of the guards looked at John kindly and said, "John, go wait in the truck. I'll bring something out to you. What do you want?" But tears filled John's eyes; he turned around and went outside, across the country road, and started throwing rocks into the field. The Germans looked confused.

One asked a guard in rudimentary English, "What was that?"

"The boy is a Negro. Negroes ain't allowed in most restaurants these parts."

The German translated for his compatriots, whose faces expressed incredulity as they looked at each other and began to talk rapidly, some clearly expressing disbelief, and the diner owner watched John cross the street and begin to throw the stones. He turned to the elegant woman: "Sorry about that, Mrs. Plymel. Boy shoulda known better." He turned around and went behind the counter to get crockery and cutlery for the men who had just filed in.

Mrs. Plymel finished what she had been chewing and said, "That's okay, Waylon. I'll go talk some sense into him. He's not from around these parts."

"Careful, ma'am. You know how they can get."

"I'll be fine. You can watch me through the window."

She looked both ways, not really necessary on such a pokey road, and caught up with John. She asked, "*Woher kommst du, Junge?*"

John, startled, stopped crying and turned to face the woman. "I didn't expect anyone could speak German here in Georgia 'cept me, my dad, and these prisoners of war. Why do *you* speak German? Is that your car?" His disturbing chain of thought had been broken.

Mrs. Plymel decided to give him as much information

as it would take to make him comfortable so he'd talk. "I used to live in Germany with my late husband, Clyde. He worked for the State Department—he made a bundle as a banker, and his contribution to the Democrats got him stationed for a few years in Hamburg. He had a heart attack last year at Oktoberfest, and I came back here to spend his money." John was silent. "What are you doing here, young man?" When she got no response, she repeated her initial question, this time in English: "Where are you from?" He told her New Orleans and how he came to speak German.

"I guess you haven't spent much time in Georgia. Most Negroes know better than to drop into any restaurants, though you don't look like much of a Negro. In Georgia, and I guess you know this from your time in New Orleans, all Southerners are not bigots and racists. It's just that the ones that are have the loudest mouths and are armed to the teeth."

"Why are you in this awful little restaurant?" he asked.

"Well, I grew up in Georgia on a plantation north of Atlanta. We had Negroes working for us, but of course, none of them were slaves. I had a mammy look after me, and she made the most delicious dishes that my father couldn't countenance. He said it was 'darkie food,' but he was unkinder with the description. In any case, she made things like catfish and cornbread and the best homemade cobbler. I drove by here and then came into this place once a few years back, and they had everything I missed from my youth. I come here now and again when I get a yearning for food as I had as a youngster. In fact, the owner loves me because once a year he locks up and caters a party at my home for me and my like-minded 'elegant' ladies. And you, young man, why are you here?"

"Another long story, but New Orleans was getting too expensive for us, so we moved with family up here in Georgia."

"Well, you'd better start thinking of another place, maybe up north or back to New Orleans, as you won't find many sympathetic people in this state."

One of the German prisoners joined them to find out what was going on, and the three continued the conversation in German.

"What was that all about?" the curious prisoner asked.

"Negroes are not allowed in Georgia restaurants unless it has a colored section," said Mrs. Plymel.

"But he is White."

John chimed in, "My skin is white. I'm a Negro. My daddy is a Negro, my mama is White."

The German's face showed disbelief as he walked back inside the diner to his anxiously awaiting comrades to share the story. Mrs. Plymel squeezed John's arm and they followed the prisoner, practicing her German, which she had not spoken in a while. The Germans were seriously dismayed.

Through it all, there was still a small positive effect to the event: though their unreasonable dislike of the Jews stemmed from a different source, some Germans received a chance to view their own country's unfairness compared to that American's treatment of Negroes, which was just as illogical.

The Germans didn't fully believe he was a Negro until it was confirmed by their southern US Army guards, and even then, they thought *jemanden auf den Arm nehmen*: that their legs were being pulled and didn't fully believe it until afterward, when John's father was waiting to collect him at the fort's gate, and John hopped out of the truck and into his dad's car.

ôôô

Not long after that incident, in early 1942, in the patriotic aftermath of Pearl Harbor, John went to enlist in the US Army, but in a subtle act of defiance (in his mind), he went to a White enlistment office in Atlanta, Georgia, just outside of Fort McPherson. Though he could "pass" as White, he never let anyone think he was, and if there was ever a question, he identified himself as Negro. While he had a lot of difficulties and challenges with the idea of fighting for racist America, he remembered how his dad had told him that the Army was a great equalizer, and he thought it would be an excellent opportunity to finally get the recognition as a patriotic Negro man that he felt he deserved.

There was a long line at the recruitment center, but his racial features were noticed immediately by most Georgians, and he faced taunts and epithets thrown at him from the good ole boys who were keen to enlist with all the hubris of similarly aged males at the exact same location some eighty years before at the beginning of the War Between the States.

He kept silent, realizing that it was, from a race perspective, a ratio of about fifty White men to just one Negro, and he wanted to end up in the military and not in Grady Hospital, the only one in town with a Negro-only ward, and that would be if he lived. Plus, the hospital was ten miles away, and there were no ambulances in town that would take coloreds.

Silent, that is, until someone said, "Your White mama clearly fucked a Negro man to get you with nigger looks and white skin."

John paused a moment and then took a violent swing at the offender. He missed, and five guys pounced on him pretty much instantaneously, only because that was the limit of the number of people with room to grab him. As a youngster, his dad had taught him *savate*, the French style of hand-to-hand combat that he had learned in the French Army, and John proceeded to make short work of the crowd. As they clawed at him, he grabbed their arms and twisted with violent strength, breaking several limbs with excruciating and awful-sounding cracks. On one attacker, a bone broke and protruded beneath the skin, and he fell in agony, then picked himself up and ran away. The crowd was thinning as his attackers were falling, and almost immediately, it was 8 a.m. A lone, uncovered bell on a temporary plywood wall rang, and the recruitment office opened with a crush toward the door.

Those intelligent enough to keep their distance from

the fight started filing into the office. A skinny-as-a-rail captain, flanked by two brutish lieutenants and several lower-ranking military police, came out the front door. The officer started calling out in a distinct northern accent, "Any Italian Americans? Yo, any ginzos, raise your hands." His accent was out of place; he sounded like a gangster from a George Raft movie. Those only moderately injured in the melee stood back in line, as did John—all wanted nothing to get in the way of their enlistment in the military.

The captain was tall with thick, dark hair and a comically big nose, even for an Italian, for Italian he was. But he held the rank of captain, and clearly, at least one good ole boy did not seem to understand the significance of that rank.

The hurler of epithets at John, the chief instigator, really, who had turned into a coward when it came to fighting him, yelled out to the captain, "Hey, Dago-boy. You looking for a new pope, or you running outta grease for that hair of yours and want some from us?"

Muted gales of laughter spread through some of the crowd, within earshot of the equally ignorant recruits.

The captain stopped in front of that recruit, just a few feet in front of John, and stared at him with clenched fists on his hips.

"You an Italian-American, cracker-boy? Because that's who I'm looking for. The Army has instructed that we interview all American Italians to put them into top-secret work." That was a lie. They were instructed to interview American Italians to evaluate their loyalty to serve America.

"I ain't no WOP," the instigator said in an arrogant voice.

"Pity." The captain glanced ever so slightly over his shoulder. The two brute MPs roughly grabbed the recruit; one hit him unconscious on the top of the head with a thick rubber truncheon and dragged him away, holding him up under each arm. Two other MPs took their places, and the remaining recruits froze. It became so quiet you could hear a mouse piss on cotton.

The captain said out loud in an affected fake southern accent: "Well, I do declare we seem to have a rabble-rouser in our midst." He then reverted to his Brooklyn accent, enunciating each word because he knew Southerners sometimes had a challenge with his manner of speaking. "My name is Captain Joseph A. Pergola—let this be your first lesson in Army discipline. You wanna fight Japs and Germans? Let me tell you something, boys, the Union Army were pussies compared to these guys—and youse gotta have discipline to beat 'em." He said the last bit in a gentler tone. "Now, any Italian-Americans in the line?" One small, obviously underage kid gingerly raised his hand.

"Who are you?" the captain asked.

"Frankie."

The captain took one look at him, grabbed him by the shirt collar, turned him around, and kicked him in the seat of his trousers.

"Get outta hee'a. Youse too young and too short anyways."

The boy, unquestionably underage, ran off, stifling tears. Seven other young boys got out of line and briskly started walking dejectedly away.

Frankie was a plant, Captain Pergola's visiting younger brother, actually. The enlistment board, no matter how desperate they were for new recruits, abhorred the arguments and lies of those too young trying to enlist before their time. And of those, there were plenty. The South was not short of cockiness. Frankie got paid ten cents from his older brother to receive a swift kick in the ass.

"We're looking for Italian-Americans. Any ginzos?" he continued. "*Whoa!*" he exclaimed loudly as he stopped in front of John. Pergola pulled him from the line and out of earshot from those queuing into the recruitment office. He looked at one of his lieutenants. "Continue, Petey. I wanna talk to this guy."

Petey continued trolling for first-generation Italians.

"You the guy who wrecked the local crackers?" Captain Pergola asked. When he saw he would get no answer from John, he continued, "Boy, what the fuck are you doing in this line?"

"I'm not a boy. I'm a man."

"Okay. Man. What the fuck are you doing in this line?"

"I want to fight for my country," John replied.

"Well, you're going to fight from inside a kitchen pantry if you stay in this line. What are you doing in the Whites-only recruitment office? Your skin color may not show it, but youse clearly a coon, as they say down here.

'Scuse my French. And these guys clearly know it. You'd be about as welcome here as a Jew in the Vatican. We can't have you becoming a cook. Youse clearly a fighter. You wanna be a cook?"

John shook his head.

Captain Pergola said in a low voice, "Look, I'm here to pull 'em outta line and interview the Italians—for some reason, they're considered 'alien threats,' like, from a different Buck Rogers planet. And they shipped me from Brooklyn to two hundred-degree, wet, sticky, hot, smelly, moolie-hating, cotton-picking, stupid, miserable Atlanta to weed out the 'dangerous' guineas. I'm here to pull out dose dagos and figure out what's what and if they can be trusted. What makes them think they can trust me?" he asked. "Do you know they tried to put Joe DiMaggio's parents into prison, and they been in the country for forty years and never applied for citizenship? Joe DiMaggio's parents!" His voice got louder.

John shook his head because he hadn't known that, though mostly because he had absolutely no idea who Joe DiMaggio was. He wasn't a fan of baseball.

"Look, I'm going to level with you kid…. You enlist here, you're going to be an Army cook or a waiter, or worse, in a *band*."

John kept quiet, not because this guy seemed to be off his rocker, nor because John didn't want to offend him, but because he spoke in a kindly, caring tone. And he was wearing a sidearm.

"Look…what's your name?"

"John."

"Look, John, I've been down South since Pearl Harbor, and I seen youse Negro guys treated like shit since I got here. I'm not a fan a moolies, but enough's enough, and if you lived in Brooklyn, you'd be packin' a switchblade, and people would show you respect, or there'd be dead crackers spread on the sidewalk. Ain't nobody gonna give you shit up dere."

The captain glanced over his shoulder and yelled, "Sergeant Pike!"

An NCO with stripes, three up and two down on his upper-arm sleeve, ran briskly as if making up for the fact that he hadn't run quickly enough in response to one of the captain's commands in the past.

"Take… Tom, is it?" The captain pointed at John, snapping his fingers absently.

"John."

"Take John inside and put him through the system: Test him and voucher him up for travel. You know where. Gimme a coupla minutes to get through the resta this line."

"Yessir."

Then, to John, the captain asked, "Kid, you ever hear of Fort Huachuca, excuse the pronunciation, in Arizona?"

John shook his head.

"That's where moolies are learning to fight. Follow the good sergeant."

John left with the sergeant, and Captain Pergola continued down the line. "Yo, any Italians? Any ginzos?"

Once inside in a smaller, side office, John asked

the sergeant, "Why is this guy sending me by train to Arizona?"

No answer—Pike was a local and didn't appreciate being addressed by a Negro.

"C'mon, give us a break for once," John urged.

The sergeant looked at him for a moment, taking in his pleading eyes and white skin, and relented. "Captain has a buddy putting together nigger soldiers in a special nigger-only regiment to fight—one of President Roosevelt's wife's special nigger projects. Like, for yourself."

Pike wanted to make the fact that he deigned to address him at all sting.

᠅ ᠅ ᠅

When the sergeant finally finished administering the testing to John and got up to find the captain to inform him, the door swung open, and Pergola was there standing in the threshold next to John.

"Sergeant, what are you doing with my boy, Tommy?"

"John, sir?"

"Yeah, John." He glanced over, smiled, and said, "Johnny-boy! What's buzzin', cousin?"

The sergeant explained he had a perfect score on the aptitude test.

"*Minchia*…," Pergola said under his breath. "Give it to him again."

"Sir, I gave it three times."

Pergola stared at Pike; his mouth hung slightly open.

"Okay, Sergeant, get me a cuppa cawffee while I look

at this." Reading the results, he didn't look up as Pike saluted and left.

"You're a real pistol, Tommy-boy." John just looked at him. Pergola caught the glare. "Sorry, Tommy...man."

A brief knock and Pike entered with a steaming cup, placing it on the table in front of Pergola, though the temperature outside was oppressive.

"Milk?" questioned Pergola.

"Yessir," answered Pike.

"Two sugars?"

"Yessir."

"Sprinkle of nutmeg?" Pergola had gotten the idea from a flyboy.

"Just like you like it, sir."

Pergola took a sip and smiled ear to ear at John without looking up at Pike. "He knows how I like it." He continued looking at John and said, now with a serious and questioning look, "You like lemons?"

"Yessir." Calling Pergola "sir" had become infectious.

"Pike, get my man here some lemonade. Make sure it's cold."

Pike returned in a few moments with a filled glass, cold moisture clinging to its sides, and placed it on the table in front of them while Pergola continued reading. John thought it strange that Pergola was drinking hot coffee but had ordered John cold lemonade.

"Okay, Sergeant, I got this. Scram."

"Yessir." And Pike disappeared out the door.

Pergola looked at John. "Look, kid... Can I call you kid?"

John knew the captain meant no disrespect, so he nodded.

"Look, kid...drink up. I ain't never seen a score this high. You scored even higher than me, which ain't saying much, but down here, my score makes me Einstein. And you can fight too. It took a lot of moxie for you to take on that crowd of dimwits outside. If you want to enlist, I'll sign you up this afternoon, but I want to send you out West where we have a camp training Negro officers and recruits. You won't be able to hide the fact you're a Negro, even if you wanted to, and it don't seem like you want to anyway. The Army don't have heaps of Negro candidates for the program. You game?"

John nodded.

"Pike'll give you a basic uniform with Georgia colors and the transport vouchers. Avoid other servicemen on the trip, especially officers, because you won't have an escort. Pike'll only have time to teach you how to salute. If you come across pain-in-the-ass, busybody officers, use the word 'sir' in each sentence. Get to Hawa...hwa...the camp in Arizona with as little fanfare as possible." Pergola glanced up at the calendar on the wall to check the day of the week and then his wristwatch. "You have about two hours to make the next train to New Orleans, which will give you time to just make a connection there for Tucson. I see you're from New Orleans. Don't visit nobody—you gotta make that train. If you're not in Huachuca..." He mangled the name again. "...in forty-eight hours, my man out there won't take you in the next basic training group, and the commander will send you to mess-cook school. Shake a leg."

"Thank you, sir."

"*Addio.*"

ఌఌఌ

In the early evening, John was driven to Terminal Station on Spring Street in Atlanta by the same sergeant who'd administered the aptitude test ordered by Captain Pergola. The sergeant had resented the command but knew that even mild insubordination was not tolerated by his captain, and at the same time, he was a bit curious about his passenger who scored perfectly on the aptitude test after the captain pulled him from the line. It surprised him so much that he administered a second time, and then a third, the last time in a closed room with no windows with the sergeant sitting across from John to make sure no collusion took place.

Pike had a doc give him a physical separate from the rest of the recruits, filled out the paperwork, swore him in, and got him his transport vouchers. Then the captain had Pike take him to the train station.

Though the sun was now very low on the horizon behind the station as they approached in a military jeep, it was still hot. Driver and passenger were momentarily blinded by the direct sun as they pulled past the northern edge of the building and into the semicircle in front of Terminal Station, Atlanta, and John saw that the stucco ochre walls and red-tiled roof gave it a more cheerful look than its government exterior exuded. The station had two tall, eight-story, gothic towers that looked as if they had been built in the style of the Jesuit churches where John spent his first formative years in the Rhineland, though these towers were spaced wider apart, with a flat roof in between them instead of an ornately curved stonework on the facade. The building's ground floor spread out like a hacienda and had about a dozen cantilevered doorways leading into a covered walkway and then into the station's waiting room proper. There were several jeeps there already waiting for pick-ups as well as some armed sentries out front holding rifles in front of them as a reminder that there was both a war ongoing and to quell any potential saboteurs, though how the guards were supposed to do that, they themselves didn't know.

Pike drove him up the ramp leading up to the station and passed dozens of parked cars in front of both the station and the parking lot. He pulled directly in front of one of the arches on the far right, above which "COLORED WAITING ROOM" was elegantly carved into marble in two-foot-tall letters. Pike pulled the emergency brake to brace the jeep from rolling.

Despite the implied insult of the sign, John was strangely pleased by its quality. Much better than the hand-painted or sloppily drawn signs that he had seen since down south.

"This is your stop, Shall-met," Pike said, not knowing the correct French pronunciation of the name, and he reflexively held out his hand but quickly withdrew it. John was used to this and ignored it. Though Pike, except for the blatant racism, appeared reasonable. He even had a twinge of regret over treating John that way that he didn't quite understand himself. Pike found this newfound attitude surprising and wasn't sure how to deal with it but offered kindly, "John, you should pick up some food before getting on the train. Likely get nothing on board."

As he handed John a manila envelope, Pike said, "The first vouchers will get you to New Orleans on the Southern Line—a train called the Washington—and then you switch to get a straight-line train to Tucson, Arizona, on the Sunset Special. Once you arrive, you'll have an hour to make the train. I say again: Buy some food in the station 'cause you probably won't be able to get any onboard or along the way. You should arrive in Tucson early tomorrow evening, and a third voucher will get you a bus to the camp. Don't miss the bus—there is only one a day, and the walk is about fifty miles."

John thanked him and was on his way after grabbing his duffel.

The waiting room was meager—and appeared to be little more than a few transplanted park benches inside a busy waiting room. It had a rough-hewn concrete floor, poured in but unfinished. He waited in line with his vouchers and got a double-take from others who immediately wondered what a White boy was doing in the colored waiting room. Though not common, Negroes who could pass for White were not unknown in Atlanta.

John looked through a door that led to the station's

central room and saw an impressive, well-appointed hall. Though the station's roof from the outside looked flat, the inside was high, with cantilevered arches, and quite cavernous. Inside were several rows, each of which held two long wooden benches with gently arched backs. The floor was shiny and being swept continuously by two Negroes in gray maintenance outfits and red caps.

Back in the colored waiting room, he got in the line for tickets, receiving another double-take from the Negro ticket man on the other side of the counter who immediately returned to indifference and handed in the voucher. He stamped it and put it in a cubby hole labeled "Reclaim from US Govt," and John was given a ticket for a one-way trip to New Orleans. He handed him back the voucher that he would need to travel from New Orleans to Tucson.

"You get this ticket in New Orleans," he said in a bored voice. "Wait. They'll call your train in about thirty minutes."

"Any place I can buy food for the trip?" John asked.

"Out the door, make a left, another left, and another left, and there are some stands where colored folks can buy food."

Out John went and found stands that were really just wooden horses covered with a plank of wood. Behind them were Negro women and men in dirty aprons selling all manner of food: fried chicken and pork ribs and sides being cooked on fifty-five-gallon drums sliced in half from top to bottom, covered with some chicken wire with burning wood beneath. There were light balsa baskets of apples and peaches as well as containers of warm milk that were not pasteurized but still in glass containers and covered with foil.

John bought what he thought he would need for the three-day trip: chicken, pork, apples, peaches, a loaf of crusty bread, a quart of milk—and a warm bottle of Coca-Cola, which the seller opened before John could protest.

She saw his look and said, "Where you gonna get it opened otherwise, boy? You got a bottle opener?"

"I thought I'd be able to get one on the train."

"Where you headed, boy?"

"New Orleans, then further west."

She laughed. "Right now, this is the closest you gonna be to a bottle opener. In fact, where you is standing now is the closest you're gonna get to the White dining car."

He picked up another large chunk of crusted bread and some small dessert cakes, clearly made at someone's home and with no icing.

"You got something to put them in, boy?"

"I have my duffel bag."

"That'll break apart. Hang on." She reached under the table and brought out a shoebox for large boots and put everything in there.

"What do I owe you for the box?" John asked.

"I usually charge a nickel, but you can have it. That food cost a dollar."

"You don't happen to have ice cream, do you?" John inquired hopefully.

The women and men behind the table working the makeshift barbecue turned around, looked at him, and laughed.

"What makes you think we got that?"

"I saw some children out in front of the station eating some," John explained.

"*Ha!* You saw some *White* chillen eatin' some. Ain't no nigger eat no ice cream I seen!"

John left a dollar for all the items and walked off toward the station. As he re-entered the colored waiting room, he heard his train, the Washington-Atlanta-New Orleans Express, being called on the public address system—it was pulling into the station in ten minutes, and the broadcast said to go immediately to the designated track.

He walked beside several wooden luggage platforms with large, Conestoga-like wagon wheels connected to each side, and the flat platforms had a short lip on each end to keep things from sliding off. The flat beds stood at a forty-five-degree angle.

The train entered the station and once there, John climbed into what he thought was his train car and met a pleasant view of comfortable surroundings. Elegantly appointed, excellent seats, luggage racks, carpet. As he stood in the entryway of the car, just alongside him, a door opened to a nicely appointed toilet for the car. In that room was a man drying his hands on a hanging towel and stepping out. Lights, mirror, and a sink with brass taps. Very nice. The lamps jutting from the spaces between the long windows and the racks above the seats, as well as the trim on the seats themselves, were polished brass. Some passengers already on the train from places as far away as its starting point in Washington gave him a glance and then put their heads back down, re-absorbed in whatever it was they were doing. John knew he was going to enjoy this ride to Tucson and then to Fort Huachuca at the end.

He looked at his ticket to find a seat number, and there was a Negro liveried Pullman attendant at the other end of the train car in a navy-blue suit including a jacket with brass buttons that gleamed, as did the racks and the lamps. As the attendant finished putting a bag on the top rack from another oncoming rider, another passenger caught the attendant's eye and said "George" to get his attention, and when he did, pointed at John.

George glanced down at John at the other end of the carriage, squinted, then vehemently shook his head no and motioned quickly for John to go outside, back on the platform. The attendant stepped out of the car just as John did, and they both met halfway down the length of the train car.

"What are you doing, boy?"

"I thought that was my car. It has the right number."

"Lemme sees that ticket." John handed it over. "You're four cars down the line, brother—in the colored car. Don't go making that mistake again, boy. We'll have a riot on our hands. Coupla peckers are in that car already, and they see you, there'll be hell to pay."

Handing back his ticket, George added, "If you need

anything, I have a small sitting room in the car next to yours. Knock on the door, ask for Cecil, but don't come in. I'll come see you."

"I thought your name was George."

"That's slave talk. Used to be that Negro slaves took the name of their master."

"You have a master? And your master's name is George?"

"George Pullman. Started the company I work for a million years ago. They control all the attendants and everything to do with the rail lines. Pays Negroes like shit, but he pays. Cheap food, a warm place to stay, for which I'm charged, but it is still cheap and warm. And I traveled more in the last two, three years than I ever did in my lifetime. Seen this whole country end to end. What's your name, boy?"

"John."

"Car four, John—down that way. Get a move on. We leaving shortly. Where you going anyway, boy?"

"Fort in Arizona. I'm going to officer training school," John said with a hint of pride.

"Hoo-wee! Don't see many colored officers." Cecil then left to look after more oncoming passengers.

John went back to his designated train car. He noticed the handrails to boost himself on the steps were noticeably grimier than the car he'd last entered. He pulled himself up and stepped into the car and was faced with a starkly different type of Pullman experience. Some seats were wooden, some wicker—there was no symmetry about them. The car was packed. No luggage racks, and people had their belongings in the small area in front of them. The car clearly had not been cleaned in a while.

He saw his seat near the toilet was still free, so he stepped into the bathroom near the front of the car where he had entered and brought in his duffel bag and box of food. The bathroom was half the size of the one in the other train car. It had a frame chair with the seat hewn out round that emptied directly onto the tracks, and a small basin with a pitcher of water next to it on a tiny shelf. There was a low-wattage bulb hanging from the ceiling by a thin wire, uncovered.

After throwing water in his face, he left the tiny toilet, closed the door, and sat down on his designated seat, which was really more or less like a lightweight park bench, barely bolted to the floor. There was a heavyset man in a rumpled suit sitting next to him; his head leaned against the window, and he was gently snoring. Across from him sat an attractive, mocha-skinned, and exotic-looking young woman wearing a white magnolia flower in her hair; he assumed she was the sleeping man's wife, though the two seemed a curious and incongruous match. She had two young boys; one was sleeping, the other quite fidgety. He handed this one a fresh peach; he looked at it and then handed it to his mother to peel. He had eaten them before and didn't like the skin. John settled down for the ten-hour train journey to his first stop: New Orleans.

ॐॐॐ

John woke up several hours later; the train was stopped. The mom across from him was gone, her two boys now on either side of John, one leaning on his chest, the other on his leg but sound asleep and drooling. The rumpled suit was still leaning against the glass, still lightly snoring.

If he moved, he feared he would wake them, and after about ten minutes, their mom reappeared. He looked at her with pleading eyes, picked one up, then the other, and sat them next to her as if they were rag dolls.

"An explosion outside wouldn't wake these kids up. We've been delayed, not getting into New Orleans till two hours late. You live in New Orleans?"

"Originally, but I gotta catch another train from there."

"What kinda accent is that, boy? Kinda sounds northern, kinda sounds southern, but really neither."

"I was born in Europe, and I grew up speaking French and German."

"Whooo-eee, you a long way from home, boy."

"Yes, but I'm American now."

"That's not exactly something to be proud of. Whatcha doing heading to Tucson?"

"Officers' training camp."

"Officer of what?"

"Officer in the US Army."

"Shit, boy, my husband is there. I just know you're gonna miss that train."

After verifying the delay and looking at the scheduled departure time on his next voucher, John got up and went across the platform between the two train cars and faced the door. He knocked lightly first, then harder. The door opened, and a Negro attendant asked sternly, "What you want, boy?"

"Cecil there?"

"Who you?" John told him, then asked again, and a moment later Cecil came to the door. "Cecil, why we stopped?" Sonny asked.

"Shunted to the side for an Army train. Could be here another hour," the porter responded.

"When are we getting to New Orleans?" Sonny was almost imploring now.

"'Bout 7:30. 'Bout an hour and a half late."

"Cecil, I gotta get a train at six to go to the camp."

"Ain't gonna happen, boy."

"When is the next train that goes to Tucson?"

"Gimme a second." Cecil pulled out a booklet from the inside pocket of his jacket and a pencil jutting out from the side of his hat and went through the schedule a few times, writing little notes; he finally whistled.

"What?" John pressed.

"Well, I checked to see if you could do it sooner, but the next direct Sunset Special train leaves New Orleans on Tuesday. You can get the milk runs—about four to five trains, Houston, Dallas, San Antonio—but you gotta keep changing, and that still gets there Monday night."

"Cecil—I have to be there before Monday morning, or they're gonna make me an Army cook."

"I'd say you're cooked then, boy. *Ha!*" He laughed at his own witticism. "Why you gotta get there?"

"I told you. Officer training school."

"You really gonna be an officer?"

"If I get there by Monday morning basic training."

"Okay. Lessee what we can do."

"Is there another train I can get?" asked John.

"Less said, the better. Forget about it," Cecil concluded.

John returned to his bench, looked at the woman sitting across from him, and reconnected with her.

"These your boys?"

"Nephews. This is Tom, and John is over there."

"My name is John."

"I'm Henny, Henny Dalton. I'm taking them here with my uncle to live on the post with my man and myself. Jimmy. Jimmy Simms. He's a master sergeant," she said proudly.

They shared stories as John saw the sun drop out of the western window lower and lower. He didn't have a watch, but Uncle Floyd next to him did, and he twisted his neck to look—it was twenty minutes after his train's departure time in Louisiana to Arizona.

As the Washington slowed down, heading into the terminal in New Orleans, John started collecting his items, gave the boys another peach, and promised to check in with Henny when he was settled at the camp.

Cecil came from the next car with an announcement. "Boy, the Sunset is running late, but you gotta make tracks to catch it."

"Cecil, I gotta get a ticket first."

"Lemme see your voucher." Cecil looked at it and said, "You ain't gonna have time, kid. Don't you worry about no ticket. Get on the car in the back next to the mail car if you can find it. Don't go walking through a White-only car like you did here."

"But they'll kick me off, probably while it is moving if I don't have a ticket."

"Nope, ask for an attendant called Cecil."

"Is there one on every train?" John paused. "Let me guess. Your brother?"

"That would be stupid, givin' him my name. My cousin."

"How will he know me?"

"Don't ask. I don't want to spend the next ten years in prison in Angola. Just tell him I sent you."

As he jumped off the moving Washington, he heard the announcement for the Sunrise's imminent departure six tracks over, and he ran as fast as he could.

As he pulled alongside the track, the train was pulling away. He jumped, slipped, and fell. He picked up some speed, jumped again, and was helped onto the back by a Negro mail sorter.

A Negro conductor working for the company helped him up the final two feet. "You just come in on the Washington?" asked the conductor.

"Yeah," John confirmed.

"You headed toward Tucson?"

"Yes."

"What fer?"

"Officers' training at Camp Huachuca," replied John.

"The Negro camps. You gonna be a Negro officer in the Army?"

"I hope so." John stepped into the last mail car and asked if Cecil was there.

They called to the next car, and he appeared.

"You Cecil?" John asked. "I was on the Washington from Atlanta."

"You John?"

"Yessir."

"You the guy gonna be an officer?"

"I hope so."

"Okay. You find a seat in the next car."

"Thanks. Why are you guys late?"

All the Pullman attendants, all conveniently named George, started laughing.

"What happened?" John asked, puzzled.

George explained, "Well, some stupid niggers, as we was described by au-gust train officials, somehow spilled the ice that was meant for the first-class air-conditioner. Wheel came off the axel of the luggage platforms we was bringing it in—for some reason. It spoiled in the mud. There happened to be a couple of drums of wheel grease that had been knocked over by the accident too. Took almost two hours to get a new batch of ice from town. The train was not gonna leave without it. And, it turns out, we took our time about it—cuz we lazy."

"I'm sorry."

A smile spread across Cecil's face. "Made the train, didn't you, boy?"

☙ ☙ ☙

When John arrived in Tucson, he ran to look for the bus. It was already late at night—hours later than when he was supposed to arrive. He had no idea how he would get to the camp with his gear by 6 a.m. He saw a jeep with a snoozing Negro driver in uniform and gave him a shake.

"You going to Huachuca?" John asked.

The driver opened his eyes. "Excuse me, sir?"

John saw the uniform but couldn't see his rank, so he wasn't sure whether the driver should be called "sir." "You going to Huachuca?" he asked again.

"I am, but I'm waiting for somebody. Who are you, sir?"

"John Chalmet," he said, with the proper French pronunciation for the surname. "Who are you waiting for?"

"Somebody named Tom. I'm supposed to get him to the camp as soon as possible. But I can't leave here till he gets here, and he's already late. I don't collect him, Captain Ventimiglia will tan my ass, and I ain't foolin'."

"When is this guy due?"

"About an hour ago from New Orleans."

John looked at him: "Tom Shall-met?" He intentionally mispronounced his surname. It was an easily inspired guess as it turned out.

"That's the guy."

"That's me."

"You said your name is John."

"Long story—here are my orders from Atlanta."

The PFC scanned them and said, "Hop in. We gotta make tracks. Captain will think we hit the town drinking up a storm."

EIGHTEEN

HUACHUCA

The private who drove John down from Tucson began to explain what would be happening the next day, relaying all manner of information about the captain of the officer candidate recruitment introductory training class and how several hundred soldiers had already arrived, including many officer candidates. However, because the weather was so mild, the jeep was uncovered and open, and he was traveling so fast that the wind whipping alongside made it almost impossible for John to hear him.

The only things John fully got were that Captain Ventimiglia—who was likely asleep at the moment—would be running the basic training and that John could bunk with the private.

John arrived well after midnight. As they approached the front gate of the camp, they passed a series of Quonset huts just outside the perimeter of the fort and made it through the front entrance; the barrier was lifted—there was an armed sentry, and they drove directly to the barracks area. John and the driver saw that a light was on in the captain's hut. The private braked, turned the jeep around, and they both went inside the office of Captain Ventimiglia, the Italian *paisan* of Captain Pergola from his old neighborhood in Brooklyn.

The private saluted and handed the captain John's papers. John looked at him, mimicked the salute, and stood at attention.

The captain read the papers and, not looking up, said with an accent almost identical to Captain Pergola's: "*Minchia*. You're the Georgia egghead." Flipping to the second page, he reiterated what John already knew: "Perfect score on the aptitude test."

The private who drove John from Tucson had been standing at attention but audibly whistled at this fact, and the captain looked at him sharply.

"Alston, wait outside."

"Yessir."

"You're late, Shall-met," the captain pointed out.

"Apologies, sir. Very sorry, sir," John said, remembering his instructions. "The train was delayed by two hours getting into Tucson, sir."

Ventimiglia continued reading. "Okay, I can see what Captain Pergola meant. I'll have Alston bring you to hut 4—everyone will be asleep. Normally, you build your own mattress with straw from out back. Take one of those against the far wall. Reveille is at zero-five-thirty—in about four hours. That's when your basic training begins."

As John walked out, the captain's light went out. He had waited up for John to arrive.

Alston took John to hut 4. A mattress doubled up under his arm (it was filled with straw), Alston showed him a bed frame, the open toilet at the end of the hut, and as he left, he whispered: "I'd go to sleep as soon as possible if I were. The bugle blows in about four hours, and it will be a loooong day."

మ‍మ‍మ

Fort Huachuca was situated near the foot of the Huachuca Mountains about sixty miles southeast of Tucson and about fifteen miles north of the Mexican border.

There was a train station just north of the town of Huachuca, about ten miles from the fort, but only one train a week arrived—usually with new Negro recruits from throughout the country—before reversing and going back to Tucson through a series of side-tracks and a small roundabout.

Fort Huachuca was truly the home of the Negro soldier in the United States. While it was a detail unknown to all the recruits at the time, it would be ingrained in them over the next several months. Beginning in 1892, when the 24th Infantry Regiment first departed through its gates, and continuing up until 1944, when the 92nd Infantry Division marched out on its way to Italy, this camp housed quite a few Negro detachments of the 24th and 25th infantries, the 9th and 10th cavalries, and the 92nd and 93rd divisions.

ले ले ले

After an early rise and a morning of necessary business, such as new uniform distribution, vaccinations, and perfunctory physical exams, just before lunch, the roughly two dozen Negro officer candidates were led into a warm auditorium, though cooler than outside. They took seats as they were overseen by a group of all-White southern officers, deliberately assigned by the military because they "knew" the nature and "deficiencies" of the Negro soldier and didn't expect much as a result. Indeed, it became clear as time went on that those racial problems were getting in the way of the soldiers' proper training within the fighting unit. Most resented the fact that they had to look after, train, and "babysit," as it were, the Negroes. All except Captain Ventimiglia, that is. He took what came to him as a matter of course, and having been rivals of the Negroes in Brooklyn, though he didn't like them, he had a certain respect for them.

After the officer candidates assembled and began chattering, getting to know each other in a mixture of accents from all over the country, a cry was heard:

"Atten-shun."

Nearly all stood statue-still in front of the nearest chair. Ventimiglia entered the gymnasium.

"At ease. Be seated."

Ventimiglia cleared his throat and began, clearly and slowly enunciating his words:

"Welcome to Fort Huachuca—Huachuca is an Indian

name meaning 'place of thunder.' Here, you will spend a minimum of what I hope is the most demanding thirteen weeks, or longer, of your lives. This post is the oldest continuously used military reservation in the nation, and it is used exclusively for the training of Negro troops.

"Though you are all officer candidates, you do not have it any easier than anyone else. You will be drilled until you nearly cry in subjects like military courtesy, discipline, sanitation, physical fitness, first aid, map reading, tank and aircraft identification, drills, and more drills. And those drills will consist of lectures, films, demonstrations, and hands-on practice to accomplish our goals." He was on a roll with what was an unfamiliar accent to most people in the room, so he spoke deliberately. "After approximately one month, you will progress to marksmanship, individual soldier tactics, obstacle courses, grenade throwing, bayonet courses, weapons care and assembly, and of course, more drills. The final month of basic training will be weapons qualification and maneuvering at the squad and certainly at platoon level. At all times, you will be kept fit with extensive PT and many marched miles. In fact, you will be expected to march carrying full packs twenty-five miles in eight hours before the end of this training."

The men sat a bit dumbfounded as the words sunk in, not so much by the skills they were expected to learn but by the physical expectations that would be made upon them.

The captain continued but shifted his tone from official-sounding to more relaxed: "Who has heard of the famous Apache Indian, Geronimo?" This pulled them out of their momentarily stunned attitude. Some men chuckled; most raised their hands in affirmation.

"Geronimo was tracked down and taken prisoner by men trained at and working from this fort, and that was the end of the Indian Wars." The captain eyeballed them. "This is the largest and most efficient training ground for Negro soldiers in the United States Military. Approximately forty thousand people live and work here. Here, we have two identical camps: one for Whites and one for coloreds. Under no circumstances, unless you are accompanied by a White soldier, and preferably an officer, are you to set foot in the White camp."

Most of the candidates were silent, taking it as a matter of course, but some, mostly from the North, committed the grave sin of murmuring in disapproval until the captain inelegantly yelled, "Shut up!" and there was silence once again. The murmuring was justified. The northern recruits, used to some segregation but not the stark level of southern discrimination, had heard rumors during the time leading up to this day as they got to know the camp: The Negro camp was missing some of the amenities, such as recreation halls, medical facilities, and expanded sports gymnasiums, that existed in the White section or cantonment. It was segregation at its worst. Yet entirely normal for the time and sanctioned by the military.

The camp did indeed have a large population, more extensive than most cities and towns from whence they came. It had its share of families (for some officers) as well as shops, traffic accidents, burglaries, rapes, and the occasional murder—as you might find with that many people in one place. In fact, one occurred not long after John arrived, but he didn't pay attention to the details.

Ventimiglia continued. "You will be officially known as Buffalo Soldiers, a name that has been around for some eighty years. Some say it was a name given to you by the Indians because you fight like buffaloes, standing your ground and charging when threatened."

This momentarily instilled pride, but he took that away a moment later.

"Some say it is because of your nappy, tightly curled hair, like a buffalo coat." He said this without shame or reaction from the assembled men, though he did get sniggers from the southern officers.

⌒⌒⌒

A local newspaper said at the time that some of Negroes that came into the camp after Pearl Harbor arrived with scars of shackles stamped into their eyes. Some came with college degrees (these were mostly the officer candidates), and others with their parole papers. Some came with pockets full of loaded dice. Many came damning America, with her Jim Crow and lynch laws. Some came cursing Hitler and Hirohito and the fascists and were eager to do battle for human rights. There were as many motivations for being in the US Army, drafted or enlisted, as there were Negroes in the camp.

For some Negroes, the experiences at the camp were

mixed. Some thought it was an oasis in their otherwise dreary lives. For others, they found the same prejudice and harsh Jim Crow laws and inequality they had left at home. For Negroes from the North, many wondered what they had gotten themselves into, believing that the bigotry their ancestors down south faced was in the dim past. Here, it was not. While discrimination did exist for the Negro north of the Mason-Dixon line, what they experienced at Huachuca was more akin to what their parents and grandparents had experienced in White southern America. In time, the facilities improved dramatically for the Negro at the fort, but it still did not even begin to erase the discrimination they all felt. Practically every kind of facility needed on a military post was duplicated so the races would not mix.

꙳꙳꙳

The next day, Ventimiglia received a phone call and announced his rank and name into the receiver. He heard a familiar-sounding voice at the other end.

"Carmine, what's shakin'?"

"Joey P! How are ya?"

"Doin' good. Hey, listen, my man Tommy arrive safely?"

"Who?"

"Tommy. Tommy Shall-met."

Ventimiglia knew who he was talking about but let him continue through the name mix-up. Joey made mistakes like this all the time.

"Tommy Shall-met. Moolie who looks White and talks White. Good man, tough as nails. If he lived up north, he be running all the moolie gangs around Howard Beach."

"Yep," Ventimiglia replied. "And it is *John* Shall-may. Made it safely and is busy first-day teaching the non-officer candidates to read and write."

"What?! I didn't send him to you for that!"

"Relax. He is doing exactly what you sent him to do." Ventimiglia continued, "Joey, it is nuts here. Most of the Negroes in the non-officer training are poorly schooled, and most are illiterate. We gotta even things out because most of these boys can't read signs on how to get to the toilets. From what I hear from recruitment leads at other camps, it ain't much better with some poor Whites, but I'm buried in them. We knew it was coming, but we weren't prepared for the numbers. Nearly half don't know what to do with pencil and paper."

Pergola listened in silence.

"Word quickly got out that your boy John had scored high on the aptitude test, which reminds me..." Ventimiglia scratched a note on the pad in front of him. "I gotta rip Alston a new one," he muttered. "Anyway, as a result, and by virtue of the fact that he was in officer training, John is naturally expected to tutor the illiterate Negroes. He spent most of his free time on day one writing letters to their families, which mostly go toward their neighbors 'cause their own family is probably illiterate as well."

Pergola shifted topics as he had heard enough. "Okay,

gotta go." His mercurial boss, Major Padgett, was standing in his doorway, fists on his hips, tapping one foot, as he suspected a personal phone call. "Take good care of my boy. I'll be there at some point and will want to see how well you train him!" With that, he hung up and addressed his boss. "Sir, checking up on an officer candidate I sent to Arizona, sir."

Padgett shook his head slightly and left.

Ventimiglia reflected on the matter. Carmine would make Joey Pergola proud. He liked John.

ॐॐॐ

There was tremendous pride and admiration of both the soldiers and their Negro officers when their training was complete, but despite their hard work and dedication to the tasks at hand, they could have performed better. Racial problems interfered. The southern lieutenants responsible for their training expected little of them because they were Negro, and as a result, the best could not be drawn out of any of the recruits.

NINETEEN

UNCONVENTIONAL TACTICS

Two days after training ended, while heavy cleaning was taking place, John was called to Ventimiglia's office. He stood to attention and saluted. "Lieutenant Chalmet reporting, sir."

"At ease."

Another officer stood up from the hut's corner and moved directly toward John, arm outstretched. "Tommy-boy!"

"John. Joey, it's John, " Ventimiglia corrected.

"Johnny-boy!" Pergola yelled.

"Hello, sir." John gave Pergola a smart salute and then shook his hand.

"I can see they're training you right out here. And lieutenant bars! Impressive."

"Yessir."

"How are ya?" Pergola asked.

"Ready to fight, sir."

"Right answer. Let's see what we can do about that."

"What are you doing here, sir?"

"I was investigating what I thought was an unsolved murder for CID, but the guy copped and has a walk planned up a short flight for a hemp necktie and a hole in the floor."

"Huh?" John asked.

"One of your *compadres* pleaded guilty, so I've got no work," Pergola explained. "A guy named Simms killed a woman named Henny Dalton." He looked at the sheet back on the desk where he was sitting a moment ago to verify the names.

"That was Henny, sir?" John asked.

"Yeah, you know her?" Pergola asked.

"Just in passing, sir. And I had heard that Simms was in trouble, but I didn't know why. Is he going to be hanged, sir?" John asked quizzically.

"Yep, and it ain't gonna be because he broke the spirit of the law. Ha!"

John went silent. He knew Simms and Henny. He had met Henny while traveling down to Huachuca on the train, and later met her partner Jimmy Simms at the fort. He was the post's librarian, and John spent whatever little free time he could there reading. When Simms discovered he was going to be hanged, he changed his plea to not guilty, and the martial court was evaluating whether or not to open up the investigation. The official story conflicted with what John knew about her and her husband (not Simms), but Negro-on-Negro killings were not terribly uncommon in the camp or in the nearby towns, and the

Whites in command wanted to have little to do with them. According to the story on the base, a defenseless woman being murdered was pretty much an open and shut case. Why it was done with a pocketknife was still a bit of a mystery. There were lots of unanswered questions about the killing, but it would be suicide for John to get involved.

"So, whatcha got planned, Tommy-boy?" asked the captain.

John looked at him and knew it was hopeless to try and correct him. "Close order drill and marching—and a boxing match in two weeks. We think we're getting close to shipping out."

Pergola looked at Captain Ventimiglia. "Carmine, you let him go for a week?" he asked, voice raised.

"As long as he is ready for the boxing match in two weeks—I got a bundle riding on him. Whaddya gonna do?" Carmine responded.

"I want to teach John what we call 'unconventional tactics' like they do with some special operations forces." Pergola looked at Ventimiglia and said to John, "He got the time?"

Ventimiglia said, "We can spare him."

అంఅంఅం

The following day, at zero-six-thirty (mess hall opened at six, and they met to get a light breakfast), they went to an indoor gym.

Both in their outdoor skivvies and standing across from one another, Captain Pergola began with a lecture.

Using a formal tone, Pergola began, "During this war, and you may have learned about this from any number of the enemy, you have to learn they'd do some of this stuff you learned from basic training, but for what we're gonna do, we've suspended the code of sportsmanship. If you're evva in the unfortunate situation where you've lost your weapon or have no weapon at all, and you're faced by a single or any number of the enemy, you have to understand the very basics of defense and counter-attack in the worst way possible. And by that, I mean, how to fight dirty.

"We're going to cover the basic and most useful tactics of jujitsu, wrestling, street fighting—in which, by the way, I have the most skill." He licked his lips. "And the very basics of *savate*, a French form of incredibly unsportsmanlike fighting that is unusually dirty, but it does the trick, and hey, we're in this to win—that is rule number one. We're in it to win. You've gotta outwit and somehow overcome the guy or guys across from you to succeed.

"We're going to learn a man's weak points." Pergola reeled them off as if he were reciting a prayer: "Side of the neck under the jawbone, Adam's apple, bridge of the nose, lip below the nose, back of the neck and skull, the spine, the kidneys at the lower edge of the ribs, the solar plexus [he pointed at his own], a direct attack at the eyes, the enemy's shin or arch, and my favorite, the instant incapacitator: his groin.

"We're gonna learn breaking grips, handholds, and breaking body blocks. By the end of this week, you're gonna master the basic techniques."

Pergola had grown up in a tough neighborhood, and he made this clear.

"Let's get started. Get in a relaxed stance and put your hands out like you're going to make a grab for me."

Pergola moved aside, grabbed John's arm and pulled as hard as he could; John fell to the ground—he was completely motionless.

Shit, I killed him, Pergola thought. He went over, pulled on John's shoulder to help him up, and asked, "Tom, you okay?"

John reached up, grabbed his arm up to his elbow, and pulled Pergola over his head and onto the ground, flipping him over his body.

Pergola had the wind knocked out of him and was breathing fast as he slowly refilled his lungs.

John explained, "When you approach a prone enemy, always assume his helplessness is a pretense."

"Where'd you learn that?" asked Pergola.

"My old man learned *savate* in the French Army. He taught me when I was ten—thought I needed it in New Orleans."

"Say honest to God," Pergola ordered.

John stared at him, confused. "Say what?"

"Honest to God," Pergola repeated sternly.

"What does that mean?"

"Don't they teach you nothing down south? It means you ain't lying."

When John didn't respond, Pergola said, "Okay, Tommy, look." He got up on his elbows. "I forgot to mention, for the next few days, we're going to be pulling our punches. I don't need you hanged for killing a superior officer, or worse, to lose the use of my 'nads."

৵৵৵

For the next week, Captain Pergola taught John all he could on hand-to-hand combat, including the use of melee weapons such as knives, sticks, batons, and anything that could be improvised for that purpose, such as army-issue entrenching tools. They covered all the things that could be learned relatively quickly.

He taught John how to act as rapidly and precisely as possible and trained him to make split-second decisions to minimize accidents.

Near the end of the second week (Ventimiglia allowed them to continue as the tactics helped John's boxing skills), he showed him how to gather and use any intelligence he could when entering a crisis situation, including the use of diversionary tactics, using diagrams to review plans, and outlining responsibilities if there were teams involved, even going so far as to conduct step-by-step walk-throughs of the process whenever time was available.

John learned that an assault can come when least expected and learned how to allow for fatigue and other things that could take away from a particular target's alertness. He was also instructed that staged "emergencies" were also helpful.

At the end of that week, John and Captain Pergola sat across from each other in the office of Ventimiglia, who was off thoroughly annoying the former recruits, now fully fledged soldiers, on the parade ground. Pergola and Chalmet were covered with grime, but they were sharing two beers the captain had grabbed from Ventimiglia's office fridge.

"Sir, the captain will have a heart attack if he sees us drinking his beer. He once made someone do a ten-mile run for just being in the office here unescorted," John warned his captain.

"Not a chance, Tommy. Who do you think gave him his first beer?"

"Sir, why do you keep calling me Tommy?" John finally decided to ask him.

Pergola stared at him for the briefest of moments with a blank look as if he hadn't realized he had been doing it.

"I dunno. I have a brother that name, and I miss him like mad, and I keep on getting you two mixed up. You remind me a lot of him," he finally admitted, then added, "You did good this week, cuz. You're ready to kill." After another brief pause, a quizzical look came over the captain's face. "Why you wanna fight? Why do you want to fight for America when this country treats you and your people, and by that I mean the darker variety, so badly? Also, to be perfectly honest, up north anyway, you have the advantage of passing as a White man. Why don't you just do that? It'd be tons easier for you."

It was the first direct question John had ever received from a White man about race. He'd been asked by loads of Negro friends why he didn't just live up north and pass as a White man, and he gave his captain the same answer he had given them: "I hope that one day, maybe when the war is over, if I work hard enough, and the Negro works hard enough, people'll start treating us like human beings. Like normal Whites. Like they wouldn't even notice the color of our skin."

Pergola replied, "I hear you, kid. I thought the same thing too about Italians. We were always put down and, in some areas, are still put down today. And the only time people thought about not putting us down was when they had somebody else to go after. Before Italians, it was the Irish, and after us, I think, it'll be the Polacks."

After a while and a few more swigs of beer, John changed tact. "Where'd you learn about this, sir?"

"Just by watching, keeping my eyes open, and listening to my family and my grandparents. They been through a lot."

"No, sir. I mean, where did you learn to fight like this?"

Pergola got quiet and lightly licked his lips as he usually did when he was about to boast but didn't want to come off like he was conceited or bragging. The latter was mostly true—the former, not at all.

"I joined the commandos and made it through their training until the last day, when I got a shot to the groin. The guy opposite me, the rat bastard, didn't pull the punch—a knife punch with his hand. Gave me a hernia, and I was laid up for the last two days of training. By the time I healed a week later, the group had moved on, graduated, and I was left behind. My commanding officer, a friend of Joey P, took kindly on me, promoted me to lieutenant, and put me in CID."

"Syd?" John enunciated.

"No, C-I-D! CID would be pronounced 'KID.'"

"So, what is kid?"

"No! CID. The US Army Criminal Investigation Division. We had become friendly, that commanding officer and me. And though he was a major and I was only a staff sergeant, he saw something in me. We were from the same neighborhood in Brooklyn. We got to talking a lot, and he said how he liked how I could solve almost any tactical problem thrown at me. And that included strategy and tactics. He said I wasn't 'elegant,' as if that mattered, but I got the job done. He wanted to put me in a group that solved crimes in the military."

"Why'd you do all this, sir?" John asked. "Why did you pull me out of the normal training routine to teach me hand-to-hand?"

"Like I said, kid, you can fight, and I expect you put up with a lot in your life, especially down south. But I'll tell you what..." Again, he licked his lips. "When I was about five, I saw my grandparents walking down across a street in Brooklyn. They didn't see me. They were walking along, minding their own business, I think going to the local grocer. A White rat bastard came up and started giving them a hard time, for fun, I guess, because they were old and short and Italian. I knew my *nonno* coulda laid the guy out because I saw him put my old man on the ground once in five seconds flat for answering back. My *nonna* was there with him, and she turned to walk away in the other direction because she knew what was likely to happen. My nonno was clenching his fists, but a few seconds later, the rat bastard's friends showed up, and it wasn't a fair fight. My *nonno* had no choice but to slink off. If he had a few seconds more, he coulda put the guy on the ground. But there wasn't enough time. Kid, I wanted to make sure you can move fast so that you can make fair use of a few seconds if you're in a similar situation."

␪␪␪

Turned out, the camp was nowhere near shipping out. They continued many, many more months, working through more tactical training and then uniform gear preparation until July 1944. The US Army wasn't terribly anxious to deploy a Negro division in which they had little confidence. John focused on his physical training and his natural leadership skills, which became apparent as their physical exertion continued. He also volunteered to assisting his fellow soldiers, writing letters for and teaching the illiterate ones to read and write.

John quickly showed his military bravery, acumen, and ability to lead and quickly rose through the ranks (as promptly as a Negro could in the current Army). He progressed from private to corporal to sergeant to lieutenant as quickly as he possibly could, all while he was still at Huachuca.

Finally, in early July 1944, they got their orders. They

were shipping off—destination unknown. When the train left the siding on the north end of Huachuca, none of the men had any clue as to their eventual destination. But after the train shifted a few tracks in Tucson, and a fresh engine was put on the other end of the long line of cars, those whose field training with their compass had sunk in and who understood geography inferred from the setting sun that their destination was likely the eastern seaboard of the US, and subsequently Europe.

TWENTY

A BUFFALO SOLDIER

After many months of continuous training in the US and then even more training, John and the rest of the Buffalo Soldiers arrived in Italy to great fanfare by the already-serving Negro soldiers in the military, particularly the Quartermaster Corps who were already there serving as cooks, gravediggers, stevedores, and waiters for White officers, though none were serving as combat soldiers.

Bigotry was predictably rife against the Buffalo Soldiers by the White military establishment, even in Italy, and many of their direct officers disliked them immensely. Their commander once they hit the ground there, General Almond, exclaimed to his Negro officers upon their arrival: "I did not send for you. Your Negro newspapers, Negro politicians, and White friends have insisted on your seeing combat, and I shall see that you get combat and your share of casualties." This was a rather harsh opinion to hold in a public arena. The Negroes had to fight, as it were, on two fronts. One against the

Nazis, and the other against the mentality of their own superiors.

The Italians, who switched sides to the Allies the year before, came to love the Negro soldiers much as the British had. They were generous with their supplies and rations, unfailingly polite, and very understanding and considerate with the populace, especially to the young and the ladies. They were also men not terribly different from all the other soldiers in the American Army except in the color of their skin.

However, most of their fellow White soldiers had several derogatory names for them, "Mrs. Roosevelt's Niggers" being the most popular, named after Eleanor Roosevelt for her public support of Negro integration. Their arrival in Italy marked the first time Negro soldiers from the US would be built into a fighting unit in Europe in WWII.

Soon after disembarking, John was given a weekend pass, and he and several of the officers hit the town of Naples to enjoy its sights, sounds, and ladies. They had already been warned to skip certain areas so as to not piss off their White "brother" officers as they didn't need or want the headache. They met a group of Negro Quartermaster soldiers at an outdoor café who had finished their meal and were in the process of lubricating themselves with beer. Once a comradery was established, the Negro officers did not pull rank very often, and information began to flow back and forth. Asked how they did by the newcomers, the story they got from everyone was always the same:

"We at the wrong end of the totem pole when it comes to getting any support. We can't even supply our own Negroes adequately. All the good stuff goes to the White soldiers. Even blood. Any of us complain, we get put on report and usually punished. We Americans got great weapons and terrific transport. In our 92nd, our Negro boys get stuff leftover from the last war—the oldest of everything. We was shipping crates of ammo up north to our guys, and I swear, most of the boxes had expired dates. I couldn't believe it, but when I got our stuff to the staging areas to bring to the front of the Negro fighters, I swear they had mules lined up, borrowed from Italian peasants—no trucks. What a crock of shit."

He got sideway glances from the Negro officers at the seeming disrespect, and the man quieted, but another officer soon continued. "You know, we have the training and the background. Shit, we trained on all the best weapons in the US during basic. Most of these White officers consider us stupider and not trustworthy, and even our NCOs are considered less than the lowest of the low. It ain't right."

Another chimed in, "I was told by a medic friend of mine that if Negro soldiers were injured or even wounded in action and required emergency blood transfusions, only the plasma of other Negro soldiers could be used to save their lives, White blood being reserved for White soldiers."

The officers flagged down a rather stunning *cameriera* so they could order the next round of drinks. After months of working, eating, sleeping, and training with men and weeks on a naval cruiser, zigzagging to avoid enemy submarines, and being under constant watch and Army discipline, she was a sight to behold. She had a killer figure, shapely legs, sultry eyes, and a full, red-lipped mouth. The entire group stayed silent and stared at her up and down while John, considered the linguist of the group, used rudimentary Italian to buy several pale lagers and a few more bottles of wine. None of them noticed the young lady's father in the doorway, leaning against the side with his arms crossed and a stern look. But when he realized there'd be no commotion and that they were a respectful bunch—and that there was hard cash coming into his café—his looks softened. It didn't hurt that most Americans ate and drank to excess. He watched while the enlisted men were thrilled by staring at his daughter, and their eyes followed her as she went back inside for their order. Her figure was good for business. In the silence, after she went inside, one of the sitting soldiers said, "In Alabama, if *we* did that, they'd find a tree for each of us."

They all had a good laugh, but not as hearty as it could have been because of the truth attached to it.

Bringing them back to reality, another said, "I heard White GIs are not allowed to reinforce Negroes on the front lines. I saw that when we had losses, we had to arrange that *Japanese* American soldiers were transferred to the front. I think they consider them as useless as us Negroes."

All this information sank into the newly arrived

officers' heads and tempered their attitude toward what they had to face. In a moment, their beer—and mostly wine—order came out, carried expertly balanced on her tray by the waitress, and they once again all stared at her curves as they did before and absorbed every move, but the officers were less gawking than absently looking, and while their gaze followed her as she waited at other tables, they were less engaged as they thought of both the dangers and the discrimination they were facing from what they just heard.

And face it they did. In addition to the discrimination among their own ranks, they faced a formidable enemy with weapons: the Germans.

☙ ☙ ☙

After the various vicissitudes faced by the entire Allied Army fighting on the Italian peninsula, some time afterward, a regiment of Negro fighting men were nearing a small Italian village called Sommocolonia, an ancient town with steep, winding roads—picturesque but awkward to move an army through. It was set on the edge of a cliff, as much a landscape painter's dream as it was a soldier's curse.

John and his captain, to keep a low profile, leopard-crawled up to the edge of one of the cliffs looking down on the town—twigs and leaves in the netting of their helmets and dulled metal binoculars to eliminate glare and avoid catching the sunlight. Their mission was to take and hold the town.

Ronald Allen, a reliable artillery captain and college-educated Negro officer from New Jersey, gave John the lay of the land he had been reconnoitering the previous week. He was an affable and tall athletic officer who was not afraid to challenge peer White officers who overstepped their boundaries with insults or insinuations toward their fellow Negro officers.

"Okay, Lieutenant, look over there. From the right vantage point, you can see the enormous valley just beyond the village. Those peaks over there, the granite ones, outline a thirty-mile-long stretch of the Serchio Valley. If we can get there, it'll get us the hell out of these awful hills. Our guys can't move in this area without being sitting ducks—and we'll have a bit of clear sailing to get the Germans. They know this too, and they're going to hold onto it like men possessed. Cutting sharply through these two mountain ranges is a valley the Germans call the Gothic Line, their main Nazi defensive line. If they hold us here, we can't get into Germany."

John interrupted, "So what do we have to do?"

"Take, and hold this tiny town, Sommocolonia, until we are relieved," Captain Allen replied in a matter-of-fact tone. "It is a perfect crossroads and necessary to move forward." He continued, "Okay, a mile to the north of Sommocolonia is the forward encampment of the German 14th Army. The word is out that their orders are *not* to take any prisoners because they got wind we're Negroes—by official Nazi standards, not fully human."

They both chuckled at this, but it still chilled them

to the bone. They knew the upcoming battle would be tough.

"How'd you hear this?"

"We captured a German taking a dump near our lines."

"When you gotta go, you gotta go."

"Yeah, great." Allan was annoyed at the stupid aphorism. "Anyway, he was near our lines at night, and we grabbed him. An arrogant prick. He spoke some English and started calling us niggers from the beginning of the interrogation and told us that their orders were to take no nigger prisoners. Sadly for him, he was shot trying to escape soon after we were finished."

Allen went on. "Six miles south of here is our Fifth Army Command Post. And I got news for you. They're refusing to provide either reinforcements for us to take the town or blood transfusions for our medics. I sent officers four times to ask. I woulda gone myself, but my major threatened me with desertion when I told him why I needed to go. I can't figure out why they won't help us."

Both Captain Allen and Lieutenant Chalmet didn't voice it, but they were facing the same issues from their own Army as they were the Germans, and though they would have been justified in doing so, only very rarely did they voice wonder what they were doing there.

かかか

On the day after Christmas in 1944, the Negro GIs in Sommocolonia were determined to prove that official assumptions made by Germans and Americans alike were wrong. When a massive German assault was launched on this windswept mountain village, two previously diminished Negro platoons comprised of about seventy American infantrymen were dug in just on the outskirts. Their own commanding officers expected them to throw down their guns and run when faced by the thousands of troops from the German 14th Army. But for over a day, this tiny group held out. Seventy GIs, all of them Negro, from the US Army's segregated 92nd Infantry Division held out against overwhelming odds, holding back an enemy offensive and very likely changing the course of World War II in Italy. Partially because of the strategic position held, and partly because the Nazis saw a level of dedication and ferocity by a race they considered inferior, news and details of the battle—some of which were certainly exaggerated—spread like wildfire among the German troops remaining in Italy, and it added an additional level of fear to the task they had at hand.

Like a thousand other battles during the war, this battle was important to the Allies, critical to the US Army's success on the Italian Peninsula, and fiercely fought with soldiers exhibiting great bravery and tenacity on both sides. And though it was said that all the Negro Americans were killed in that battle, they were quickly forgotten by most Americans, and certainly by their German attackers. Not because it was an insignificant battle but because it was fought primarily by Negroes.

Not all seventy of the Negro Americans were killed, however. In this horrific pitched battle, one GI lived.

༳༳༳

John managed to avoid the shelling that the artillery captain had intentionally called down around their ears to salvage the situation. That officer was killed, and John was concussed and knocked against a wall in one of the ancient narrow streets. That wall was blown open, crumbling onto the road where he was lying, and a pipe from an indoor toilet broke and covered his jacket with excrement.

His head and vision soon cleared, and when he came to, he was staring down the muzzle of a German Mauser pistol. He grabbed air with his arms and submitted. He had no idea the Germans were so close.

His captors held a conversation in front of him, unaware that he spoke German.

"I was told that all the soldiers were niggers and were to be shot. This guy is White," said one of them.

"Yeah, don't waste the bullet. *Diese Soldaten kämpften heftig.* These guys fought fucking fiercely, and it looks like he is the ranking surviving senior officer." Germans, for some reason, respected officers above all other soldiers. "Let's take him to the prisoner area. Corporal, grab the field coat off that body..." He pointed to a man whose head had been cleanly blown off. "...and give it to this guy. He smells like shit."

The blood at the neck of the acquired jacket, supplemented by bullet holes on its back, was not much of an improvement over his old coat, but it certainly smelled better.

And hence, John was the only Negro survivor of the battle of Sommocolonia and was taken prisoner by German troops.

TWENTY-ONE

ROAD NORTH TO CAPTIVITY

John was shoved into a cattle car going north toward a German POW camp, and to his disadvantage, there was a good ole boy from the race-obsessed South in the car with him who started to "wind up" the other members of the boxcar against John.

The trains were standard for shipping cattle and had built into the top of them an indented box, though reinforced with metal, and a wooden roof; the box above had enough room for a small bench, and it was here that the German soldier responsible for that car guarded the prisoners.

The cars were not packed as tightly as those departing the Ardennes, but there was still an unreasonable amount of prisoners in each one. At one spot, moving north toward Germany and their final destination, the train made its first stop to take on a little coal as well as watered-down wood because coal was scarce. The guard came down from his perch, and he had the look of a man not happy unless he had a reason to harass his prisoners. Many a backside and arm were pricked by the tip of his bayonet. He, like his compatriot guards looking after prisoners on trains up north in Belgium, was evidently annoyed to be guarding prisoners instead of fighting them.

かかか

The ride was tedious but not horrific. The weather was much better this winter, and an ample but not overdone amount of food was given to the prisoners. When John's ethnicity dawned on some of the White southern soldiers in John's cattle car, at least those who could discern his race because of their decades of doing so growing up, they started to kick up a ruckus. They didn't want a "nigger" in the car with them. They knew by now the guards would listen to nothing they said; so, after they had the opportunity to disembark and relieve themselves while under heavy guard, when the time came to re-enter the cars, they crowded John away from the opening, shoved him a good couple of yards out onto the layby, then jumped in and shoved the door closed.

A guard saw what happened, ran up to the doors, and said in a loud voice in English: "Open!" It was ignored. Though the latch lock was on the outside, soldiers on the inside were holding the door fast.

"I shoot!" he warned them. And he pumped a round into the car, high enough to not hit anyone but low enough to get their attention. Still nothing.

A piercing train whistle announced the impending

departure, and rather than miss it, the soldier poked John roughly ahead to the next car that was still loading, allowed him to climb in, and the door was slammed shut. The car was filled with English soldiers.

"We caught ourselves a Yank!" one called out. Despite the occasional enmity between British and American soldiers, those in the train car were happy with the US contribution to the war effort, and they quickly got to know John.

After some banter, one asked him, "Hey, mate—are you a Negro?"

"What?"

"Are you a Negro, mate?"

"Why would you ask that?" John was terrified that his race appeared to be exposed.

"I heard a guard say it last stop. My German's a bit rusty, mate. I was raised in Germany, you see. When I was a lad, my dad was sent to—"

"Yes, please, tell the story in a bit," John interrupted hastily. "What'd the guard say?"

"After the doors shut, I was looking out the scuttle. I heard the one guard normally planted in the box on top of this crate scream at the guard who shoved you in here."

"What'd he say?" John asked impatiently.

"'Can't you tell that Yank was a nigger?' he said to another guard. 'Why didn't you shoot him?'"

John couldn't fathom how he knew, but he later learned there was a bigoted German-speaking Pennsylvanian in the previous train car with them—a whole enclave of those speakers lived in the state, and he never knew it. The Pennsylvanian Dutchman had proudly told his train car comrades that he caught the attention of a guard and tipped him with a wink with a comment through the scuttle about John being a Negro. When these same comrades in the boxcar discovered what he said, they beat him unconscious. John was a Negro, but he was "their" Negro.

"Don't you tell the Germans nuthin," one soldier warned the Pennamite with a final kick.

The Brit in John's car continued. "The Nazi guard said he would take care of you at the next stop. At least that is what I think *Mit ihm umgehen* means. You'll cop it the next stop." John knew he was correct but didn't need to explain his knowledge of German to his new friends.

"When will that be?"

"I ain't the train manager, mate. Any gate," he said to some laughs to those within earshot.

They all heard the final doors slamming shut along the length of the train. The train whistle blew again, and a few moments later, the car jerked forward as they moved toward their destination.

"Who is the guard?" asked John. "You said he was at the top of this car?"

"That's right, mate."

෨෨෨

The British, always thinking of escape, had managed to release one of the floor panels beneath the cars— large enough for a man to crawl through to the outside of the rolling stock. Though they had no clue where they would go once escaping the car. They had only planned it out as far as getting a release from their immediate incarceration.

They were continually scheming and, to mine some possible new ideas, shared the car's weakness with John.

"Where did you think you were going to go once you got out?" John inquired.

"Not a clue, mate, but we absolutely hate the guy sitting on top. He's a right bastard. He shot Kieran Prince two stops ago for taking too long to piss. Right in the head. He's gotta go, but we haven't figured it out yet."

Knowing full well that he'd probably be next, John eagerly joined in the plan to "snuff him" as the Brits were saying.

Once they showed John the opening and where it led, John concocted a plan.

"Give me about five minutes and then start banging on the bottom of the guard's box—I'll take care of the rest," John instructed.

He climbed through the bottom of the moving train, hanging from the supports holding up the floor, and crawled to the end of the back of the train car. He then carefully supported himself as he shimmied around the corner and climbed up the side on a ladder installed for the guards to the top of the car. It was good that there was no moonlight, and he was conscious that they were going through a series of tunnels. He peeked over the edge of the car and saw the roofed box that the guard was sitting in, facing forward in the other direction. He was poised to move.

John waited for what seemed like forever. *Where's the planned distraction?* he thought. In a few moments, the banging started from inside the car below the box, and the guard started yelling and rapping the butt of his rifle on the floor of his enclosure. He turned the gun around and was about to shoot into the boxcar when John ran crouched along the roof, grabbed him, and snapped his neck as Captain Pergola had taught him. John had no remorse. The guy certainly deserved it according to some of the prisoners, and John also knew the guard would be looking for him at the next stop. Without a second thought, when the long train got through the next tunnel, he threw the guard over the side and into a deep valley adjacent to the tracks, and the lifeless body quickly disappeared below into deep drifts of snow on the mountainside, likely not to be discovered until spring if at all. They were now in the pre-Alps, approaching the Alps proper in South Tyrol in Northern Italy.

He made his way back down the side, under the boxcar, and into the interior, where the other prisoners were intently staring at him. Most were surprised that he had made it back. He looked up, smiled, and said, "Done," to the loud cheers of everyone in the boxcar, though it could not be heard as they were going through yet another tunnel, and the engine whistle sounded its warning.

"The sonofabitch had his rifle lying to the side, and he was staring away from the wind trying to light a cigarette.

I couldn't do it—I couldn't risk him seeing and shooting me. I kept on peeking over the side, and he was staring intently at the cig and the lighter, which kept on blowing out. I was going to climb over and help him get it lit," John said to the men's giddy laughter.

"He finally got it lit; you guys started your noise. He was about to shoot through the roof. I quickly crawled over, snapped his neck, and flung him and the gun, including his blanket, over the side before we entered the last tunnel."

One man cried, "You should have kept the blanket. It is fuckin' freezing in here."

Several soldiers looked at him, and one smacked him on the back of his head for his stupidity.

At the next stop, he overhead the Germans' surprise that the roof guard was missing. They searched the area but found no blood, and so determined he either absconded or fell off taking a leak from the side of the train. In any case, they had no time to deal with it, and they replaced him with another guard, who was cursing his ill luck as he went up the side of the car as he had to exchange his place from a warm passenger area.

They arrived at Mühlberg near Stalag IV-B in the evening—and they began the long walk to the POW camp from the station. At camp, John sadly had to separate from the British and was put in with the Americans again. Once again, someone from the South immediately recognized his features. They started calling him John Redbone, but he really wasn't. Though one prisoner hit closer to home when he saw John and called out, "High yella."

"What's that?" a soldier standing next to John asked, not knowing they were referring to him.

"A light-skinned person of White and Negro ancestry," John explained.

"Like a half-breed?"

"Quiet, shitheads," the prisoner's commanding officer yelled at no one in particular. "The last thing we need is another North versus South Civil War. The Germans will exploit that, and we'll all be at each other's throats. Anyone caught doing it will be skinned alive…by me. And you will be outcast to another camp. I don't care which one."

All the soldiers, including all those from the southern states, complied. They felt that once they were made prisoners, they completely lost control of their own lives: what to do, what to eat, where to go, and when. They complied because they could not bear to be separated from the group and American military orders. They feared that more.

Though occasionally, when some were certain it would not be detected, John once again experienced both subtle and wild discrimination by many until he was billeted in another barracks and was bunked directly below Sonny.

TWENTY-TWO

NEWARK CONTINUED

Yet another expulsion from the threshold of an un-
welcoming tavern. Sonny was perplexed. He had
never visited a bar in Newark that didn't accept him or his
money readily. as most times he brought in a gang from
the brewery and they received courtesy discounts because
they not only delivered their kegs of beer for customers but
also spent their paychecks on beer and food into the night.
Another reason he was troubled and incredibly stressed:
Sonny was missing Christmas Day with his family.

æææ

How can people act this way? Sonny mused to himself
about the ejections from the taverns. Did they see something he didn't?

Of course not, he concluded. They simply held what
they considered reasonable convictions against Negroes
that they had learned from their parents and friends, who

had learned it from their parents and friends, who had learned it from their parents and friends, and so on, and all that would not be at all easy to overcome. People felt entitled to these views even though they were wrong. As Sonny pondered this question, he heard John in his head, explaining something from his past that Sonny never realized.

Sonny spent what seemed like hours trying to find a place for himself and JC to sit down and have a coffee and get something to eat, partially because it was Christmas Day and most establishments were closed, but mostly because JC was a Negro, and this was Newark, and they met with nothing but bigotry. Nor could Sonny bring JC home to his family. And though Newark had many ethnicities in neighborhoods right next to one another, but still autonomous, Negroes were placed at a disadvantage in the pecking order and were expected to stay in their own neck of the woods.

And JC was truly *black*: almost blue-black. African Black. But Sonny didn't know where he was from. If John had mentioned it, Sonny certainly never would have remembered the name of his country of origin. But JC had actually been born in New Orleans to Senegalese parents, brought over as servants along with a French family decades ago.

Sonny was cordial but somewhat uncomfortable by his own prejudice of not wishing to bring John's father to his own bigoted family home. Though his color didn't bother *him* much, he knew there'd be hell to pay if he brought a Negro home to his grandparents. He likely wouldn't make it up the front porch steps on Fabyan Place without being turned away.

ཙ ཙ ཙ

JC had been to the North infrequently, but he knew that even in a mixed-race city, he stood out—mostly because he was blacker than most other Negroes, which, in his own mind, impacted by decades of racial mistruths, somehow seemed to make a difference.

At the next tavern he planned to visit, Sonny knew he had frequently seen a Negro bartender working there. Driving along, Sonny swung south until he reached Washington Street, made a left toward Bridge Street, and then headed to the aptly but not terribly cleverly named Bridge Street Bridge and drove across the Passaic River onto the main street in Harrison, the next town over and the tavern and bar capital of the state of New Jersey. A last chance.

The windows were moist and clouded on the inside from patrons' breath and the steam that emanated from a cast-iron potbelly stove. The drops of condensation collected and dripped from the bottom rung on the small tri-circle neon sign of the Ballantine beer logo.

The sign looked like bright-colored fuzzy cotton from the outside. Sonny led the way inside and was relieved that Amos was behind the bar, a man whose father moved to Newark during the Negro Great Migration from the South twenty years before.

Inside, the wooden floor let off the not unpleasant

smell of spilt beer when mopped up, a familiar scent in all old taverns. He recognized his man behind the bar, and he looked at them briefly and returned to wiping the bar top. They were not turned away.

They went to hang their coats on wooden pegs near the small stove. Sonny's coat was heavy and wool, and JC's, thin cotton. A newspaper strewn at the end of the bar showed soldiers standing at attention at a flag-covered coffin. The article headline read: "Gen. Patton Dies Quietly in Sleep: Burial in Europe." They warmed their hands on the stove, and as the blue-black man sat down, he glanced over and saw Sonny still warming his hands, staring into the cherry-red glow through the holes of the stove grate. Though warm and comfy, he continued to stare at the deep orange embers through the spaces in the oven door. As he gazed into the open fireplace in the tavern, Sonny's strong memories mentally transported him once again from Harrison back to Barracks 11 at IV-B.

☙ ☙ ☙

It was his turn to stand in front of a similar stove, not nearly as hot as the one in Newark, with some thin wood that had been stolen from the pile collected by the work detail bringing back fuel for the stoves in the guards' barracks. Because it had not cured or aged since it was carried fresh from the woods, the pile let out a tell-tale stream of smoke through the hut's chimney—more so than the other barracks. The guards' huts, on the other hand, let off the same type of exhaust.

Two German guards walking along the camp periphery saw it, burst in the cabin, opened the hatch door, and saw a remnant of the white-barked wood in the last moments of being consumed by the flames. One kicked the stove over, bringing the red-hot pipes down to the floor, billowing carbon dust from old fires. It would have ignited the straw used in the mattresses except they were too wet from urine. The guards found the men from the work detail and made them stand outside for several hours, then confiscated the rest of the wood they found inside the prisoners' mattresses.

Sonny began to think about what had previously been explained to him in the camp. The Germans developed their institutionalized racism using the American so-called Jim Crow laws as models. And Sonny had no idea because he'd never heard of Jim Crow nor knew of his laws.

Although the American brand of racism didn't put into practice the institutionalized killings that were undertaken by the Nazis, there were still "sanctioned" murders, called lynchings, which were not usually done with the ruthless efficiency of Teutonic organizations. As with most racism, though, the cultural results were pretty much the same: gradual and planned exclusion from all elements of life, discrimination against that race's ability to exercise life's opportunities, and the denial to mankind of their humanity, all because of their origin of birth.

ಶಿ ಶಿ ಶಿ

As JC put his coat on the peg, he removed a dog-eared envelope from the inside pocket of his thin jacket and carried it over to the table he had found. Inside was something that would change how Sonny looked at life and race forever.

"Sonny, what can you tell me about a place called Berga?" JC asked as he placed the envelope down on the table in front of him.

Sonny stopped moving abruptly and thought about the question. It was strange to hear the name again and re-experience the emotions he felt when he first heard the word a year ago. He was not anxious to talk about it and wondered why John had never shared his experiences there with his dad.

When Sonny had returned home after the war, after a decent interval had passed, he had sat the family down in the kitchen at Fabyan Place, where he spent several hours telling his mother, father, and two sisters of his wartime ordeals post-capture. When he finished, there was silence. Both his sisters and his mom had tears streaming down their faces, and his dad sat there with his mouth slightly agape. Sonny looked at each of them, got up from the table, and hoped never to speak of it again for the rest of his life.

In the tavern in Harrison, though, Sonny once again recounted to JC some of what he had experienced in the camps and told him that the Army felt it shameful that

American soldiers had been forced to endure such horrors after IV-B, specifically Berga. A death camp. After his release, US military officials required all survivors of that camp to sign an affidavit pledging not to say a word about what they had witnessed there. It was meant to be a temporary injunction because the military didn't want to have the US public try to process what American soldiers in a Nazi death camp had experienced as they were preparing for a possible conflict with Russians, where the remaining German military there would be needed as allies.

However, Sonny and other prisoners interpreted this agreement as a lifetime oath of silence. Sonny assumed that no one would believe it anyway.

The printed guidance on the affidavit said: "You must be particularly on your guard with persons representing the press. You must not give an account of your experience in books, newspapers, periodicals, or in a broadcast or in lectures."

As Sonny told his painful story one more time, he saw JC's eyes become teary once again for what his son had privately experienced and never told him. Sonny had seen similar weeping on so many faces these past months since the war ended, especially from former prisoners. Partly from joy, but mostly from incredulity for the pain they'd suffered for which there seemed no reason. There was so much silent suffering and so many tears to shed from pain endured, lost loved ones, and disruption of life in general. Such things became commonplace to witness right after the war and for quite some time thereafter.

TWENTY-THREE

FEAR OF WORSE

Sonny was not sure of the first time he heard the name of Berga at Stalag IV-B or initially what it meant, though every time the word was uttered, prisoners within earshot—and even Germans—stiffened, and he soon came to understand its power. The prisoners used the name sparingly because they knew without equivocation that it was the stuff of which nightmares were made. One soldier made it back from Berga, a Yank who was a nephew of one of the American commanding officers at IV-B, and while the story was that he was sent there in a rare German clerical error, it was generally assumed it was intentional so that "teeth" would be associated with the name of that camp.

The stories with which he returned made the soldiers' already irregular heartbeats skip: Berga was modeled after all the Germans' other work/labor/death camps in the east of Germany and was almost too tiny to show up on most maps because it was in a particularly hilly area and the nearby town had less than a few thousand souls. The men at IV-B were not usually accustomed to fighting over crumbs, chewing pieces of wood or charcoal to staunch diarrhea, eating snow, clean snow if they could find it, or coughing blood from throats lacerated by rock shards in the mines where they were forced to work. But they were in *Berga*, and there some slipped away from life silently in the night, while for others, the shame of survival was sometimes too much to bear. But those incarcerated there were told to get used to it at Berga. It was considered the place of no return. When the Germans did manage to identify an *Untermensch*, a common pejorative meaning "subhuman," they marked him for transport to Berga.

It was a place the temporary residents of IV-B could not comprehend, an ephemeral little hell for the men there for which they had no preparation or instruction.

It was with the fear of always being sent there as a backdrop that on a freezing winter morning, Sonny was called to the commandant's office. One was rarely called to the commandant's office, so this was indeed peculiar.

Trager, the unusually friendly guard, showed up one day with two other goons at the barracks door. The Germans were mainly reluctant to enter the barracks because of the smell and the possibility, though remote, that one of the lice would spring through the air and land in their own hair.

In a brusque voice, Trager called out: "*Angus Jacobs!*"

The men in the barracks looked at each other and said nearly simultaneously, "Who was that?"

Again, Trager called out, "*Angus Jacobs*," pronouncing the name Hane-Goose Yaah-Kobs.

Sonny stood up.

"Sonny, what are you doing?" O'Mara asked him.

"That's my name, genius," replied Sonny as he shuffled toward the door.

Trager was disappointed that the prisoner the commandant had summoned, Angus, was the one he knew as Sonny. Trager looked kindly upon Sonny, and being called to the commandant's office was tantamount to getting either heart-wrenching news from home (though only if it came through official channels such as the Red Cross and the Germans were bored enough or mildly motivated to pass it on), or the result of having done something terrible while someone had seen them do it—or occasionally, because the commandant decided that it was time to have a bit of fun and randomly give someone a hard time to see if they could uncover an escape attempt or glean some other useful information.

As he was led out, some of his fellow prisoners practiced their wit on Sonny:

"It's Berga for you. It's curtains!" he heard as he closed the barracks door behind him.

Some of the soldiers gave a weak laugh, though they actually felt terrible for him. But the barb hit its mark, and Sonny was somewhat terrified as he was led through the mud of the muster yard toward the commandant's outer office. As horrible as his life was, though, the thought of ending it, or conversely, more potential torture, was excruciating.

Trager, too, had a sympathetic look as he brought him to the foot of the four short steps to the front door of the commandant's building and slowly led Sonny up them. After a knock, he was met by another guard, a liveried soldier with clothing light enough to indicate that it was exceedingly warm inside.

With his heart beating rapidly, he was led through the door.

Sonny was surprised when he entered the commandant's anteroom. It was akin to walking into another surreal realm and not at all unlike dropping into the British barracks in the camp. It was warm...very warm...comfortably warm. And the smell of food, wonderful food, hit his senses like nothing he had experienced for months. The aromas blasted him in the face and his brain had trouble processing them.

The room was wood-paneled; clearly, the frame was constructed of wood, but the walls themselves had a higher-quality paneling that went to the ceiling. There were *two* potbelly stoves identical to the ones in the prisoners' barracks, only these were clean, very clean (superlatives came easy since he had been living in filth) and obviously scrubbed to a shine regularly. The wooden floor had none of the grime of the prisoner barracks, and in fact had a bit of a gloss like the stoves. A cherry-red flame showed through their front grates, and the air in front of it was distorted, wavy.

There was no one in the room, though a sideboard against the far-left wall had all manner of food on it—in amounts he had not seen in a long while. He looked around and over his shoulder, then immediately went over and plucked and pocketed several rolls, put them into his trousers and overcoat pockets, and then picked up a sliced piece of chicken and shoved it into his mouth and tried to swallow it whole before someone came in.

As Sonny did this, the door to the next office beyond opened, and the camp commandant walked in the anteroom wearing his army uniform but without his officer's cap. His boots up to his knees had a high polish, his Army uniform impeccable. He was slightly balding and had a slight paunch, which made him look much older than 40. As well his tone of voice was very slight, almost as if he was speaking in a very loud stage whisper, but this was due to a wound to his throat in the Great War. He was with another person wearing a kindly smile but with a pinched face like a judgemental policeman. He sported a double breasted civilian suit, the likes of which Sonny had not seen in many months. He had thick hair and what looked like an honorable dueling scar, but was actually from a broken glass bottle from a street fight many years ago. The suit had a small gold ring swastika badge on his lapel, and both Germans were chuckling as they walked in the room. The person in civvies identified himself as Major Sneyder of the *Gehime Staatspolizie* (the Secret State Police, otherwise known as the Gestapo).

The civilian said to Sonny, "Yes, good. Eat. I'm sure you're hungry. Don't eat too quickly, or you will become ill." His English was perfect except for a slight accent while enunciating the "W" in "will."

"Good, Sergeant Yaa-cobs. Good for you to eat. And here, here is a warmer jacket for you when you go outside," the commandant offered.

Sonny's eyes narrowed slightly as his mind worked to figure out the reason for such largesse. It was thick and wool and looked warm. Very warm. And almost good enough to eat. He eyed it both with suspicion but with intense curiosity, like looking at a fine piece of art in Newark Museum. But he wasn't going to question food right now, and anything he was able to swallow before whatever they wanted in return was fair game. He took the overcoat and put it on immediately over the thin one he had—they'd have to wrestle it from him if they wanted it back. Though he was weak, and ripping it right back off of him wouldn't pose much of a challenge, he reasoned they probably wouldn't want to risk a lice attack. The coat was a prisoner's winter wool coat that had been somewhat washed. Not terribly fashionable to begin with, but an extra piece of clothing was an extra piece of clothing.

"We are not much different, the Americans and the Germans...," the commandant began. "We—"

Sonny swallowed the piece of chicken he was chewing before he interrupted. "Huh? First, you treat your prisoners like shit—you starve them." Sonny's own directness surprised him, but the contrast of where he was presently versus where he had just come from made him angry.

"No," the commandant interjected Sonny before he could go on. He began raising his voice. "We feed our own people first. If it wasn't for Allied terror bombing on civilians—civilians and their children, not war targets—you would likely have all the food you could eat. But your leaders have decided to kill family farmers and take food out of your mouths. Come now. Do you think we feed *you* before our own people?"

It didn't matter; Sonny was on a roll. "And speaking of your own people, I don't believe you. You take your own people and shove them in camps because of their religion."

"To whom are you referring? What do you mean, religion?"

"I mean how you treat Jews."

"Who is being naive now, Sergeant? It is not a religion. It is a type of creature…a type of animal, like your Negroes. A type of rodent."

The commandant's eyes were gradually taking on a wild display—almost fanatical in appearance. His high forehead started to show mild red blotches from from the annoyance he felt, and his voice started to sound metallic.

"How should you treat rodents? You know from the way you treat your own Negroes. What about how your country treated your own native aborigines, your so-called American Indians?" The commandant smiled as Sonny stopped talking. Perhaps the point hit home, the commandant thought.

Here, though, Sonny kept silent and quit speaking. It was not because he agreed with the German or the idea of mistreatment of the Indians seriously dismayed him. In his own mind they probably were, but that event was as far in the past as the Revolutionary War to Sonny, when the British were mortal enemies of his young country. And, to be honest, he only thought of aborigines as a term applied to the natives of Australia, having read a *National Geographic* magazine about it, and his mind was still processing the comparison. He stopped so he could continue to shovel food into his mouth and his pockets, holding the commandants gaze, staring directly into his eyes so perhaps he did not notice.

Sonny became more frightened because he knew how the Nazis reacted to racial "impurities," and he remembered the abuse flung at him in grammar school in Newark as an "injun" and a "dirty redskin" after he innocently told a friend of his family's background.

He was afraid that somehow his racial background was compromised. But it did not seem to be as the commandant continued, further encouraged by his silence.

"We Germans learned how to treat our Jews from how you treated your Negroes! We copied your so-called 'Jim Crow' laws in how we treat our Jews. In fact, we treat our Jews better than you treat your Negroes."

Sonny had no clever retort but continued to eat as much of the different foods as he could stuff into his mouth. The commandant, once again emboldened by Sonny's silence, continued on a different tact.

"Sit down, Sergeant, and talk to us. Tell us how you are doing. How are you getting along?" Sneyder from the Gestapo implored.

Sonny, his energy starting to mount from the meager bits hitting his stomach, let fly with: "Seriously? Your camp stinks and probably is breaking every law in the world—the food, such as it is, also is terrible, and this might sound stupid, but there is not enough of it. And you're going to lose the war, and if we bother to give some of your guards a trial, it would surprise me because I'm sure you and most of your soldiers will probably be shot on sight the minute the prisoners get ahold of guns. The Russians will be here soon as I'm sure you know."

The civilian and the commandant again looked at each other. They knew the nature of the last comment and that it was probably right, and it made them hesitate in taking the "bad cop" approach with Sonny.

The commandant and civilian Gestapo policeman were not so terribly stupid. They could see the handwriting on the wall relative to the war's outcome. But they reasoned if they could gain some reasonably good intelligence, they figured it might allow them to gain both an audience and considerable favor with their superiors, which they could then use to gain promotion *away* from the advancing Russian Army. As it was, they were preparing to pull up roots from the camp, and they were under long, set standing orders to, if the Russians came too close, evacuate every prisoner further west inside of Germany. They thought this was absolutely ludicrous, particularly as they were saddled with thousands of ill and seriously handicapped prisoners who would be incredibly challenging to move. They may as well just shoot them rather than let them be repatriated to the Allies, and they half expected that is what would be required of them. Essentially, the commandant had been given veiled instructions to leave the "scene of the crime," making sure he took all the evidence of it with him. The motivation the commandant could not see was that the German high command was hoping to use the prisoners as a bargaining chip to save them from the Russians.

The Gestapo major placed a sheet of paper in front of Sonny, shoved a pencil in his hand, and after a moment their tone changed. They began asking him questions about his work prior to his capture:

"What was your job in the Quartermaster's Division?"

"For what were you responsible?"

"How much…?"

"How many...?"

"In what volume…?"

"In what ships…?"

"At what rate…?"

The questions went on while he stared at them and continued to put food in his mouth with his left hand now, holding the pencil in his right lest they stop him from eating.

The nature of the questions posed along with the abrupt change from false concern about his well-being to this logistical interrogation startled him, but not so much that he could not slip yet another piece of food—which looked like beef—from the table just next to him into his mouth and rapidly chew while they were talking. His mind focused on his hunger as what he was munching only minimally quelled the rumblings in his belly. But through the questions, he vaguely realized the familiarity of this conversation compared to another one he had several times over the last few days in the barracks with his fellow prisoners. Sonny had enjoyed sharing with his barrack mates the sheer volume of supplies, adding in gleeful detail what was entering Europe and where, certainly improving spirits in the same fashion that his Fabyan Place Christmas meals stories had brought light and gave hope to the souls of his "charges" over the last few months.

His mind went astray since he knew the barracks building had already been thoroughly investigated by his fellow prisoners to check for listening devices, though not because they had anything of use to say for the Germans. It was known that the Germans used personal family information and anecdotes to gain an advantage with the soldiers and also listened for escape plans. And the men were thoroughly bored with their existence in the barracks and wanted to feel useful in blearing their captors' eye.

What the commandant and major wanted from Sonny was information about the nature of the material and food/rations under his purview: volumes, how it was being shipped, and what type of security was involved in protecting it. Even the amount of food Sonny had transported could tell the Germans how many more troops to expect.

"Good luck with that," Sonny said to them, and the Gestapo major produced a six-inch truncheon that had been clipped to a metal rung on his belt underneath his double-breasted coat that was now open, hit him on the side of the head, and knocked him on the floor.

It was painful. Blood started pouring from the side of his head, but he didn't stop chewing the food still in his mouth. And as he got up, he made a surreptitious grab for more off the table and jammed it into his mouth and the pockets of his now new overcoat.

In his slightly accented English, the Gestapo major said, "We [which he pronounced "Vee"] have ways to make you talk," and Sonny chuckled because he remembered that line from a Gary Cooper movie he saw a while back. Against this latest insubordination, the commandant took out his own truncheon from his desk drawer, walked over to Sonny, and walloped him on the other side of the head. Once again Sonny fell to the ground, still chewing.

"Look, Sergeant, I will make this very clear to you. We want that information, and we want it straight away." The Gestapo agent's voice was clearly menacing now.

The commandant contributed in a softer tone, his voice slight once again. "If you give it to us, we will provide coats like this for everyone in your barracks, wood for your stove, and a crate of food for everyone there. If you do not, I cannot answer for what will happen to you," his voice raising near the end.

Sonny picked up two chicken legs and placed them in his overcoat pocket while picking up another piece of bread and stuffing it into his mouth. Given his condition and the fact that his teeth were all loose, this was the easiest thing to consume immediately. The two Germans hardly seemed to notice.

The commandant stood straight, indicating the

meeting was over, and said to Sonny, "Go back and discuss this with your fellow soldiers in the barracks—tell them what we will provide and see if they cannot be more persuasive with you."

"If that does not work, the only choice for you is one you do not wish to contemplate. You will be sent to Berga," the Gestapo major said with finality. Sonny stopped chewing. It was the first time he heard a German say that word, and he didn't like it.

On the one hand, he was fearful of the unknown; the Germans rarely disappointed with their threats. They certainly hadn't whenever Sonny had been faced with some wicked or painful punishment. On the other hand, he knew if he went back to the barracks with that offer, he could likely be killed on sight because no matter how hungry the men were, they hated a traitor and a rat bastard even more.

The commandant finished with "You have twenty-four hours for your comrades to convince you." And the two German interrogators turned and went back into the inner office.

As the commandant departed out, he snapped out loudly, "*Bewachen,*" and Trager entered the room from the outside freezing porch. A blast of cold air hit Sonny in the face. Trager gently led the frail prisoner back, and having listened at the door of the commandant's office, was perplexed. Trager didn't want anything to happen to Sonny or his good friend John, and he began to noodle on ways he could help these two men.

Once back at Barracks 11, it was clear to Sonny's fellow prisoners that something was different. Sonny's newer, warmer jacket and slight glow on his skin (a sure sign of having eaten something more substantial than a scrap or two) couldn't have stood out more. The men saw this, and Sonny was promptly excoriated for clearly giving in and telling the Germans what they wanted to know, whatever that might have been—the men didn't waste time trying to get an explanation out of Sonny. Clearly, they felt the conclusions they had drawn were solid.

John had a commanding presence, which he used to distract their now-belligerent colleagues, loudly asking Sonny for an explanation of what had happened in the commandant's office.

Sonny explained what had happened and the food available, and as he did so, he passed out what he had managed to stuff into his pockets, bidding the men to share. Nothing he said from that point was heard as the men focused on the food, but John asked him to explain again after Sonny's supply was devoured.

When he had finished, the men were too exhausted, and further craving more food, to continue to rebel against him.

John spoke up. "Jesus, Sonny, tell them what they want to know. Anything you knew is out of date now anyway, and it wouldn't make a damn bit of difference in any case."

Another prisoner spoke up. "Maybe you're saying that because you're a Nazi yourself, Shall-mat." (No one ever saw the last name written down.)

"Your German *is* pretty good," someone else volunteered.

"I never hid that fact," John pointed out.

"Maybe too good," someone else chimed in.

The men revived and started verbally ganging up on John, and as they moved closer to him, with two prisoners holding shivs fashioned from part of the interior door frame, Sonny barked out, "Will you idiots stop this? You think the Germans are going to care if we kill each other? We'll be doing their job for them."

The prisoners' anger was feeding on itself, and while they were all relatively weak, so was John. A fight with the entire barracks' population would have overwhelmed him. Just before it became ugly, Sonny spoke up even louder and revealed what he said he wouldn't.

"You think the Nazis would have anything to do with him? Can't you tell he is a Negro?"

The men went silent and backed off. They stared at John, starting to discern some of his physical attributes. Some who couldn't make out his physical features previously because it confused them now understood. Others couldn't comprehend anything that went beyond skin color.

"No way. All the Negroes were shot when we were taken prisoner," one man said.

"Jesus. You dickhead. Does he look like a Negro?" Sonny asked.

The men noticed a resemblance, but the skin color still threw them off.

"But if there ain't any microphones in the barracks,

then how do the Germans know what Sonny was talking about?" inquired another prisoner, clearly baffled.

Indeed, now both Sonny and John faced the prospect of Berga. Sonny because he would not share useless information, and John because of his race. If there wasn't a small microphone, there had to be a traitor, and that information would certainly be shared—of this, the prisoners were sure.

Sonny and John were now quite motivated to find whoever it was.

ॐ ॐ ॐ

The next morning, well before first light, the men already awake in the barracks saw John surreptitiously come in the barracks' front door and quickly lay on his straw mattress. The entry door at the back of the barracks opened up quickly and closed just as promptly against the cold, but since that end of the barracks had no windows, and most of the men were lying huddled toward the front for warmth, they could see nothing.

Many of the prisoners were light sleepers and two of them woke up immediately at the noise to see what was about. John confided to them where he had been. He was glad one of them wasn't Sonny because they had defended each other all too often recently, and he didn't want the barracks to think they were colluding. John told the two men that he had seen one of the other prisoners, a GI captured in Belgium named Jim Preun, slip out of the barracks way before sun-up, and John had followed him.

John explained that he had snuck behind him, keeping at a distance as Jim walked to the commandant's office's back door. Jim knocked, the door opened, and the commandant's adjutant, whom John recognized as a monoglot, opened the door; the two spoke for a moment. Preun was given a piece of bread, which he stuffed into his mouth and walked away.

The men were incredulous. John wanted to break Preun's neck straight away, but the two men with whom he was talking thought better of it and decided to set a trap, so they would know for sure that he was a traitor. When Preun came back inside the barracks, after a short amount of time passed, John asked him where he had been. Preun's reply was that he couldn't sleep and needed to take a walk around the barracks to tire.

When the exchange ended, Preun's face took on a deathly pall. The brief conversation, which only lasted a moment, had taken place entirely in German—which didn't dawn on Preun until he said the last syllable of the last word. Chalmet just stared, and Preun knew it was over and was petrified as to what would happen next.

Some of the men in the barracks already knew John could speak German, but no one knew that Preun could. Indeed, Sonny had told the barracks about the salvation from the dogs and how John came to speak in the Rhineland when he was young. Previous to that moment, the two men had a dilemma over whom to trust: John or Preun. Now, the choice was easy.

ಊ ಊ ಊ

During roll call and muster thirty minutes later, the cries came along the line as the prisoners were being counted. After a few more loud orders shouted in German, it was discovered that Barracks 11 was missing a prisoner. Several guards with dogs (now under strict orders not to unhook their leashes under any circumstances) converged on the front of the barracks.

A few moments later, a German guard came to the barracks' prisoner leader at the head of the muster and asked what had happened to Preun, who was inside, badly wounded. Those standing at attention seemed in disbelief, and doubt was shared all around.

The barracks leader began to run back—shuffle, really—to the barracks in a panic but was held back by the men.

"I was next to last out for roll call, and Preun was just behind me." The barracks leader insisted on going inside to look after his man, but the Germans refused to release him. He had to play along and express dismay and concern. He knew Preun was in the barracks, not only badly wounded, but his neck had been broken and his skull smashed.

The official German explanation was that Preun had tripped and fell violently on the corner of the concrete plinth on the barely used potbelly stove.

TWENTY-FOUR

JIM CROW *IS* IN GERMANY

Now sitting in Newark with JC, contemplating the tears and still looking across the tavern floor at the potbelly stove in the establishment, Sonny's mind returned to IV-B...

For once, the potbelly stove in Barracks 11 was not quite hot but still extremely warm, thanks to the thieving competence of the last group of soldiers who were assembled to collect wood for the Germans outside the fence. They were still efficient smugglers. The now meager flame was dying out, and because of the poor insulation of the barracks, the cold once again permeated the walls. It started to become nearly as cold inside as outside, so when a radiant sun peeked through the clouds, Sonny and John decided to take another of their long walks, though more carefully this time. The sky was blue, and the sun gratefully was beating down on the camp, providing some unusual warmth. It was still cold, and the color contrast was great: Cast your eyes up and be met with a bright sky seemingly washed with blue, then lower them and take in the almost monochromatic scene of prison life with nearly everyone and everything covered in a fine film of dust and grime. In the distance toward the north, south, and west on the horizon, billowing dark smoke almost the same color as the dominant one in the camp was rising from the earth and, from what Sonny and John assumed, were German cities targeted by Allied airpower, and they were correct.

The sun felt wonderful, and for a moment it distracted them, though it did not erase their continual hunger, and they continued a conversation that had been interrupted the day before.

"Johnny-boy, why did you break Preun's neck?"

"I didn't just break his neck. I bashed his head against the concrete floor and cracked his skull," John clarified.

"Why did you not just break his neck but then bash his head against the concrete floor and crack his skull? Happy?"

As it happened, John had gotten up off the end of the bunkbed, gone over to Preun, and put his arms around his neck. Preun was dead by the time John forcefully banged the front of his forehead against the corner of the concrete base that held the cold stove. It created a gash on his forehead and drew blood. The gash made the "accidental" broken neck more believable.

"Right after you were taken to the commandant's office to spill your guts for food, I saw him leave. I've been watching him for a couple of days. He didn't complain as much about hunger as everyone else and was not looking too bad, health-wise. I slipped out the front door to follow him and saw him go to the back door of the commandant's office. He knocked, and when the door opened, he spoke to a guard I knew spoke no English and was given a handful of food. He stuffed half in his mouth and half in his pocket and walked back to the barracks. As he returned from behind the barracks, I saw you thrown out the front and brought back by Trager about a minute later. He is possibly the only considerate guard in the whole fucking camp."

"Not to everyone," Sonny pointed out.

"Maybe. He treats us both like we're human beings, though."

"I'm surprised he didn't poke you on the way over with the commandant looking out the window," John muttered. Anyway, I saw the same thing happen with Preun yesterday morning. He's the rat."

The men walked in silence for a moment, then Sonny asked, "Shouldn't we have had a prisoner trial for him?"

"What would be the point?" inquired John. "We would have had to get rid of him anyway. The Germans weren't going to protect him, and no barracks would take him once word got out."

"Yeah," Sonny went on. "That's another thing. How'd you learn to break a neck like that, and why did you feel the need to bang his head on the side of the stove? You didn't learn that in basic," Sonny said declaratively. "Not my basic anyway—we learned how to shoot and throw grenades and dig foxholes, but we didn't break any necks that I recall. It appears to have come in handy."

"I had a guy who showed me the right friendship—he showed me how to do it. A White captain. Good man."

"John, how do I know you're not the spy, and you bumped off the one guy that could rat you out?"

"Fair point, Sonny, but you heard the Brits tell you about the guard I 'knocked on the head' for them coming up from Italy."

"Another fair point in your favor. In any case, I suppose I knew you spoke some German. Otherwise, the dicks in the barracks might have suspected you. You didn't hide that. Evidently, the Germans have forgotten about Preun already because they delivered a bread ration for him by mistake this morning. Red Cross coming this week, so they beef up food distribution."

"Nice. In any case, given half a chance, there are several guards I'd like to take out when this war is over—trial or no trial. I'll do the same thing," John confided.

"Anybody I know? Don't take out Trager. He's been one of the good ones," Sonny entreated.

"And he protects me, I suppose, by proxy because I'm friends with you. He seems to look after you. A friend from the past?" John inquired.

"I can't figure it out," Sonny admitted, "but he has been friendly. And he likes you a lot too, I think."

"Agreed, but that bastard Schwartzie is the first one. Did you see how he shot those Russians he found taking the shoes off the guy that fell dead next to them in muster?"

"Johnny-boy, how many guys you think you killed so far?"

"During the war or not in the war?" he asked. "And don't call me boy. I'm a man."

"Well, I'm saying it in a friendly way."

"People use that term 'boy' for Negroes all over the US. Especially adults—it's insulting."

"I wouldn't mind if you called me boy!"

"That's because you've heard it before, and no one was insulting you."

"There is a guy at work who is a Negro, and I call him Mikey-boy. He never complained. And an Italian that I call Tony-boy—no problem with him."

"Sonny, with Negroes, it is just one small way they push us down and keep us in a box and not give us the same opportunities"

"Johnny-b...John, so why don't you do something about it? You musta been thrilled to fight the Germans. Finally giving it to someone where—"

"Sonny, have you heard of Double-V?"

"Is that a munition I've never heard about?"

"It is a slogan from a Negro newspaper, I think in Pittsburgh, printed just before I enlisted. It explains that we should be pushing for both victory in the war and victory for fighting for Negro rights at home."

"You *have* rights," Sonny said definitively.

"Says who?"

"Says *me*. I know you're picked on, but so was I when people found out I was an Indian. It went on for years until people got tired of it. The same thing will happen with Negroes—you watch."

John looked at him with something approaching annoyance. "Sonny, it is not going away. First, you can hide you're Indian. And there are laws in the US that prevent people from treating Negroes as normal. You ever hear of Jim Crow laws?"

"Nope. Never.... Well, yes, I did hear about it from the commandant."

"You're kidding? *Seriously*?! The Nazi commandant here in the camp? What did he say?"

"He mentioned something about it. Let me tell you about the food first. The table was a couple of feet long and was covered with sliced chicken; fresh, warm bread; beef chunks; some pastries—"

"Which we're never gonna see unless you tell them what you know. It's all dead information anyway."

"Bad as it is, I prefer this life than getting beaten to death by the rest of the camp."

"Okay, so tell me what the commandant said about Jim Crow."

"Yes. By the way, who is Jim Crow really?"

"Doesn't matter. Just tell me what the commandant said."

"He said the Nazis copied the laws in place in the States when they were putting the laws together to put down Jews."

John paused, thinking a moment, and then continued. "Well, if that doesn't take the cake. But it doesn't make any difference. Jim Crow was a White entertainer that mocked Negroes, so they named the laws meant to put us in our place after him."

"Baloney. There are no laws in the US to keep Negroes 'in their place.'"

"It's true, Sonny."

"For example...?"

"After the Civil War..."

"When the slaves were *freed...*," Sonny reminded him.

"When holding slaves was illegal. But lots and lots of people couldn't stand that idea. The slaves were freed on paper, and suddenly, former field workers were just as good as the best White people. We could buy things just like White folk if we could find a job, and we could walk about the streets with Whites, and we didn't have to step out of the way and go into the muddy street if they were coming toward us. For a while, it lasted, and things started to be normal. But the Confederates who lost, particularly the slaveholders who lost everything, went crazy with hatred and wanted things back the way they were. And some entered politics where they put laws in place to keep us Negroes down."

"What laws?"

"Like making it impossible for Negroes to vote—which means we can't get Negroes into government or serve on juries that always convict Negroes."

"Look, I don't vote anyway—and if I live to be hundred, I never want to be on another jury."

"Negroes can't vote."

"Yes, you can."

"The laws make it awfully difficult to vote. The

majority of us can't. And laws on the books that say we can't marry who we want to."

Sonny's protests were dying down at this point.

John continued. "Sonny, it's starting to make sense to me. Why can't you accept that Hitler's anti-Jew laws are based on American anti-Negro laws. They're practically the same."

"Bullshit. No way."

"Absolutely, asshole."

"Prove it."

"I can't, but it makes sense." John was getting angry as Sonny remained obstinate. Until, suddenly, Sonny finally realized what the commandant had meant while he was stuffing his face. It all fell into place.

Sonny grabbed John's arm and said, "Stop…I believe you."

"Why now?"

"The commandant told me himself. He said the Germans knew how to treat Jews from a guy called Jim Crow. I remember now. I'm sick and fucking tired of talking about this. Lemme tell you about the food."

"Got any left?"

Sonny took from his pocket a squashed slice of now stale bread he'd been saving and handed half of it over. John shoved it into his mouth.

TWENTY-FIVE

WORSE

The men in the camp believed that as long as they could avoid being sent to Berga, they would at least probably make it through the war in one piece.

But as a result of Sonny's recalcitrance during his interview with the commandant two days earlier, and his apparent disrespect, in late April 1945, Sonny was roused out of his sleep in the middle of the night to be taken to Berga.

And because Sonny had blathered the news about John's race in front of the now-dead Preun the Snitch *and* because *he* had blithely passed it on to the Germans (though they hadn't really believed that he was a Negro), John was roused as well; he had no idea why, nor did any of the hundreds of their fellow prisoners gathered up at the same time. In the group that was being assembled were suspected Jews, Italians, argumentative Americans, and others who were considered "troublemakers." The commandant had been given an order to replenish some of the workforces at Berga, which were engaged in important war manufacturing, as soon as possible. This was the perfect opportunity, the commandant had realized, to rid himself of some "uncooperative" prisoners.

These men were going to Berga, the place they all feared as the camp of "no return."

❧❧❧

"We're headed to Berga," Sonny said.

"Shit." John added nothing after that. Nothing could be said, really.

If they could have, they would have collectively dry-heaved from fear, but their weakened bodies didn't have the energy.

They made sure they had what little they owned on their person and headed outside to join a growing group of sickly prisoners.

Sonny and John were to be part of a group of several hundred soldiers; some looked like Jews, others were "rabble-rousers" (John and Sonny were in this classification), and still others had just been grabbed randomly on a whim. They were the first Americans taken to an actual Nazi death camp during the war.

❧❧❧

The initial rations were hearty, and the prisoners were seduced into thinking things would not be that bad, but it was a hollow enticement, merely intended to give them initial energy to start the journey. And the little food they gave them—bread and some lukewarm soup with some meat (probably horse)—was still meager. As their horses were less precious to the Germans than petrol for truck transport, it was a more cost-effective solution.

They marched twelve hours a day—followed by twelve hours of rest just sitting in the open with no shelter by the side of the road. The journey became a blur for the men, with many marching while sleeping, keeping step with their eyes closed, sometimes with a hand on a shoulder in front of them. Scores dropped dead from exhaustion and exposure along the way. Any conversation was forbidden, but they grabbed snippets here and there. They were at times holding each other up as they walked, going back and forth when one had the energy to hold the other up, afraid to look in each other's faces as they were sure to see a reflection of how they looked themselves.

The awful smell of their unwashed bodies and dirty clothes somehow became negated after being in that state for so long. Occasionally a breeze carried the smell of evergreen from the nearby woods under their noses, but was quickly replaced once again by their own stench once the waft passed. The scent from the forest evoked strong memories of Christmas trees past at Fabyan Place, and it gave him the energy to continue. It was Sonny's turn to support them both, emotionally and physically. He had his arm under John's supporting him as they walked.

"Sonny, I'm not gonna make it," John muttered.

"Great, more food for us," Sonny replied, practicing his wit.

"*What*?!"

"Are you ready to drop on the ground?" Sonny asked sternly.

"Almost," John decided. "Not quite yet."

"Then hang on till just before you go down and then let me know. I want to grab your coat before you fall into the mud."

"That's pretty awful, even for you."

Sonny just looked at him. "John, you have to hang on. We're almost there!" After a moment, he continued with, "Hey, John, did I tell you my uncle died in a WWI concentration camp?"

"*What*?!"

"Yeah. He fell drunk out of a watchtower," Sonny finished, deadpan.

John stared at him for a moment and broke into his first smile in an age, followed by convulsive laughter, followed by a coughing fit.

John, now slightly invigorated, hunched over and leaned on his knees with his hands to catch his breath until they heard the guards coming closer, and then both returned to silence. John was lucky. The column had stopped moving for a few minutes' rest, giving him a much-needed reprieve. In due course, they began moving again.

Almost there they were not, but at that moment, a hand-held whistle was blown far in the front, and the trudging group of men slowed to a halt. That had continuously passed fallen soldiers who were just left by the side of the road, dead. Some made a slow dash to take their clothing. Sometimes they were allowed, sometimes not, and when it was the latter, it was always the guard Schwartzie who penalized those wishing to be warmer with a bullet or crushed skull beneath the butt of a rifle. The prisoners doing the walking just stopped looking at their fallen comrades after a while out of fear of seeing a friend.

The men moved off the side of the road, did what little business they could, looking for fresh snow to eat. Some of the more adventurous among them ventured off a few meters into the woods to grab some leaves to munch on. This went on for about fifteen minutes as the men saw no German retaliation—until very abruptly, Schwartzie grabbed a rifle from one of the guards standing next to him, took a bead on one of the soldiers, and shot him in the back of the head.

The prisoners promptly got back in line, and almost immediately a whistle was blown again and the men resumed walking. And walking. And walking. Of the over three hundred US soldiers transferred to Berga at that time in 1945, due to marching through the snow and cold for over two hundred miles for seventeen days with little shelter, only 120 survived. Sonny and John were among them.

ॐॐॐ

And those who did survive the journey lost another unaffordable 10 percent of their already paltry body weight during the journey. Those who did not survive the first day after arrival were stacked like cordwood before being thrown into ditches laboriously dug by exhausted camp inmates who had arrived previously, and the bodies were covered with lime and some sawdust. The Germans had anticipated their demise. Another ditch was being dug as the first order of business by the newly arriving prisoners in anticipation of the next group to come.

Ostensibly, the camp was constructed for prisoners tasked with building caves into the side of a mountain to protect the Germans' rapidly diminishing armaments manufacturing capability from air bombardment. Still, it served an additional purpose, already perfected at their other death camps: *Vernichtung durch Arbeit*, or annihilation through labor. The prisoners were intentionally worked and starved to death to maximize the energy they could get out of them at next to zero cost with minimal expenditure (the guards had to eat).

As time passed, the prisoners came to be rarely stunned at how low their captors could sink below the norm of common decency. They were already steeled against all manner of disgust but were still utterly appalled by the appearance of the camp, even with the anecdotes and horrific stories already spread back at Mühlberg. Naturally, they were shocked by their accommodations.

Though their low expectations had been met continuously and even had occasionally exceeded how bad things could get, they reached a new low with Berga. The site was attached to a bona fide death concentration camp—a prison for those considered to be political prisoners, those who had boldly defied the Reich.

Trager was one of the guards reluctantly dragooned into joining the contingent taking prisoners to Berga, though he did it less reluctantly when he realized some of the prisoners considered "his own" were among the selected. Trager figured he could at least do his best to look after them and hopefully protect them from Schwartzie's excesses. He was one of the friendlier guards (meaning he didn't arbitrarily beat prisoners, nor prod them very stiffly with the bayonets) and explained quickly and quietly to "his prisoners" it was a work camp for political types and mostly Jews to try and dampen the fear they held.

There were hundreds of incarcerated already at Berga, thinner than the incoming group if that was possible, all jammed against a mesh wire fence. The gaps in the metal mesh were big enough to put their hands through, but none of them dared. They stared standing in their striped prison garb, their personal civilian clothing having long since been taken, deloused, and—if not completely in rags—redistributed among the German populace there.

The scores had turned out to stand by the wire fence to see the newcomers walk in—yet as the Americans marched by in broken ranks and disordered lines, no sound was made, not even a whimper. The prisoners merely stared and looked at the group of IV-B prisoners, mostly Americans still in the odorous uniforms they had been captured in months or years ago. The *in situ* prisoners were first horrified at the sight of the newcomers but then calmed at seeing additional prisoners from countries they didn't recognize in military garb. It was proof to them that many different forces were fighting the Germans, a scrap of hope to which they clung, the idea that the walls were closing in on their captors. Though that was only a small relief. Their real concern was still hunger, and they were verily worried that the new prisoners would diminish the food pool, which, in fact, they would.

To the incoming prisoners, apart from lack of food and the fact that their long journey had ended, the only saving element was that what little bodily warmth everyone possessed was shared among the men as they were placed three to a bunk bed. The beds were stacked three high, one on top of the other. No one took off his clothes as they were afraid they'd be stolen while they slept, and a single bucket was on the side interior wall next to an open cesspit in their new barracks. The smell permeated the poorly insulated barracks.

John was first in the shelter, if you could call it that, and he spied the open pit in the cabin.

"Sonny, you're not going to believe this. The cesspit is *inside!*"

"Say honest to God?"

"If I had a scrap of bread every time you said that phrase, I'd be the fattest guy in the camp."

"What do they want us to do here?" wondered Sonny.
"Who knows?"

❧ ❧ ❧

The following day, they were sent into deep caves
that had already been dug with a massive auger and were
instructed by a non-military foreman to begin drilling
holes.

Sonny tried to pick up the drill. "The damn thing is
too heavy."

It weighed only twenty pounds or so, but their muscles had so atrophied during their time in Mühlberg that
they could barely lift it.

"Let me see if I can help," John offered.

The drill, powered by a thick electric cable connected
to a diesel generator only run when drilling was taking
place, was placed against the wall, and four men pushed
their weight against it, holding the side handles until it
vibrated like hell. Two of the vitamin-deficient men had a
tooth immediately fall out from the shaking.

The sound was incredibly loud, and it injured their
already weak ears. Another two had blood pouring from
broken eardrums.

"Stop. Stop! Stop!" everyone yelled.

Their bones were still vibrating when the machines
were turned off, and a third man reached up and pulled
out a tooth that was hanging by a thread. He promptly ate
it in an attempt to staunch his hunger.

"What is the point of drilling these holes? It is going

to take months to get this done. We'll be dead before then, " John said to no one in particular, but Sonny was there with him, holding the heavy drill.

They looked at one another, sure that that was the plan.

They were instructed to put the holes in ten to twelve feet deep, each hole three feet apart or so, and then shove in sticks of dynamite. Though they were sheltered from the outside elements, the men inhaled granite dust with each breath.

The shifts lasted twelve hours a day. The Americans worked from 6 a.m. to 6 p.m., and then the political prisoners took the second shift. The Americans could see that the political prisoners were as weak as themselves.

They all knew the Geneva Convention of 1929 stated that "it is forbidden to employ prisoners of war on unhealthy or dangerous work." It would have been less than useless to complain.

An SS foreman came back in because he heard the drill stop, and when he realized the men were not working, he proceeded to beat them.

ॐॐॐ

Sonny and John had always been able to avoid Schwartzie and his arbitrary beatings; he took his sadism out on the political prisoners for some time as a change of pace, and his rounds took him to different caves to supervise and beat the occasional Jew, taking out on them some unknown anger the guard harbored.

Sonny and John knew that if he happened into their cave and had the slightest inkling that John was a Negro, there would be no saving him—not this time. They weren't sure if Preun's discovery about his race had reached his ears.

John didn't know that Trager had engineered keeping Schwartzie away. There was so much pain and death, and Trager was pretty sure he was going to hell if not a thousand years or two in purgatory. Perhaps to assuage his conscience, Trager made John and Sonny his particular project, keeping them away from the murderous elements, particularly Schwartzie. Then Trager abruptly received new orders: He was to return to IV-B camp in two days' time to help organize an evacuation west, deeper into Germany.

The next morning during muster, a guard came up behind John in the back row. He moved up close to one of his ears and said:

"John, don't turn around—it'll give me away. Kratzer wants to kill you. He's heard that you're an 'undesirable.' He knows you're here; he doesn't know precisely where or who you are yet, but he is in no rush."

It was Trager, who had broken all convention by telling John this plainly. John kept facing forward but felt a rush because it was the first time a German had used his given name.

"Keep out of his way if you can. I'm sorry," Trager said.

ॐ ॐ ॐ

Marcus Trager was an interesting fellow and considered an anomaly among the SS: a compassionate guard. Born in Munich, he moved with his mother to Vienna after his father abandoned them and took his younger brother and sister to parts unknown. Ostensibly it was because of domestic disagreements, but he could not understand why his dad, Stanislaw, took his youngest two siblings but left him with his mom.

Trager was a decent man, and though still the enemy, there were no arbitrary killings or torture under his watch. He could be rough, but as long as a prisoner performed as a prisoner, Trager served as the perfect jailor, was decent, and did his best to limit the gratuitous sadism undertaken by some of his fellow guards. If a defenseless prisoner was being beaten unnecessarily, Trager either stopped it outright or distracted the perpetrator long enough for their attention to wander elsewhere.

He was raised a devout Catholic—one of the reasons he took a shine to Sonny when he saw him participating in mass and using the rosary. By extension, Trager also took a liking to Sonny's good friend John as he discovered more of his background, and it verily intrigued him. Though Trager was a dedicated and dutiful Nazi, he didn't see the difficulty in being loyal to both his military duties and his faith. In fact, Trager knew it was Hitler's first major diplomatic coup that lent enormous legitimacy to his cause in overwhelmingly Catholic Austria: an agreement negotiated by the future Pius XII, Eugenio Pacelli, for religious autonomy for Catholics in Germany.

Trager learned Catholic doctrine and ultimately joined the Hitler Youth, where he learned Nazi ideology in detail, though he dismissed its more radical views as being only politically expedient.

In contrast, *Sturmbannführer* Kratzer "Schwartzie" was also schooled in Vienna at exactly the same time, though he didn't know Trager and mainly absorbed the bigotry of Hitler's teaching. Kratzer joined the Hitler Youth, but unlike Trager, became an adherent to its more racist and radical views.

ન૦ન૦ન૦

Schwartzie was on the prowl at Berga, taking his time finding John because he had no need to rush. They were both in the same camp, and the capricious nature of an unexpected murder would please him.

Around this time, John realized that if something was going to happen to him at Schwartzie's hand, he was going to make sure he either killed him first or took him with him by shivving his throat. Either way, Schwartzie was going to die at John's hands.

ન૦ન૦ન૦

Their days at Berga were brutal, even more so than at Mühlberg, and the evenings of hunger even more painful because there was far less food than at IV-B. Though welcome sleep did provide some miserable escape, it was not enough to stem their pain.

They foolishly wondered why their captors would want to work them till they dropped, though the answer was quite simple: The Germans saw them as a slow but renewable source of work, easily replaceable and quite deserving of the pain being meted out because, of course, they were enemy.

When fuel was available, trucks came daily, often bringing additional prisoners from different nearby prison *Lagers* for the work. They returned to camps sometimes empty, sometimes with guards to offer a change of venue for the sentries, and yet other times with favored prisoners or decent workers who could use some time back at camp. The Germans did not want to kill off all the skilled laborers.

John and Sonny used the drill together with two other prisoners in yet another portion of the cave to bore in several yards. The vibration of the drill shaking loosened their phlegm, which they freely coughed up when they were not guarded by the SS. They breathed in the granite and sometimes spat out blood, the air itself acting like sandpaper on their lungs. The caves protected them from the elements but offered little respite from the cold, the walls seeming to emanate freezing air.

When the guards were looking in the direction of the ringing bells of St. Martin's Church in the tiny, nearby town of Schlieben or lost in the moment talking among themselves about better days, all the prisoners made it a point to rest on their tools or the side of the cave wall. In addition to the drilling, they had to carry out the chunks of incredibly heavy granite stone broken apart by the explosions and place them on a small flatbed train built for that purpose. If there was a hell, this was it. They were so far removed from the real world that this was now reality, though they had only been here days. John and Sonny had luckily avoided any inspections by Kratzer.

Schwartzie with his rank had the talent for making everyone's life miserable, even that of some of his fellow Germans. They detested "picking up" after his fits of outrage. Shooting people for no reason, gratuitous torture, and treating prisoners in a wicked fashion was a way of life for him. Once at IV-B, when two hundred eyes in the barracks were trained on two soldiers carrying what was passing as soup but was, in fact, rancid water with the standard mint leaves strewn in, the sloshing of the heavy twenty-five-gallon drum had slopped some soup into a deep footprint frozen in the mud. A Russian prisoner nearby from an adjacent national camp, seeing the guards either absent or otherwise engaged (for when food was being delivered, many boundaries fell), broke ranks and ran to stick his nose in the rancid mixture in the ground to suck it up greedily. Unluckily for the Russian, Kratzer turned around at that moment and spied him. He strode to the prisoner, pulled out his Walther, and shot him in the brain.

He was so near death in any case, Kratzer resented wasting the bullet. He glanced toward the other prisoners attempting to stand at attention and pointed to two of them and then at the dead man whose face was in the mud. The two men ran over as quickly as they could—though they could manage nothing more than a hobbled stride—grabbed the corpse under each arm, and dragged him away to a cart behind the barracks. As they rounded the corner behind the barracks, one cupped and drank the blood still coming out of the bullet hole in his head, and in the few minutes it took to bring the body to the dray, long strips of what was left of his leg muscles had been expertly sliced away with a shiv fashioned from a sharpened piece of wood and devoured on the spot, such was their hunger. Had he seen their deeds, Kratzer would have shot them as well—not for their cannibalism but for satiating their hunger.

ॐ ॐ ॐ

One afternoon, Sonny and John got a short break and were leaning on the walls. If they sat down, it would expend too much energy to stand back up again, so this was what passed for relaxation. The guards were having a smoke—they also were not too rushed as they could hear the guns in the east coming closer, and the SS were discussing their own escape plan: Shoot the prisoners, change their uniforms for civilian clothes, and head west. Many of the guards already had fake army identification papers because they knew that the SS had a somewhat "unsavory" reputation on the entire continent.

Break over, Sonny and John continued to drill holes for dynamite.

Barely able to lift their arms, let alone their drill, they heard the guards being harangued outside the cave entrance. It was Kratzer. Schwartzie.

"*Christ!* What are they saying?" Sonny asked in a low tone.

John whispered, "He's giving them an earache about not being in the tunnel supervising and letting the Jews probably stop their work. He doesn't hear the drill working. He expects them to beat one and shoot another as motivation."

Sonny froze still at first then sat on the ground—since he knew he was the most fragile and would finally be chosen—with relief. He had about reached his own breaking point and was ready for it all to end. The cold, the hunger, the loose teeth, and breathing in the granite dust that was scratching his throat. He knew he stood little chance, and he accepted what was about to happen.

The guards shot the first two prisoners near the mouth of the cave, and then as Kratzer moved farther into the cave and approached Sonny to shoot him in the head, John screamed: "*Schwartzie, nein!*"

The German guards and Kratzer, overcome with incredulity and amazement, froze at John's arrogance and loudness. All this…from a prisoner. A Jewish prisoner at that, they assumed. Kratzer stared, and one of the guards moved toward John and Sonny with his un-holstered pistol to finish them off, while Trager, the second guard, looked on helplessly. The SS guard casually held up his weapon to the side of John's head as he stared at Kratzer.

The report of two gunshots could be heard outside the tunnel. Everything began to move in slow motion. John and Sonny initially didn't hear the weapon's report, but they knew they would be "transported" to a place of no pain and be released. They had reached the "end of the journey" that they were resigned to accept.

TWENTY-SIX

JEAN-CLAUDE

When the Great War began, all the participants started to scour their colonies, territories, and diaspora around 1917 looking for soldiers who could serve their cause, and France was no different.

Jean-Claude Chalmet, John's dad, was brought to the United States and to New Orleans while in his mother's womb in the 1890s. His parents were born in Senegal into a prosperous family and became highly rated servants for a French family who moved to New Orleans. The wealthy White French citizens had wished to settle in Louisiana's French enclave. He grew up speaking French, obviously, but soon learned Creole, a local mixture of French and English in New Orleans, as well as native Senegalese, only spoken at home with his parents.

JC had an easy life at first, but by the age of ten, his exposure to the vicissitudes of discrimination in the Deep South of the US began.

He was drawn to enlist in the US Army when WWI

broke out, much as his son did in the subsequent war, and JC was sent to Huachuca just as John was when he enlisted twenty-five years later. Fort Huachuca, which had involved training soldiers (mostly Negroes) since the 1800s, was involved with the fight against the Apaches and Pancho Villa, which were fascinating in themselves as both were known as historical figures. He was trained in the 93rd Division, one of two trained at the camp comprised entirely of Negroes.

The 92nd and 93rd divisions were shipped over to Europe at the same time, but the 93rd had been neglected during training. The 92nd had been trained exclusively by White southern US soldiers (the standard theory at the time being that Whites from the South "understood" Negroes), while the 93rd was treated as an afterthought.

The 92nd Division performed badly in various battles, including the Battle of the Meuse-Argonne, where their casualties were relatively high.

The 93rd, on the other hand, was turned over directly to the French upon arriving in Marseilles, who needed the manpower, where they were trained by French and given French equipment.

By war's end, the *entire* 93rd had performed so well that they were collectively awarded the Croix de Guerre. Three specific Negro officers won the Legion of Honour, one of the highest French decorations. Over 120 rank and file won individual Croix de Guerres for valor, and twenty-six won the Distinguished Service Cross. *There is a lesson here somewhere*, JC thought at the time because the

Negro division outperformed nearly all the *White* French and American divisions.

JC fought bravely for the Allies and was awarded a personal Croix de Guerre for bravery for taking out a German machine gun nest single-handily, proving at a minimum his own bravery as well as further demonstrating the daring and skill of an adequately trained Negro soldier.

After the war, JC was given the option of returning to the US, but he was disdainful of the discrimination he was sure to encounter back home and embraced the relative freedom he enjoyed as a Negro in Europe. Subsequently, he was sent as an occupying guard to Mainz in the Rhineland, a narrow strip of land, formally German territory, that had been ceded to France postwar as reparations and would act as a physical buffer to prevent a surprise invasion by Germany upon France. It was occupied by Entente forces and had been demilitarized under the 1919 Treaty of Versailles and then the 1925 Locarno Treaties.

JC showed his gift for languages by picking up German rather quickly.

Several months after arriving, JC was billeted in the city next to the Rhine River in a youth hostel that was commandeered by the occupying French forces, where he was befriended by a German couple living right next door whom he saw very early each morning on his way to the military parade ground. They at first appeared exceedingly amiable, and their acquaintance made his being posted in a far-away country more endurable. He met them in an interesting fashion.

While on a routine patrol with another French soldier one Saturday, JC happened down near the river in
front of the baroque red sandstone buildings near Mainz
Cathedral after taking a walk through the nearby museum
under the guise of making sure all was in order. He loved
museums. Rifle slung over his shoulder, JC spied a miniature boy of barely one, toddling as if he had just learned
to walk, dash in between two vehicles: one an automobile,
the other a horse-drawn wagon owned by people out for
the day going for a stroll along the river. JC dropped his
rifle and sprinted toward the street. Without looking for
any autos or carriages, JC scooped the boy up and continued across the narrow road, one fast-moving car just
missing them both, which then proceed to swerve and hit
a parked automobile. The smell of a burning rubber hose
filled the air.

Smoke rose from the car's engine, and the sound
of the crash was so loud it drew a crowd. The little boy
laughed as if nothing had happened and proceeded to
rub JC's face and then check his own hand to see if JC's
darkness had rubbed off on him.

A woman came through the crowd screaming a name,
spied her son and JC, whom she recognized from their
early morning encounters near the hostel, and laughed
with relief, grabbing both and hugging them. They had
not been properly acquainted but recognized each other
as neighbors, and Anna insisted JC come to dinner that
evening to meet her husband, Max.

Both JC's neighbors, Anna and Max Schmidt, taught

geography and mathematics respectively, and JC became quite friendly with them in just a few days. Anna was a young, attractive, new mom devoted to her son, and Max was a bespectacled math teacher whom JC learned was severe with his slower students and possessed a sullen demeanor, seemingly harboring some type of ill-will toward something.

These Germans were quite different from other people JC met in the city in that they didn't recoil from him because of his race as some people did. In fact, they seemed to find him charming and exotic, partly, JC suspected, because he was a soldier of an occupying force and partly for the spare rations he gladly shared with them. It came to be that they invited him as a guest in their home time and again—a very modest setting, but it made the distance between home in New Orleans and where he was billeted much easier to bear.

కికికి

To Jean-Claude, initially, this family setting of Max and Anna seemed idyllic, almost like paradise.

But no sooner had he come to that conclusion than he began to peel back the surface of his new friends, the elder Max and Anna. Indeed, there seemed to be some unsettling tension in their home. Their first meal went well enough. Both were clearly grateful to JC for saving young Max's life. Though it was clear that Max Senior was initially delighted at the rescue, it was just as clear as the meal progressed that he felt uncomfortable by

JC's presence—perhaps due to another male being in the house, or sharing their own precious food rations, forgetting what JC was bringing, or the change in attitude Anna was now expressly carrying: Max had not seen her this animated since before they were husband and wife.

JC had also overheard him challenge Anna on nearly everything about the dinner, whether the soup was hot or the bread stale. He also contradicted everything she brought up by way of conversation at the dinner table to the point where she was diminished into silence, looking down at her plate during the sometimes hastily served dinner (expedited by her husband). After the meal, JC would depart, pleased at having new friends but confused by their attitude toward each other. Though he was uneasy with their relationship, it was balanced (in his own mind) by their acceptance of him within their family setting and the home-cooked meals he got so far away from his home.

అ అ అ

Several weeks after they met, JC was on yet another early evening of patrol, just along the Rhine near the Main tributary. The sun had not entirely gone down, and JC told his fellow soldier that because it was part of his duty area, he had decided to walk north along the Rhine, which gently merged with the Main, to hopefully catch a cool breeze because though it was early autumn, it was unusually warm that evening, and he and his partner could meet up again by the Gutenberg Museum.

As JC walked along the quay near the western shore,

he saw some sort of an altercation up ahead and to the left. Four youths were beating up one other kid. Sadly, an unfair fight. *Kids*, he thought, but as he got closer, still undetected because the thugs were consumed with the task at hand, he heard:

"Do you talk to the nigger? Does he understand? Does his color come off when you shake his hand?"

JC figured they had to be talking about either himself or one of the other several Negro soldiers from the French garrison in the town.

As he came upon the scene, the thugs saw him and dispersed, running up the steps and into the ancient city's narrow streets. He screamed for them to stop, leveling his rifle (as an empty threat), but they scurried off. As he hurried toward the heap they had fallen upon, he saw a bloodied pulp not of a child as he expected but of a man. He turned him over and saw the face of Max Schmidt. Before he could take action, he heard his fellow patrol soldier call out: "*Jean-Claude, ça va? Comme vous aider?*"

He screamed for him to call an ambulance and for help. As the soldier ran off to make the call, two other soldiers hurried down the steps of the quay to assist and carried the bloody mess up the steps.

With German efficiency, an ambulance arrived almost immediately just as other patrols were converging on the scene, and they began searching the streets for the thugs based on JC's brief description.

As they piled Max into the back of the ambulance, JC asked the driver: "Closest hospital?"

"*Universitätsklinikum Mainz.*"

"Take us there." JC grabbed a junior French soldier before they departed and asked him, "Do you speak German?"

"*Ein kleines Bisschen*—a little bit."

"Go to this address." John wrote it out quickly on a scrap of paper. "And tell Frau Schmidt to go to *Universitätsklinikum Mainz*. Her husband has been injured. Tell her this message is from JC Chalmet."

చించించి

When Anna arrived at the hospital after she was summoned by JC, she found him looking after her husband, and he immediately took charge of Max Jr. so she could go to her husband's side. To distract Max Jr., JC asked one of his comrades to bring a small burlap bag hanging from the headboard of his barracks bed, wherein he had a work in progress—a carving of a little wooden doll for the child of another soldier. He had begun to paint it blue and was preparing to paint the rest the next day; at the moment, the doll's skin tone was the color of the wood.

He gave it to Max Jr., who squealed with delight, not having any idea of the peril that his father was in a few feet away.

JC stayed with his friends as he had time off from his duties, and after a day or so, Max Jr. became a bit more colicky. JC took him aside to an empty parlor near Max's hospital room and started to gently sing to calm him down. Senegalese songs, such as "*Fatou yo*" and "*Sama raka modou,"* had been sung to him a thousand times by his parents, used to soothe him during his infancy. He segued into French songs he had learned as a toddler, such as *"Tout le monde aime Samedi soir,"* sung by his parents, having learned them after they reached New Orleans. Finally, he switched to Christmas carols in both French and German, which he had been learning as part of an impromptu choir set up by the French troops. His gentle singing voice was angelic.

Max Jr. stared with what appeared to be delight at JC, and at some point, he gently cooed and fell fast asleep. JC smiled down at Max, and when he looked up, he saw Anna in the doorway, leaning against the frame of the open door with tears running down her face. Though JC was perplexed by Max's roughness toward his wife, he also knew that he was confused continuously by who people chose to love, just as he was surprised by what they chose to read. Taking into account her tears, he said, "I can tell that you love your husband very much."

Anna gave him a bemused look and decided it was time to tell him the truth. "JC, Max has quite a temper."

JC said nothing; it was not his place. He had seen Max sometimes berate her when he visited, when they thought they were out of eye and earshot of others within their small flat. He continued to play occasionally with a clearly delighted Max Jr., who seemed pleased with the dark-skinned man with the wide, toothy grin and ebullient attitude—very different from his own live-in male role model.

During an early visit to their home, JC noticed that Anna was wearing a long-sleeve blouse; he saw the bruise when her sleeve had pulled back as she drew out her arm to pass a plate, as well as a swollen bit of her cheekbone poorly covered with more than a bit of powder makeup.

That latest wound she received when her husband learned that she had once again invited the Negro French soldier for dinner. Though that time, to Max Sr.'s surprise, it also ended up being a welcome visit because of the food JC had managed to take from his own canteen—including some dairy products for young Max—which supplemented their own meager supplies.

In that nearly empty hospital parlor, he continued to entertain Max Jr., apropos of nothing while Anna stared at them. After a silence lasting more than a few moments, during which JC allowed Anna's exhausted mind to be alone with her thoughts, she looked at him and continued: "There was a boy back in my hometown of Gelsenkirchen. He was several years older than me, actually. A young man more than a boy. He taught art, history, and language—at the same school where Max was teaching. They were colleagues but never really friends.

"Dieter—his name—was a charming young man, actually. Friendly, polite, a beautiful singing voice, and also clever with children. He was the youngest by far of his four older sisters, so he was one of the youngest 'uncles' in the town. And he was oh so talented with his nieces and nephews, playing games in the park and constructing small toys from the simplest of objects. His exhausted sisters regularly and gratefully used their youngest brother as a babysitter for their children for only a few *Groshens*, but Dieter would have done it for free. I would see him with a couple of children almost every day in the park after his classes were over."

Jean-Claude could see that Anna was seeing Dieter in her mind's eye as she stared at another young couple in the waiting room fussing over their own young child as they awaited word on the status of the husband's father, who had suffered a heart attack and was being looked after by the doctors. The couple and their young child soon left the room.

"And Dieter could sing!" She smiled at the memory. "I used to go hear him even during his choir practice at the local church. I would sit under the balcony, so he didn't know I was there. Sometimes, when I would listen to the choir, I was sure I could make out his voice among all the others."

Anna continued, "Most evenings I went, I saw Max too in the church, though he was sitting on the opposite side from me. Max tried to hide who he was, though it was challenging to do with his thick glasses. I thought he loved music like myself, but I later discovered that he was there not for the music but to follow me. But I did not wish to spend time with him—my heart belonged to Dieter."

Anna went on, "After a while, Max became bolder in the church, moving closer to me after several rehearsals until he came up to sit next to me one day and asked to take me for a walk, and I agreed that he could walk me home. He was delighted, and in the vestibule of the church, he recited a short, practiced speech, clearly rehearsed, though he stumbled over the words a few times, beginning again and again until he said it perfectly to his satisfaction, professing his love to me. I told him I already had a young man, and he abruptly stalked off, his body wrenching in a way that convinced me he was furious. As he stormed away, he slammed the heavy church door behind him, echoing in the church, the loud bang ending the choir singing above."

In the waiting room in the hospital, Max Jr. began stirring in the pram while his mother spoke, and JC took the small wooden doll that was now under his leg. The toy was the first thing the little boy saw when his eyes opened. He smiled, grabbed the toy, closed his eyes, and within a moment, was heavily breathing once again, resuming a deep, contented sleep.

JC remained silent.

"I had to move fast due to Max's persistence." Anna again smiled, swept up in another memory. I walked to the balcony steps in the church's foyer and intercepted Dieter as he left his rehearsal. I quite promptly told him that I loved his singing and had been listening in the church that evening. I asked if he would walk me home. He was taken aback, I suppose, by someone showing him that much interest. He walked me home, and though I lived less than a mile away, and the sun stayed up very late at that time, it took him hours to get me there. We became very close friends and very exclusive. From that day on, he led me to sit upstairs in the balcony during both his rehearsals and their Sunday performances at church, and soon we were both having meals with our parents in each other's homes. I loved him very much. I barely saw Max at all after that. In his embarrassment, he kept his distance from my sight and from my memory."

Anna was quiet as that feeling sank into her. Finally, she sighed and continued, "Dieter went to war. All the young men in town did, but Max was spared because of his eyesight. The military couldn't take a chance on his spectacles being knocked off in battle, so he stayed home in Gelsenkirchen where they still needed teachers. His workload nearly tripled, and that didn't help the anger he carried—the anger at having to miss the war and his anger at my rejection.

"When word came back that Dieter was missing in action and later killed, I was heartbroken. Max, on the other hand, was delighted by the loss of his colleague and rival. He thought this gave him free rein to pursue me, and his entreats and attentions became more and more unwelcome. At one point, as I was leaving the church after listening to a *Liederkranz* by the remaining choir, now seriously diminished in membership due to the war, I was set upon by Max, once again professing his love, and once again, he was angered by my refusal, though this time, JC, he pulled me into an alley near my home and set upon me."

Max Jr. slept, and Jean-Claude was sitting down next

to the pram in front of her, as still as a statue. He dared not speak, but at the same time, he didn't want to hear what would come next. Yet his silence invited her to continue.

"Soon, I was expecting a child. My parents were furious with me, thinking I had led Max on. When gossip began to travel that I was expecting, and it became clear to the town that I would be with my darling little Max any day, a hastily arranged marriage took place, and we moved in together in a two-room flat attached to his parents' home and previously occupied by his recently deceased grandmother."

We lived together, but not happily. Max was angry about everything: his job and the fact that he had to look after an unloving wife and a young child and that his anger caused him to get fired by his school because of his temper—apparently for the second time in his career—thus forcing us to travel here, far enough away so that the reputation of this temper did not follow him. The school that now employed him paid a fraction of what he was paid before, so I had to teach as well, though I could only do so when Max was still young enough to sleep in the classroom or I could find another mother who would watch him for me.

"Thank you for calling me here, watching Max, and listening to my unfortunate story," she finished.

JC had been sitting motionless the whole time whenever he was not glancing at Max to ensure he was still sleeping well. He stood up and gave her a warm hug, which she clearly needed.

She asked, "What happened to Max, and how did you happen to be there?"

JC proceeded to tell her what had transpired that evening, including what the thugs had said to Max.

తతత

Both JC and Anna sat by Max in the hospital for three days before he died of his injuries. JC received permission to stay at the hospital during this time from his commanding officer. Nobody saw anything, and it was impossible to identify the perpetrators, though JC suspected some of Max's students.

JC helped look after little Max while Anna dealt with the funeral arrangements; he spent a good deal of time looking after her as well to help assuage her grief—which seemed not to stem so much from losing her husband as it did from being a single mom with little income. Having just arrived in the Rhineland with her husband only a month before they met JC, she really knew no one except him, and most of the other locals kept their distance from her because she and her husband entertained a Negro at their home.

As they spent more time together, Frau Schmidt soon fell into JC's arms because of his kindness. She did not think about his race because so few Negroes were ever seen in that part of the world, and race relations were rarely a topic of conversation anywhere. As time went on, it became clear to both JC and Anna that their relationship was not blessed by anyone. It was not even acknowledged by her racist neighbors.

෨෨෨

John was born to the couple a little more than two years after Max Jr., and he was given the American spelling of his dad's name: John. As he got older, Anna thought he would eventually look more like his father than herself, though he looked more and more like a White boy as he aged. In fact, the older he grew, the more easily he could pass for a White boy.

Initially, JC thought nothing of his light-skinned child—indeed, in New Orleans, he had seen many classmates of mixed-race parents grow darker pigmentation as they grew older. Just as the contradiction in the back of his mind started to take shape that John's skin color was not becoming deeper, John emerged from an early puberty with JC's distinctive nose: slightly wide at the base but as straight as an arrow from the bridge to the tip—almost pointy. He maintained many of his mother's features: straight, fine hair, though black like JC's, and his skin was not brown or black at all: more light-olive than brown. When he was thirteen years old, many thought him an Italian lad.

JC understood from his own mom, who, among other things, was a midwife when she was not a servant in both Senegal and New Orleans, that when Negro children were born, they had a decided lack of pigmentation for the first few weeks before the rich color set in. But this did not happen with John. As his facial features and body morphed into that of a standard toddler, it was unmistakable that JC was, physically, a copy of his dad as he had had his same fine features. JC had a photo of himself as an infant, taken in New Orleans from a famous photographer, and the picture was the spitting image of John except for JC's much darker complexion.

JC was among the very residual French soldiers left in the Rhineland as the French started removing troops as a cost-cutting measure. His pay was quite enough; he could speak English, French, a smattering of Senegalese, and he was initially provided German language lessons by the French Army, which he assimilated quickly—and of course, he had help from Anna Schmidt.

࿒࿒࿒

As Nazi political fortunes changed in Germany, and they began to get bolder with territorial demands and intrusion into German cultural and racial life in the early 1930s, John's dad could plainly see the handwriting on the wall.

It was clear from the newspapers that the Germans were systematically beginning to persecute their own Jews just across the Rhine, and the occasional story was reported that other minorities, including some Rhineland bastards—mixed-race children fathered by Negro French soldiers who had "infected" Germany from Mainz—had been thrown in jail.

The French Army had quit the Rhineland around the time John was born. JC was honorably discharged and easily found work as a cabinet maker, his race not being a hindrance to employment because the French and the majority of those living in Mainz saw national identity tied more to language than ethnicity. Other allies stayed in the Rhineland to pick up the occupational duties left by the departing French, but they, too, were preparing to depart as the political climate in German changed and it appeared that the area would once again belong wholly to Germany.

Things changed abruptly when the German Army marched in to occupy the Rhineland in 1936—and following close on their heels was the Gestapo. Chaos ensued among those who were non-ethnically German, and many who had been part of French families for generations pulled up roots and moved west.

JC and Anna were torn. JC wanted to leave and go to France and then America, but in the hope of reconciliation with her family, Anna could not move away from her estranged parents and siblings, and she refused to depart.

On a cataclysmic day in March 1936, JC was arrested by the Gestapo, who were surreptitiously infiltrating the Rhineland and thrown in jail for cohabitating with a White German. Anna panicked—she could not bear for herself or her boys to be arrested as well, and while she had a German passport for Max, she never got one for John.

She visited JC briefly in prison, not knowing what to do. It was dangerous to remain in Mainz during this time of upheaval, and she knew that while she had to leave, it would be difficult for her and John because he would forever be known as a "Rhineland bastard" and she a "Rhineland whore."

"I'll be out in a day," he told her. "The French still have some pull in local government here, and they're negotiating with the Gestapo to let me loose as long as I move back to France. The fact that I am an American helps with that case a lot. Take Max, move back to your parents' home, and leave John with the school. I'll arrange for you to come to France in a few weeks when I plant myself across the border. The French take care of their veterans." This was true, and arrangements were indeed being made to set him free the next day.

Anna and JC could not embrace as they were separated by a mesh screen, and JC watched as she walked out the door. It would be the last time he saw her.

He was indeed released the next morning. He collected a delighted John from his school, the understanding headmistress having kept him for the evening, and headed west into France via train. He was told by a neighbor that Anna left the night before on the last train that had departed, heading for North Germany and an uncertain future.

Anna left the Rhineland, bereft, towing a teenage Max with her to live with her family up north, but they turned her away at the door because they had heard with whom she had been keeping company in Mainz. She did an about-face and traveled to her cousins in Munich, her own family wanting nothing to do with her for giving birth to her second son—a Rhineland bastard born not even a year after her husband died—and with a Negro father, at that.

JC stayed only briefly in France as he could not get back into Germany. He wrote desperately to her family in Gelsenkirchen, to no avail. Letters were neither acknowledged nor returned, her parents burning them in the hearth unopened when they read the return address.

German forces remilitarized the territory in 1936 as part of a diplomatic test of wills before war hostilities started not long afterward, but by then, JC and John were long gone to America.

TWENTY-SEVEN

NEWARK, FINALLY

In this last tavern across the river from Newark in Harrison, JC continued his story. "When things started to become 'troublesome' for anybody who was not a White German or who was a Jew in the Rhineland, and the Nazis started picking up steam, I begged Anna to come back with me to France and then to the US because I didn't think it was wise to stick around to see how it turned out. The Nazis were clearly pretty violent, and John was already being called a Rhineland bastard. He was almost a teenager. He knew what that meant."

While they were waiting in the tavern for their food, Jean-Claude opened the packet he had taken out of his jacket, and he started rifling through photos he brought along to show Sonny, occasionally stopping at one to stare and smile at it before handing it over. They were all shapes and sizes—some with straight edges, some serrated.

"Here is John when he was five, reading in the

backyard. God that kid loved to read. And he could read equally well in French and German."

"Here he is, about the same age, with his first fishing pole. He'd go to the nearby river when he wasn't reading and caught a brace of fish that he'd bring home for dinner."

More and more, the photos were of a happy family before the upheaval. John's mom was White, which Sonny expected.

"Here's one when we were in Georgia." John had a stern visage, almost angry. "John wasn't happy then. Angry at the world or so it seemed. Joining the army was the right thing for him. Helped him to work out all that rage I think he had."

JC returned to talking about Anna. "She couldn't bring herself to leave Europe and always hoped to make peace with her family. Though she was intelligent, she never learned any languages other than French and German and did not want to move to America," JC repeated, almost as a way of asking absolution for leaving her behind.

"She and Max moved—I'm guessing to Gelsenkirchen to be with her parents—and I said I'd send an address when I got settled. I wrote a dozen times to her parents, but I never heard back.

"I never found out what happened to Anna or the boy. Looked there for them for years. I later learned her parents worked in defense and were killed during a bombing raid. By chance, I discovered from one of their neighbors that she moved to be with a cousin in Munich."

"How did that happen?" Sonny asked.

"The neighbors were nosey, and they got one of my letters by mistake, being right next door, opened it and read it. They took pity on me and my letter and briefly answered it. Anna and Max, they disappeared into Germany, and after that, it became impossible to find out anything. I couldn't locate them in Munich. Her sisters were as good as her parents were in answering my letters. In the run-up to the war, there was no way a Negro could visit or would be able to investigate what happened, and I could not take John, really. Anna and the boy just disappeared into Germany," he repeated.

"She was German, right?" Sonny asked after a pause.

"Yeah."

"Tell me about her."

JC thought a moment, unsure whether knew Sonny well enough to share all the details of that relationship, so he somewhat abridged the story.

"I chose to be stationed as part of the occupying French Army in Mainz after the first World War for a couple of years. When I met Anna, soon afterward, her husband, who was their primary source of income, abruptly died, and he did not provide for her at all. And to be honest, I don't think he treated her terribly well. There were sometimes smiles and affection in front of others, but I spent a little time with them, and I don't think they were aware of just how much German I could speak. I treated her right, probably unlike any other man she had ever met. When her husband died, she had pretty much only known me less than a few months. Same with her husband Max. They had a very short courtship, a boy, and not long afterward, her husband was killed. When I met her, we fell in love—or, at least, I thought she loved me. Let's say it was a relationship born out of love as much as necessity. We didn't marry. John was born nine months later.

Sonny asked, "How'd her husband die?"

JC pondered before he told him, wanting to limit how much he disclosed because of his relationship with the couple and their child. "He was beaten to death by thugs one night on his way home from his school."

While he was talking, JC continued leafing through the pictures that were in the envelope he brought.

"My stepson Max didn't think there was anything strange about having a Negro stepfather until other people, specifically school chums, told him it was. Since his own father died when he was an infant, I became his dad."

JC showed Sonny photos of John as a young boy in Germany and several pics of John's mom and of JC with John's older stepbrother—a handsome, blond-haired young man.

JC went on: "The boys adored each other—Max was enamored with his new brother, and they became very close. They got into everything, even after John injured Max during a mock sword fight. They were born less than two years apart.

"I took John with me to America when he was thirteen years old. The political situation was as chaotic there as it was in most countries, but as the Nazis' presence grew more substantial, racial and ethnicity problems came to the front."

JC had filled Sonny in, in that toasty warm Harrison tavern, on a lot about John's life that Sonny hadn't known: the origins of his excellent, multiple language skills, his history, his family, and most of all, his skin color.

చాచా

JC came across a certain photograph and handed it to Sonny while talking. "When Max was eight, as I said, John injured Max's eye horsing around using blunted wooden dowels as swords. Stupid thing. Problem was that Max needed an eyepatch after that. He didn't blind him, mind you. Just damaged a small part of the retina."

The photo was a dog-eared, yellowed image of an eight- and ten-year-old boy, one he recognized as John the youngster, looking a lot like his dad, though obviously dark hair with what looked like light-colored eyes, before studying the boy with the eyepatch.

"They nicknamed Max 'Blackie' at school because of me, which we all thought was funny because both my boys were as White as they come."

TWENTY-EIGHT

END IN BERGA

One of the two remaining guards was deciding how best to shoot the remaining two prisoners so the bullets would not pass through their emaciated bodies and ricochet off the granite walls into themselves, so the guard grabbed them both by the scruff of the neck to kill them outside the tunnel entrance. The other guard, Trager, was thinking furiously about how to stop his comrade from shooting his two friends. But his thinking abruptly ended.

Kratzer shot both guards in quick succession before they could react, and darkness filled their eyes quickly as they crumbled to the ground, oblivious. Trager was an easy kill for him. Schwartzie had recently been advised by his commanding officer that, though Marcus had been raised a Catholic, they had reason to suspect that his father was, in fact, a Jew who had abandoned his family so they would not suffer whatever fate chanced upon himself. It didn't matter that Trager was a guard—a Jew was still a Jew to Kratzer.

Sonny had heard the two shots moments before and wondered if he was dead. Sonny then heard John yell, *Schwartzie, nein!*" And though it was simple German, he had no idea what was said because he didn't know the language well.

As Sonny slowly turned around, he thought it was a dream that, after a moment, John and Kratzer were embracing.

A conversation ensued in German, which Sonny could not understand.

John and Max, who had been nicknamed "Blackie" while growing up, looked at each other. Max got the name because his stepfather was black—and he hated it.

John, when he finally had a look at his face close up, realized that Kratzer was the stepbrother he had not seen in years. And Kratzer too, shocked by boldness of the screaming of the prisoner, peered through the grime on John's face, and recognized his younger stepbrother.

Because of prior slights he had received in his life, Kratzer had ended up becoming a particularly brutal SS guard—singling out those who were Jewish or even had Jewish names—in fact, anyone that did not meet the Aryan ideal. He was resentful that his father had been killed; he was embittered that his stepfather, whom he had loved, had taken away the brother whom he adored and had left his mother, who he thought died of loneliness. He hated being considered as a lesser being because of that same stepfather, and he loathed being called "Blackie" growing up.

He had to vent his anger somewhere as he grew older, and when he reached adulthood the SS was the perfect place.

Kratzer hated John as only a family member could, for through the filth and face covered with granite dust, he saw his brother that he loved and missed. A thousand memories flooded back, particularly his shame of cruel treatment of the people he had killed and tortured whom he had defined as the dregs of society—as he imagined his brother at this moment.

"Why are you with the Jews?!" was his first question.

John was surprised by the question but answered. "I made friends with this guy, and he is not a Jew. And some snitch at IV-B told them about Dad, I think. And what if my friend is a Jew?" John demanded—a rather bold thing to do to a German officer. "He showed me the 'right friendship.'"

Kratzer was silent.

"How is Mom?" John finally asked.

"Dead for years—almost just after we left you. Tuberculosis. I grew up in Vienna with her cousins."

"Daddy was looking for you in Munich."

"Her family there didn't want her there either. Nor our grandparents in Gelsenkirchen. They knew she had a Negro child." Schwartz seemed apprehensive as he asked, "How is Daddy?" Though he felt abandoned, he needed to know.

"Okay, I guess. In Georgia, but I doubt he got any of my letters from Mühlberg, and I never heard anything after I arrived in Italy in September. I was captured there."

"Why did Daddy leave Mommy and me?" That question had plagued Schwartz's mind for over a decade.

"If he hadn't, we'd both be dead by now—and you know that. He begged Mommy to come."

John's dad had told him the story of their exodus often and asked John to look for Anna and Max after the war in Europe ended when the time was right.

Schwartzie sighed. He knew John was right.

John repeated, "Daddy tried to find you over the years but couldn't. He wrote to people all over Munich."

"Mom's cousins in Munich wouldn't have us, so she changed our last name, and we moved to Austria. She couldn't use Schmidt because they'd have just traced it back to Chalmet. Why do people call you Shall-met?"

"Some idiot when I joined the Army wrote it that way. Daddy was looking in Munich because he knew Mommy's sister lived there," John repeated again. After a pause, he asked, "Max, what are you doing here?"

His certitude left him. "I don't know. It just happened. It happened to everybody."

"Before today, to be honest, I wanted to kill you first chance I got," John admitted. "Now I can't."

"I wish you would have killed me," Max replied with a severe look.

The brothers stared at one another: one emaciated and ill-clad, the other well-fed and in an immaculate but evil uniform.

"What now?" John asked, looking down at the dead German soldiers in the cave.

After a moment, Max stood up straight, holstered his weapon, and helped Sonny to his feet. He draped John's arm around Sonny (appearances were important) and led them to the tunnel entrance. He dragged the other two guards deeper into the tunnel so they wouldn't be easily seen right away.

Max flagged down an empty truck leaving the camp and to the soldier driving he said, "Take these…Jews back. They're engineers, and I need them to rest a few days."

"Which camp, *Herr Sturmbannführer*? the driver said awkwardly, saluting with one hand on the wheel. "We can't take them back to IV-B—that's 150 kilometers, and we don't have the petrol."

"Take them to Chemnitz to the *Rathaus*. They've got POWs working on rebuilding parts of the local waterworks, and turn them over to *Oberst* Krehel there. I know him. Ask him to protect them as engineers and to hold them until I can collect them—probably in a week's time. Both these Jews are critical for building this factory. What are you waiting for? *Now!*"

"I don't have anyone to guard them."

"They can barely stand. They'll give you no trouble. That is a direct order."

The truck pulled away, with John and Sonny leaning against empty boxes in the open back of the truck.

༐ ༐ ༐

As they drove away from the caves in the back of the truck, Sonny was exceedingly confused. He had no idea what John and Schwartz had spoken about, but he was too weak to ask.

He thought for a moment that this might be death because what was happening seemed bizarrely sweet and surreal, but the pain in his head and stomach told him he was very much alive. Sitting in the back of the truck, he leaned against some boxes. John was already fast asleep, overcome emotionally. In the back of the truck and at the expanse of the face of the mountain and the tunnels, what he saw would have made the little energy he had make his heart beat faster. But he thought it was all part of a dream as the truck drove over the bumpy road, the first conveyance he had been in these many months, and he fell fast asleep.

☙☙☙

As the Russian Army came close to overrunning the camp and were about to arrive, the Germans started mustering the men. They broke them down into two groups to be moved out.

As they approached the end of the war, the prisoners from both Berga and IV-B were subjected to yet another forced march to keep ahead of the advancing Russian troops. Because they had been sent to Chemnitz to work on rebuilding City Hall, both John and Sonny missed that.

When they arrive in Chemnitz and turned over to *Oberst* Krehel, he immediately placed them in the town infirmary, already burgeoning with wounded German troops. But he knew Kratzer would not have sent them unless there was something important about them, and in any case with the allies coming closer having important prisoners, particularly living Americans could be used as a bargaining chip.

Luckily for them Chemnitz was declared an "open" city, and the wiser German soldiers dropped their weapons, changed into whatever stolen civilian clothing they could find, and scurried west. The remaining citizens and prisoners waited to be liberated, by whom they did not know: either the Russians or the Americans, during which time the prisoners threw themselves on whatever food they could find until a US medic arriving in a scouting group the next day forbade it and told them of the dangers of doing that. General Patton had targeted that city as an objective, and his troops started to pour in unchallenged, but he was told to cease as it was due to be turned over to the Russians. The group the general sent forward he said was a reconnoiter group in force, but it was really only two platoons ordered to liberate what prisoners they could and bring them west. There were rumors that the Russians were holding onto US prisoners longer than they should. Patton, too, was thinking about a continuation of hostilities, and like the Germans, he was sure the Russians would want to use them as bargaining chips.

They were freely turned over to Patton's soldiers by the Germans guarding them, who at the same time begged the Americans to take them too as they did not wish to fall into the hands of the Russians. The Yanks obliged many, as they did need help with stretchers. In fact, the few prisoners they did get out then were the last to be released for many months by the incoming forces. Krehel supervised and joined the group.

Patton's men took them immediately to their field hospital forty miles west, where they were well looked after. John and Sonny were so malnourished and weak that for quite some time, they were on their backs, taking as much sustenance as their bodies could gradually handle. When Sonny awoke after what seemed like days of much needed sleep, he discovered that John had been forwarded to England by air for treatment as his physical challenges were more significant. He met up again ever so briefly with John at Fulham Hospital in London with British war veterans weeks later.

えべべ

Telegram 1945 10 May 5:42 PM
WESTERN UNION
MRS. MARY JACOBS – 50 FABYAN PL NEW-ARK NJERS

THE CHIEF OF STAFF DIRECTS ME TO INFORM YOU YOUR SON MSTR SER-GEANT ANGUS F. JACOBS JR IS BEING RETURNED TO THE UNITED STATES WITHIN THE NEAR FUTURE AND WILL BE GIVEN AN OPPORTUNITY TO COM-MUNICATE WITH YOU UPON ARRIVAL. J A ULIO, THE ADJUTANT GENERAL

TWENTY-NINE

FABYAN PLACE

At the moment of JC's last reveal from the photos, Sonny abruptly stood up, grabbed their coats, draped his own over his companion's meager covering, and gently shoved him toward the door.

Sonny had thought so much about the fact that he had failed to protect John, he didn't even realize that it was John who had saved him. He wanted so desperately to grab him and hug him and thank him.

Sonny hopped into the driver's side of the car while JC jumped through the passenger door. He started up the engine, and while it was warming, got out with a straw broom to clean the accumulated snow on the windshield.

Sonny knew that only a direct personal epiphany could take away his family's ingrained bigotry.

He was convinced of the need to give his family their own individual personal revelation. It was the only thing that had worked for him.

The photo JC showed him helped Sonny understand

the exchange between Schwartz and John. It was of two boys, arm in arm: one clearly John, and the other, his brother with a patch over his left eye from the makeshift épée.

Sonny thought back to the scene at the tunnel entrance at Berga.

Before the truck had pulled away, as he looked out of the open back of the truck toward the tunnel entrance, he had seen Schwartzie put the gun muzzle into his mouth and pull the trigger. A pink mist formed in the air behind his head, and he had fallen to the ground.

It hadn't been a dream. Clearly, Schwartzie—or Blackie—had been unable to live with his *own* epiphany and had put a bullet in his brain.

At the time, Sonny didn't know how he had been saved or that John had saved him, but now he did. And he knew he could never tell JC, who Max had become as he couldn't be sure whether John had told him.

ॐॐॐ

The seriously injured former POWs were mostly transported by ground livery, but those from Patton's field hospital were transported by aircraft—a luxury. Both John and Sonny were in bad shape, but they had one lie-down cot available for transport via air ambulance and DC-3s back to England. Since John was conscious when they were looking for someone to take the spot, he was chosen promptly.

Getting shipped in the direction of the US so quickly did him little good, though. He was transported to the

Fulham Hospital in London, where soldiers, mostly former prisoners with limb injuries, were sent. Sonny was sent there several weeks afterward, having taken a very bumpy land ambulance to France, a boat from Le Havre to England, and an over-ground train to London.

When Sonny arrived at Fulham Hospital in London, it was early morning, and he was placed in a comfortable bed with clean sheets and a delightful breeze coming in through the window next to him. It was early summer.

He was lying there for only a few hours, both legs elevated, reading a newspaper with weird spellings of familiar words to see what was going on, and a lovely young nurse reading from a list announced, "Mail delivery." Sonny ignored her and buried his nose in his paper. He had just arrived at the hospital, so, surely, no mail would be forthcoming for him.

She wheeled down the aisle of beds with her stacks of mail on a small dolly, some tied with string, others singular small parcels. She looked at the number above his bed, then at the back of the newspaper covering his face, and called out, "Angus Jacobs?"

The newspaper came down quickly, and he stared at her.

"Angus Jacobs?" she asked again.

"Can I help you?"

"Mail delivery, Sergeant."

"For who?"

"Are you Sergeant Angus Jacobs?"

"Yes, but there must be another one."

"Quartermaster Corps?"

"Yes."

"Previously at Stalag IV-B?" She read out the Roman numerals rather than saying "four."

"Yes."

"Well, sir, you have mail."

Without saying thanks, he grabbed the envelopes tied carefully with string. He was bewildered to find that mail from home had caught up with him, though he should not have been so terribly surprised. The Quartermaster Corps looked after their own, and prioritized mail addressed to soldiers in the corps, particularly former prisoners. Though often unpredictable and chaotic, this time, the US Military displayed its efficiency. Sonny's mail had been no farther than two or three trucks behind him since he left Mühlberg and Patton's field hospital. It finally caught up with him at Fulham Chelsea Veteran Hospital, designated for the most seriously wounded and debilitated former POWs recently released.

He looked at the covers. Written several months ago and postmarked Newark, New Jersey, they were directed to Angus Jacobs, 89th Quartermaster Corps, German Stalag IV-B, Germany. It had ink stamps from the stations through which it had traveled, including the Red Cross in Switzerland, and someone had misspelled his first name on the upper right-hand side: AGNUS.

He opened the one with his mom's handwriting immediately, with all the covers addressed to Stalag IV-B. Professions of love, of missing him and praying for him (incessantly, Sonny was sure, the note omitted) and that the entire family was happy to receive word that he was alive through the Red Cross, though there was no mention of any letters he'd sent to them. They hoped he would make it home in time for Christmas. It was signed with much love from his mom and, in his father's own hand, simply "Dad."

A note from each of his sisters was included. Mostly neighborhood gossip and Eileen being incredibly excited about the fact that they had a telephone installed.

She had written, "Here is the telephone number," and then begged Sonny to call her when he received the note.

Where he was supposed to get his hands on a telephone in IV-B, he didn't know. He smiled to himself and gently and affectionately shook his head. "Eileen…"

The young orderly had distributed her mail and was departing the long-aisled ward, inhabited by dozens of beds spaced five feet apart and across from one another, that held over one hundred patients at present.

Sonny called out, "Excuse me, what patients are at this hospital?"

"Sick ones!" she replied.

Some of the soldiers who had been staring at the orderly laughed. It had been so long since they had seen a pretty, young girl that she could have said, "Hopeless, soon-to-die cases" with a smile, and she would have received the same reaction.

"Really, please tell me."

"If you must know, mostly those with ambulatory illness who were prisoners of the Germans."

"Did any arrive by air ambulance?" he asked.

"I'd say most of them."

He very briefly cursed his bad luck. "Do you have a list of the patients?" he inquired. "Can you see if there is a John Chalmet?" after she nodded affirmatively.

She perused her mail list, wrinkling her brow and moving her lips at each patient named "John." She was about to say no when Sonny interjected, "It looks like it would be pronounced 'Shall-Met.'"

"Yes, Lieutenant Shall-Met. In Building 4, two buildings over. Bed 11B."

"Young lady, please call an orderly for me," requested Sonny. "I need a wheelchair."

❧ ❧ ❧

While he was being wheeled over to Building 4, he wondered if the size of the war effort was deceiving him. There had to be as many John Chalmets as there were men named Angus Jacobs (though probably not as many of the latter).

And *his* John was not a lieutenant as far as he knew—unless he had been promoted on the way to the hospital.

Though his John was, in fact, a lieutenant. While in Sommocolonia, Italy, his field jacket was swapped by the Germans, who had decided they didn't want to march with a prisoner who smelled like fresh shit from a broken refuse pipe; the new coat had displayed the rank of sergeant. While he proved to the Germans he was a commissioned officer and could produce his identification, guards taking

341

responsibility for prisoners measured people's worth usually by their uniforms, and they still shoved him with the NCOs when he arrived at IV-B. John never bothered to correct anyone after that because he knew most thought he was White, and he didn't want to draw attention to himself, particularly from the Germans.

When Sonny and John finally did reunite, and they were before each other, Sonny in the wheelchair with the high back, sitting on comfy pillows, John prone, flat on his back in a hospital bed, his head propped up by pillows as well, both offered each other somewhat hideous grins, as they had lost a lot of their front teeth to malnutrition at Mühlberg and Berga, and they began to cry.

"John, why are you still here? You left weeks ago."

"Sonny, I got here a few days after we split up from Patton's hospital. Sonny, it was like a dream. From Berga to Patton to London in a matter of days, Sonny."

They didn't tire of using each other's names because it was so incredible that they had reunited; using their names made it even more real.

"John, what is this place?"

"A hospital for those with messed up feet and legs and plenty of other problems. Pretty girls; nice people; entertainment; clean, clean sheets; and excellent food, but I could only watch the grub go by the first week or so. They told me I had to go slow or my stomach would explode. And the physical therapy is excruciating, but they say it is necessary if I want to walk normally again."

"I thought you'd be home by now," Sonny said.

"Me too, Sonny, but typical snafus in the military. Sometimes it works. Sometimes it doesn't."

"Well, you say that, but I just got mail addressed to me at Berga."

John replied, "Say honest to God?"

They looked at each other and laughed, as only people could who had dodged death's "bullets" together.

"I hope you remember Christmas at Fabyan Place," Sonny reminded him promptly.

"How could I forget, Sonny?"

"Look, my family got a telephone." He wrote the number on the envelope from Eileen's note, tore it off, and handed it to John.

"I'm sending a note to my dad today. I'll put it in so I don't lose it."

"You won't forget the address in any case?" asked Sonny.

"It's 50 Fabyan Place," John recited.

They were situated in oversized wheelchairs on an outside porch in delightful July weather, just getting into their delicious personal debriefing.

"Fabyan Place kept me alive in Berga too, Sonny."

"John, about Berga. What ha—?"

Just then, a captain showed up to collect an Army VIP major who was in John's ward. He had been due to be transported to the US via air but had died of circulatory complications an hour before. Thus, the captain asked the patients on the floor: "Which one of you wants to be a major and fly home to the US?" Sonny raised his hand first, and the captain, in a hurry, ran over and proceeded to take the handles of the high-backed wheelchair, but Sonny stopped him, pointed at John, and said: "Take him. He has been here weeks."

Sonny let John take the flight—or flights, really—consisting of a transfer from England to Iceland to Greenland to Nova Scotia and, finally, to Maine in the good old USA. He would be back in the States in four days, then a two-day trip via train to Atlanta, and then on to home—after a likely stint at Walter Reed Hospital in Washington, DC, if the medical personnel transporting him felt it was necessary.

They were together barely minutes in the hospital and really had no time to talk, but their friendship didn't need the words, and there would be time later to catch up. They knew each other's address and could write.

Sonny would take an ocean liner converted for military use, which had quadrupled its capacity, to get home. The trip would take weeks and weeks. John would be home in a matter of days.

As they parted, John said, "I'll see you at Fabyan Place for Christmas!"

"Looking forward to it. Save some backpay and give me a call when you figure I've arrived back in the US!"

❧ ❧ ❧

After all those different flights and planes, while on the final leg of his journey, on a small Howard DGA-6 single-engine air ambulance taking him to New York and then onto Atlanta via train passing through Washington, DC (so he could go to Walter Reed), the plane crashed and disintegrated at the end of the runway. Of course, there were no survivors.

When Sonny discovered this the following week from a small story in *Stars and Stripes*, he became very angry with John—as the living sometimes do against those who die and leave them bereft and alone and with unfinished business. He wept bitterly and asked himself his perennial question whenever he was dismayed or heard of something incredibly useless or wasteful: *Was there a reason for this?* And he kept on coming up with the same answer.

"No. No lessons to be learned here."

෬෬෬

After he learned his son had been killed, JC received three letters in quick succession from him through the Red Cross written from Germany, then France, and finally the United Kingdom, where John had last written while convalescing, telling JC about his months in captivity and about Christmas at Fabyan Place and how John planned to bring him along. The last had Sonny's family's phone number in Newark, mailed from Fulham Hospital. As he was being driven in an ambulance to the airport, John had smacked his head, thinking, *I should not have mailed that letter. I'll probably be home before it even leaves England!*

❧❧❧

Sonny was ashamed of all the times he had tolerated the jokes, the lack of acceptance, and the ignorance of so many people with whom he was friendly with or loved. He knew better, way better, and had done nothing to correct his own faults. He realized by not challenging bigotry and prejudice, he had perpetuated it. He also became ashamed of the way he had treated the women whom he had met during his life—as things for pleasure, not as individuals. Much the same way he thought about Negroes. Not the pleasure bit, but not as people: not individuals.

He knew he had to begin with educating his own family members, one at a time, and share the revelation of his own shame on Christmas Day on Fabyan Place as he walked in his front door pulling Jean-Claude in, his arm around his shoulders.

He had to change how others looked at people around them.

There was no excuse not to.

Sonny realized that things don't happen for a reason. They happen at random.

Sometimes the things that happen are good, and sometimes they are bad.

It depends on what you do *after* those things happen.

He owed it to John's memory to try to make the outcomes good, and the bad voices quieter.

AFTERWORD

*T**his story's genesis began with a grandmother telling her ten-year-old grandson, me, the story of her own son, Sonny, my uncle, who was captured by the Germans during WWII. She shared all the trials her son faced with her grandson, especially the hunger—or, at least, the stories the son had decided to share with his mom when he returned home. He left out many of the more horrible events.*

Among the things she stressed in the retelling was that her son promised God that if he returned to America safely, he would go and pray in church no matter the day or the hour; and second, he would take the first homeless man he could find in his hometown of Newark on Christmas Day and take him to dinner in a restaurant. He was remembering his own Christmas in captivity.

He did both those things (though I think Grandma shared the first story as his priority because of her piety). The very first homeless man he found on the streets was a Negro, and he took him to an unexpected, delightful Christmas dinner.

The story got fuzzy after that, with her recounting that he would eat grass and scraps out of his captors' rubbish bins if they were available, eventually losing half his body weight and withering down to eighty-five pounds. She talked about how, when she had opened the door and first saw him after his return from the war, she had fainted, noting that his thick mane of black hair had nearly disappeared during his imprisonment.

As I researched some background information around this brief tale of my ancestor's past, I came across many things I had not been aware of, which surprised me as I am a schooled historian of that period. I was not aware of the pervasiveness of the Jitterbug dance, or how it became prominent in England before America because of Negro soldiers. I had also been unaware of the mixed ethnicity of Newark, New Jersey, the home of my grandparents; and of a variety of other things, such as Fort Huachuca, Rhineland bastards, Buffalo Soldiers, the fact that the Jim Crow laws had been copied by the Nazis, that American soldiers had been imprisoned in a Jewish concentration/death camp, the institutional challenges and prejudice faced by Negroes in the United States, and the mixed but mostly positive reaction to American Negro soldiers in wartime Britain.

I also discovered quite a bit about my own family's North American aboriginal roots and how the Indians were sympathetic but remained mostly silent about Negro discrimination in America at the time because while they were themselves minorities, they eluded strict scrutiny and prejudice because of their nearly Caucasian skin color.

AFTERWORD

Except for Sonny and John's story, the Jacobs and their ancestors' autobiographical nature in Newark is as real and as accurate as I could make it.

By including the historical narrative into the story, I hope the reader might investigate further if their interest is piqued and perhaps search through these topics and their own family history as well.

ACKNOWLEDGMENTS

*W*hether or not they spell it out, all authors owe a debt of gratitude and acknowledgment to people who help bring their work to fruition. I'd like to hold some up to the sunlight and thank them.

I don't purport to even begin to understand the Negro experience in America or throughout the world in the 1940s. My research only scratched the surface and was initially inspired by my uncle's anonymous Christmas meal with an unknown homeless Negro in Newark upon his return from incarceration.

That said, I wish to acknowledge someone who helped me understand the journey, a man named **Walter Francis White** (1883-1955), who was an African American civil rights activist who led the National Association for the Advancement of Colored People (NAACP) for a quarter of a century. **John Chalmet's** character is based loosely on this individual (and incidentally, John's name in the book and that of his father's are stolen from a dear and brilliant friend of mine).

ACKNOWLEDGMENTS

I first became acquainted with White from **Doris Kearns Goodwin's** *book,* No Ordinary Times. *I was fascinated with White because he was one of the few people on the planet who came face to face with FDR and could resist his charms, insisting that several civil rights issues be addressed. I was impressed because there were very few people who had that reaction to Roosevelt. It was only years later that I learned that White, while indeed a Negro, could easily pass for a white person yet refused to. He was constantly being asked in university settings when he showed up with his wife why he was married to a Negro. The brief persuasive argument that John gives Sonny in Chapter 15, when wondering what would happen if all Negroes would turn White overnight and what would become of bigotry, was largely from an obscure article written by White in the now-defunct* Look *magazine in 1949 entitled, "Has Science Conquered the Color Line?"*

Jean Wisner Dupon, *a prolific reader I have known for years, was my initial muse and harshest critic. She kept me on focus and encouraged me along the entire journey.*

Ann Howard Creel, *who has a pile of books on Amazon, was my initial story editor, and while I kept the tale identical to its original narrative, she gently persuaded me with her critique to rewrite nearly half the story to make it easier to read, changing nothing but telling the story differently. She is great!*

David Aretha, *a stellar copyeditor, helped me not look foolish with the finished manuscript. He and his collaborator,* **Andrea VanRyken**, *did a fine job, I hope, in making me seem intelligent.*

A prudent first-time author, afraid of his or her skills, will have a challenging time sharing their work with beta readers and supporters to see which storylines work and which don't. These readers must be sincere, patient, and discerning, and I had an excellent group to help me complete this novel. Some read the whole thing, some just portions I had questions about, but they all added value.

Laura Von Ahn, *a first cousin and Sonny's daughter, who let me portray her dad in the book and allowed me to adjust his character for story purposes.*

Kathie Rooney, *a third cousin who helped me with family background.*

David Adams, *a newly "discovered" fourth cousin found for me by RelativityDNA.*

Stephen Corcoran

Mark Trager

Greg Krehel

Susan Padgett

Carly Plymel

John Devaney, *yet another cousin who is an attorney at the International Criminal Tribunal at the Hague, who helped with bits and bobs.*

You may recognize some of the surnames listed above!

Lisa Von Ahn, *an excellent editorial writer (and Laura's sister-in-law).*

Marla Lowenthal

Brenda Champion

Maureen Gazzara

Lisa Schreiner

ACKNOWLEDGMENTS

Patrick Bucek
And thanks to:
Richard DiClemente, *who gave me an enduring appreciation of history.*

Dr. Lavan Varathan, *just because...and he knows why.*

And Kay Williams, *the first professional author to read my completed work and who got me to change large portions of it (again, not changing the story!) for the better.*

It goes without saying that Wikipedia was an online Godsend. Contribute when you can!

Other sources I used to verify some details: The New Yorker, The Atlantic, The Telegraph, *Ellen Knight's article,* "Black Veterans Earned Respect During WWII" in the Daily Times Chronicle, *timeline.com, Jim Crow Laws and Racial Segregation from the Social Welfare History Project,* Liverpool University Press, *and various WWII prisoner diaries.*

Doug George-Kanentiio, *Akwesasne Mohawk, is the vice president of the Hiawatha Institute for Indigenous Knowledge, a former trustee for the National Museum of the American Indian, and is the author of numerous books and articles about the Mohawk people. He provided details of Mohawk cuisine!*

Finally, the publisher who engineered my landing in the "self-published" world, **Jose Ramirez** *from Pedernales Publishing. He let me focus on writing the book, and he took care of everything else.*

Grateful thanks to all.

Any errors or historical misinterpretations are mine and mine alone!
Peter Angus, London, July 2021

If you enjoyed the book, please take a moment to write a review of it at:

www.peterangus-author.com

Featuring information and previews of my latest novel